Her Dear & Loving Husband

Meredith Allard

Copperfield Press
Las Vegas, NV

Copperfield Press
Visit our website at www.copperfieldpress.com

First paperback edition: April 2011

Cover design by Dara England

Publisher's Note: This is a work of fiction. Names, characters, businesses, places, and events portrayed in this book are a product of the author's imagination or used in a fictitious way. Any similarity to real persons, living or dead, places, events, businesses, or locales, is entirely coincidental.

"To My Dear and Loving Husband" by Anne Bradstreet and "Ode to a Nightingale" by John Keats are in the public domain.

Her Dear and Loving Husband/by Meredith Allard. – 1st ed.

{1. Salem Witch Trials—Fiction. 2. Vampires—Fiction. 3. Salem, Massachusetts—Fiction. 4. 17th Century—Fiction. 5. Literary—Fiction. 6. Historical—Fiction. 7. Paranormal—Fiction.} I. Title

ISBN-10: 0-615-45422-4
ISBN-13: 978-1-615-45422-1
LCCN: 2011903368

Printed in the United States of America

Contents

PROLOGUE

I am looking lovingly into the eyes of a man, though I cannot see his face because it is featureless, like a blank slate. We are standing in front of a wooden house with narrow clapboards, and there are diamond-paned casement windows and a steep pitched roof with two gables pointing at the laughing, hidden moon. I am certain I hear someone singing sweet nothings to us from the sky. From the light of the few jewel stars I can see the halo of his hair, like the halo of an angel, and even if I cannot see his eyes I know they look at me, into me. I stand on my toes, he is much taller than me, and I point up my face and he kisses me. As the warmth of his lips melts into mine, making me weak from the inside out, I feel my knees give from the thrilling lightness his touch brings. I know the face I cannot see is beautiful, like the lips I feel. His hands press me into him, clutching me closer, closer, unwilling to let me go. I grip him with equal strength, wishing he would carry me inside, yet I cannot bring myself to break our embrace.

"I shall never leave you ever," he whispers in my ear. I promise him the same.

I do not know how I have been so fortunate to have this man in my life, but here he is, before me, wanting me. I am overcome with the joy of him.

CHAPTER 1

Sarah Alexander didn't know what was waiting for her in Salem, Massachusetts. She had moved there to escape the smog and the smugness of Los Angeles, craving the dulcet tones of a small town, seeking a less complicated life. Her first hint of the supernatural world came the day she moved into her rented brick house near the historic part of town, close to the museums about the witch trial days, not far from the easy, wind-blown bay. As the heavy-set men hauled her furniture inside, her landlady leaned close and told her to beware.

"If you hear sounds in the night it's ghosts," the landlady whispered, glancing around to be sure no one, human or shadow, could hear. "The spirits of the innocent victims of the witch hunts still haunt us. I can feel them stirring now. God rest them."

Sarah didn't know what to say. She had never been warned about ghosts before. The landlady peered at her, squinting to see her better.

"You're a pretty girl," the old woman said. "Such dark curls you have." She still spoke as if she were telling a secret, and Sarah had to strain to hear. "You're from California?"

"I moved there after I got married," Sarah said.

"Where's your husband?"

"I'm divorced now."

"And your family is here?"

"In Boston. I wanted to live close to my family, but I didn't want to move back to the city. I've always wanted to visit Salem, so I thought I'd live here awhile."

The landlady nodded. "Boston," she said. "Some victims of the witch trials were jailed in Boston."

The landlady was so bent and weak looking, her fragile face lined like tree rings, that Sarah thought the old woman had experienced the hysteria in Salem during the seventeenth century. But that was silly, Sarah reminded herself. The Salem Witch Trials happened over three hundred years ago. There was no one alive now who had experienced that terror first hand. Sarah wanted to tell the landlady how she believed she had an ancestor who died as a victim of the witch hunts, but she didn't say anything then.

"Yes, they're here," the landlady said, staring with time-faded eyes at the air above their heads, as if she saw something no one else could see. "Beware, Sarah. The ghosts are here. And they always come out at night."

The landlady shook as if she were cold, though it was early autumn and summer humidity still flushed the air. When Sarah put her arm around the old woman to comfort her, she felt her skin spark like static. She rubbed her hands together, feeling the numbness even after the old woman pulled away.

"It's all right," Sarah said. "I won't be frightened by paranormal beings. I don't believe in ghosts."

The landlady laughed. "Salem may cure you of that."

For a moment Sarah wondered if she made a mistake moving there, but she decided she wouldn't let a superstitious old woman scare her away. She thought about her new job in the library at Salem State College—Humanities I liaison, go-to person for English studies, well worth the move across the country. She saw the tree-lined, old-fashioned neighborhood and the comforting sky. She heard the lull of bird songs and the distant whisper of the sea kissing the shore. She felt a rising tranquility, like the tide of the ocean waves at noon, wash over her. It was a contentment she had never known before, not in Boston, never in Los Angeles. She was fascinated by Salem, looking forward to knowing it better, certain she was exactly where she needed to be, whatever may come.

Sarah's first days in the library were hectic since it was the start of an autumn term. She spent her shifts on the main floor, an open, industrial-style space of bright lights, overhead beams, and windows that let in white from the sun and green from the trees abundant everywhere on campus. Across from the librarians's desk, a combined circulation and reference area, was a lounge of comfortable chairs in soothing grays and blues where some students socialized using their inside voices while others stalked like eagle-eyed hunters, searching the stacks or the databases.

By Wednesday afternoon, as she saw the short-tempered rain clouds march across the Salem sky, Sarah thought she would have to buy a car soon. After driving and dodging in nail-biting Los Angeles traffic for ten years, she liked the freedom of walking the quiet roads from home to work, watching in wonder as the leaves turned from summer green to an autumn fade of red, rust, and gold. But she had been living in the sunshine on the west coast for ten years, and she had forgotten about the sudden anger of New England thunderstorms. They could appear just like that, a crack of noise overhead, then a gray flannel blanket covered the sky as fast as you could blink your eyes, water splashing all around, wetting you when you did not want to be wet, and she was caught unprepared. She held out her hand and shook her head when she felt the drops splash her palm. Jennifer Mandel's voice sang out behind her.

"Need a lift?"

"Please."

Sarah wiped her palm on her skirt, grateful once again for Jennifer's assistance. Jennifer had been the head librarian at the college for five years, and she had taken Sarah under her wing, showing her where everything was, introducing her to the rest of the staff, answering her questions. There was something almost odd about Jennifer's intuition—she always seemed to know when Sarah needed her, like a clairvoyant magic trick. They sprinted to the parking lot, trying to avoid the sudden splats of rain soaking their thin blouses through, and they clambered into Jennifer's white Toyota, laughing like schoolgirls jumping in puddles. Jennifer drove the curve around Loring Avenue to Lafayette Street, the main road to and from the college.

"Where were you before you came here?" Jennifer asked. "You're obviously not used to the rain."

"I worked at UCLA."

"A small town like Salem must seem dreary after living in the big city."

Sarah looked at Jennifer, saw the compassion in her eyes, the understanding smile, so she said just enough to make herself understood. "I'm recently divorced."

Jennifer held up her hand. "You don't need to explain. I have two ex-husbands myself."

They drove quietly, letting the sound of the car's accelerator and the rain tapping the windshield fill the space. As Sarah watched the small-town scene drift past, she thought it might not be so bad to drive in Salem. Everything back east, the roads, the shops, the homes, was built on an old-time scale, narrower and smaller than they were out west. But here people slowed when you wanted to merge into their lane and they stopped at stop signs, so different from L.A. where they'd run you over sooner than let you pass.

"Why don't you come over tomorrow night?" Jennifer asked. "We're having a get-together at my mother's shop." She leaned closer to Sarah and whispered though they were alone in the car. "I should probably tell you, and I'll understand if you think this is too weird, but my mother and I are witches."

Sarah studied Jennifer, her hazel eyes, her long auburn hair, her friendly smile. "You don't look like a witch," she said.

"You mean the kind with black hair and a nose wart? The kind that fly around on broomsticks? Not that kind of witch."

"You mean you're Wiccan?"

"Yes, I practice the Wiccan religion, among other things. I'm the high priestess of my coven. I'm also licensed to perform weddings here in Massachusetts, in case you ever need someone to preside over a wedding for you."

Sarah laughed. "I just got divorced. I won't be getting married again any time soon." She paused to watch the drizzle slip and slide on the windows. "I'm surprised there really are witches in Salem."

"Ironic, isn't it? The city known for hanging witches is now a haven for mystics." Jennifer shook her head, her expression tight. "Is this too much information? I don't usually tell someone a few days after I've met her that I'm Wiccan, but you have a positive energy. You don't seem like someone who's going to assume I'm a Satanist who loves human sacrifices."

"I don't mind. I'm just surprised. I've never known a witch before."

"There are all sorts of interesting people you could meet around here." Jennifer nudged Sarah with her elbow. "So will you come tomorrow night?"

"I don't know, Jennifer."

"You don't need to participate in the rituals. Come make some friends. I think you'll like the other witches in my coven. They're good people."

A Wiccan ceremony did sound odd, Sarah thought, but she had always been fascinated by different religions and cultures. Librarians had to keep learning—a healthy curiosity was a job necessity. And it would be nice to know some people in Salem, even if they were witches.

As they continued down Lafayette Street, Sarah saw the sign for Pioneer Village and she added it to her mental to-do list. "I haven't had a chance to see much of this part of town since I've been here," she said.

"How about a quick tour then?"

"What about the rain?"

Jennifer turned right down Derby Street. "I've lived here my whole life. A little water doesn't bother me."

Jennifer drove down one tree-lined street, then down another street, and another until Sarah didn't know where she was. Though Witch City was small, Sarah was still learning her way around. She tried to gauge her surroundings and saw the tall, white lines of the Peabody-Essex Museum, then further down was the Hawthorne Hotel. Past that was the brick, colonial-looking Salem Maritime National Historic Site. As she watched the history flip past, like a stack of photographs from time gone by, she noticed a house she thought she knew though she was sure she hadn't been down that way before. The one that caught her attention had wooden clapboards, diamond-paned casement windows, and two gables on the roof. It was old, though it didn't seem to be a museum as the other old buildings were.

"What is that house?" she asked. "It looks familiar."

"James Wentworth lives there."

"Do you know him?"

Jennifer's answer was stilted, as if she considered each word, weighed it, measured it, decided yes or no about it, before she let it drop from her lips. "He teaches at the college. He—his family—has owned this house for generations. It's over three hundred years old, one of the oldest standing homes in Salem."

Jennifer slowed the car so they could get a better look as she drove past. "Does it still look familiar?" she asked.

"Yes. Even that crooked oak tree in front seems right. I can picture the man I dream about standing in front there kissing me."

"What dreams?" Jennifer gripped the steering wheel more tightly and her eyes brightened. "My mother's friend Martha is great at dream interpretation. She's done a world of good for me." She winked at Sarah. "And you dream about a man? Is he a good looking man?"

Sarah pulled her arms around her chest, wishing she could take back her casual reference, afraid she had already said too much.

"Do you have a lot of dreams?"

"Yes," Sarah said. But that was all she could manage. When Jennifer had waited long enough and Sarah had to offer something more, all she could say was, "It's not a big deal. I just thought I knew the house from somewhere."

"A lot of houses around here look the same," Jennifer said.

Sarah looked at the houses, the tall, Federal-style ones, the Victorian ones, the brick ones, the modern-looking ones. Suddenly, as they drove around the green of Salem Common, the rain cleared, the sun brightened, and the clouds flittered away across the bay.

"That must be it," she said.

She lowered the car window so she could smell the wet air. Though she missed the rain when she lived in Los Angeles, at that moment she was glad to see the serene blue reflection of the northeastern sky again.

They drove the rest of the way in silence.

CHAPTER 2

Thursday night Sarah was slow with her steps, savoring the town. She turned from Washington Street and wandered between Front and Derby, past the old-fashioned Salem Marketplace where people window shopped through the narrow lanes, gazing at the painters and sculptors in Artists Row, imagining what it must have been like living there centuries ago. She continued to the watery expanse of the bay where the breeze blew lazy laps in the water, postcard perfect along the natural coastline beauty. Rising above the water, towering above the sailboats, was the 171-foot-long, three-masted ship the *Friendship*, an emblem of Salem. She saw the white lighthouse, waiting patiently, beckoning sailors home. She stepped onto Pickering Wharf, a harborside village of gray-blue buildings with white trim, the hubbub of local seafaring activities, and she paused to admire the slick boats parked in neat little rows. She breathed in the wholesome air, exhaled, and relaxed. She felt comfortable, as if she had found a childhood friend after many years. More than anything, she loved the peace she felt. Her thoughts had been congested so long, the ten years she spent in Los Angeles, to be exact, and with every step she took she felt her muddled worries clearing away, lifted from her shoulders by the sauntering wind.

The Witches Lair, Jennifer's mother's shop, was located on Pickering Wharf, tucked in alongside the clothing, gift, and antique boutiques. Sarah arrived before everyone else since she was still on an L.A. schedule where you had to leave an hour early to get through the traffic to get anywhere on time. A tinkling bell rang as she pulled open the door, and when she walked into the shop she said hello to the woman behind the counter and glanced around. The Witches Lair was a perfect name for the store since it was stocked with any accoutrement a witch or wizard might need: altar supplies and incense, aromatherapy oils and diffusers, cauldrons and tarot cards, crystals and gems, and books about subjects ranging from the kama sutra to kabbalah and from magick and spells to dream interpretation. It was dark inside, with dim overhead lights and flameless candles in the sconces on the walls, the shadows adding to the mystical ambiance.

Sarah paused by the bookcase, searching the titles. She was intrigued by one, about dream interpretation, and as she scanned the back cover she wondered if the information inside could help her unravel the dreams that plagued her. There were nights when the images were so intense that when she woke up it took some time to distinguish between the scenes in her head and the reality in the world outside. With the book forgotten in her hands, she remembered her latest nightmare, the one that staggered her awake the night before. She was so lost in thought she didn't notice the older woman beside her.

"Would you like a psychic reading, dear? I can read your palm, or perhaps you'd prefer a tarot card reading?"

"Oh no." Sarah returned the book to the shelf. "I'm waiting for Jennifer Mandel. We work together at the library and she invited me here tonight."

The woman clasped her hands together, and she smiled in warm greeting. "You must be Sarah. I'm Olivia Phillips, Jennifer's mother. Welcome to the Witches Lair."

Olivia looked like a fortune-telling gypsy with her hoop earrings and peasant-style skirt. Her steel-gray eyes and the wisps of silver in her close-cropped red hair were striking. Sarah and Olivia shook hands, and Sarah gestured at the store around her.

"Your shop is fascinating. I've never seen one like it."

"Shops like these are a dime a dozen around here. Everyone in Salem thinks they're a psychic or a mystic or touched by the supernatural somehow." Olivia waved her hand in a firm dismissal of those who would think that way. "Jennifer tells me you're new to Salem."

"That's right." Sarah began to explain about her divorce, but Olivia held up her hand.

"You don't need to explain, dear. I have four ex-husbands myself. But why Salem?"

"I've always felt drawn here. When I was growing up in Boston I asked my mother to bring me to the Halloween festival, and we lived so close, but somehow we never made it. My mother always had one excuse or other to skip the trip. Just the thought of this place made her shiver."

"Has your mother ever been here? There's nothing to be afraid of, at least not for over three hundred years. These days it's more of a tourist town than anything."

"I've told her that, but she still won't come. I thought she'd want to know more about our ancestor, but she's not interested."

"Your ancestor?"

"When I was a girl my great-aunt told us that someone in our family died as a victim of the witch hunts, but my aunt didn't know anything else about the woman, not even her name. I started working on my family tree when I was in L.A., and I thought if I were here I could do more research at the Danvers Archival Center. At least I'd like to know her name."

"A mystery to solve. I love it." Olivia looked at the book Sarah had slipped back onto the shelf. She turned to Sarah, her face fixed, like a detective gathering clues where no one else thought to look. "Jennifer tells me you have dreams." She took Sarah's hand and patted it in a motherly way. "Would you like to tell me about them?"

Sarah shook her head. She had never told anyone. Nick, her ex-husband, knew, but only by default. He would yell and bitch and moan whenever she woke screaming in the night, clenching her jaw tight until the bones popped in her ears, her muscles like sailors's knots. He told her she was weak for giving into the internal heckling, but they were her dreams. She couldn't control them. They would have their way with her, picking and pulling at her, though she didn't want them to. Because of Nick's impatience, and her own disappointment with how easily she was jolted awake by the clear-as-day images, she kept her dreams a secret from everyone else. Instinctively, she felt she could trust

15

Olivia, that Olivia might be someone she could confide in about the teasing games her subconscious liked to play when she was sleeping and defenseless, waking her with nervous, earthquake-like tremors. She had the clothbound notebook where she recorded her dreams there with her in the Witches Lair, in the canvas bag hanging from her shoulder. She could have pulled it out to show Olivia. But she didn't. She shook her head again.

"Whatever you wish, Sarah. Just remember, I'm here should you change your mind. And my friend Martha, you'll meet her tonight, is excellent at dream interpretation. She's an expert at past-life regression as well."

"You're very kind, but you don't need to trouble yourself over it."

"But dreams are our subconscious whispering truths in our ears, Sarah. You should pay attention. You'd be amazed at what you could learn."

Olivia gripped Sarah's hand tighter and led her past the book-cases and displays to four cubby-sized rooms separated from the rest of the store by black velvet curtains.

"Come. I'll give you a reading for free. Any friend of Jennifer's is a friend of mine." Sarah tried to protest, but Olivia wouldn't be swayed. "Really, dear, everything will be fine. Perhaps I can help you understand your dreams."

Sarah relented, telling herself she didn't believe in psychics, extrasensory perception, mysticism, or anything like that, so the reading didn't matter. And she did like Olivia. There was such unconditional warmth in the older woman's manner. Besides, in a tarot reading didn't they just pull three cards from the deck and make guesses about your life based on the pictures? She would humor Olivia, pretend to be startled by the revelations, then join Jennifer and the others.

Olivia pulled aside the curtain to the cubby on the end, fringed with more black velvet. Inside there was only enough space for a small round table covered with white linen and two folding chairs while a candle and spiced incense burned on a shelf. Olivia sat in the chair behind the table and gestured for Sarah to sit across from her. She took Sarah's hand and looked at her palm.

16

"Have you had a psychic reading before?"

"Once, when I was in college. I was taking a religious studies class and one of our assignments was to have a psychic reading and write about our experience."

"And what was your experience?"

"She seemed very young, the psychic, just college age herself, and I wasn't impressed with her predictions since everything she said was generic and could have applied to anyone."

Olivia dropped Sarah's hand to study her. Again, that detective seeking clues look. "What did she say?"

"I was getting ready to move to Los Angeles where my fiancé had a job in the film industry. She told me moving away would be a mistake because L.A. was not my home. She said my husband was not my husband and I was not who I thought I was."

"Who do you think you are?"

"I'm Sarah Alexander."

Olivia was in deep thought as she considered.

"Yes, well, let's see what else we can learn."

Olivia took Sarah's hand again and stared deeply into her palm, as if her eyes were x-rays and she could see through the layers of skin past the veins, the blood, and the muscles to the truth within. Her eyelids shuddered as she went into a trance. Her head bobbed in a rocking motion, and she breathed loudly, exhaling from her mouth and wheezing in through her nose. Sarah became nervous when Olivia seemed to expand to twice her size, though it must have been the flickering candlelight playing tricks on her sight.

"Yes," Olivia said, her voice a whisper. "Yes, I am beginning to see. You are hard to read, there are many layers to you, but I am beginning to see." She was silent again, though she kept nodding. Sarah's head began to bob along, like when you're on a boat and your body sways in time with the rhythm of the waves.

"Who you are is not yourself. The secret to the puzzle is there. The other psychic you saw was very good. Very good. She could see that who you are is not yourself. Yes, I can see that he will find you. He is here and he will find you."

"Who?" Sarah asked.

"He will. The one who is waiting for you. He has been waiting for you for oh so very long. You will be afraid. He is not what he was. You will find your way home again."

Sarah tried to pull away, but Olivia kept a tight grasp. Sarah leaned forward, not breathing, struggling to understand what Olivia was saying because her words sounded like they should make sense but they didn't. Suddenly the black velvet curtains scraped against the rod as they were tossed aside, and Sarah jumped. Jennifer, in a flowing black robe, stood in the fluorescent light shining in from the store, one hand on the curtains, her other hand on her hip.

"Mother! I asked Sarah to come to the Harvest Moon ceremony to introduce her to some people. We're about to start."

Olivia pulled away from Sarah, covering her face with her hands until her breathing slowed. The overwhelming psychic who had expanded to twice her size was gone. When she opened her eyes she looked as she did when Sarah first saw her in the store, friendly and motherly. After Olivia composed herself she smiled.

"I'm sorry, Jennifer. I lost track of time." She stood up from behind the table and pulled the curtain aside for Sarah. "I hope I didn't frighten you too much, dear. I should have warned you that I go into a trance when I'm in tune with the spirit world."

"I wasn't frightened at all," Sarah lied.

"Good. Now did I say anything that made sense? Sometimes when I'm with the spirits I begin speaking in tongues and no one can understand what I'm saying."

"She's a great psychic," Jennifer said. "Her clients don't understand her half the time, and she can't help them because she never remembers what she says."

"I'm in a trance, dear. What do you remember from your trances?"

"Nothing. Just like you."

Olivia turned to Sarah. "Did I say anything that helped you understand your dreams?"

"No," Sarah said. "Nothing."

"I'm sorry. Perhaps we can try again another time."

Sarah looked through the store to where the sliding glass door was open. In the courtyard outside she saw a grotto with rose trellises, scented lavender shrubs, and a cherub water fountain spitting in an arc in the air. There was a covered altar set against the brick wall and about twenty people in black robes mingling while drinking tea and eating cakes. Sarah stopped suddenly, her feet leaden, as if there were iron chains around her ankles.

Jennifer grabbed her arm. "What did my mother say to you? Sarah? What did she say?"

Sarah looked at the people in the grotto and realized she didn't want to go out there.

"I'm sorry," she said. "I don't feel well. I think I should leave."

"What did you say to her, Mom?"

"I don't know, Jennifer. I wish I could remember."

As Sarah walked home, passing the same historic sights she had seen on the way, she was oblivious to everything but Olivia's reading. She was unnerved by the whole experience, seeing what had happened to Olivia, hearing that someone, some man, was going to find her. Olivia didn't say what would happen once she was found, and frightening visions flashed behind her eyes, images of being stalked. Attacked. Or worse. Slowing her steps, forcing herself to think logically, she reminded herself that she didn't believe in psychics, extrasensory perception, mysticism, or anything like that. She didn't understand why Olivia's words struck her so deeply.

Once Sarah was home she was exhausted, though she wasn't afraid any more. Being away from Olivia, away from the cryptic message, helped her feel better. Sarah knew she wouldn't be getting another psychic reading any time soon. Olivia brought up too many uncomfortable emotions, and Sarah had moved to Salem seeking peace. She didn't need the headache of illogical puzzles in her life then.

When she woke up at three a.m., she turned on the light by her bed, grabbed her clothbound notebook and a pen, and wrote about the dream that had tapped her awake. This was a pleasant vision, one she was happy to write down, unlike some of the more frightening nightmares she had been having. It was hard to write those down even with the lights on. But this one she was glad to remember.

19

I am sitting at a table surrounded by people who look like they should be part of a Thanksgiving Feast tableau with their modest Pilgrim-style clothing, old-fashioned manners, and antiquated way of speaking. There are pumpkins, pies, roasted game birds, and mugs of ale set out on the table. I am included in this gathering, the people seem to know me, and I seem to know them though no one looks familiar—everyone's face is a blank slate. A girl about ten years old is talking to me like she is my sister perhaps, showing me her cloth doll and telling me how her doll helped with the sewing, the cleaning, and the cooking. She asks what I did that day.

"The same as I do most days," I say. "I went to the spring to get water this morn. Then I milked the cows and gathered eggs, and later I shall finish spinning yarn."

She puckers her adorable cherub-like face. "Did you know I asked Father if I could help him this day?" she asks.

"Did you?"

"Aye. I am no longer a babe in long clothes. Now I wear upgrown folks clothes, and I asked Father if I could help with mending the fences and reaping the rye. He said nay! He said I am too small and a girl at that."

"Father is right," I say. "You needn't worry over such things. 'Tis grueling work. Best to let the men have at it. Besides, the sickle is dangerous. You could lose a finger or even your arm, and I am not enough of a seamstress to sew it back for you."

"But I want to help! What if the harvest isn't gathered before the weather turns and we have nothing for winter?"

"That won't happen," I say. "Father has always provided well for us, and he shall continue doing so even in this new land we now live in."

"I shall be the greatest soap maker in the village, and I shall make enough money selling my soaps to buy my own horse and plow. Then Father must let me tend to the upgrown folks work."

"Shall you make some soap for me? I am in need of it."

She laughs. "Of course I shall," she says.

She is a sweet girl, so even tempered for one so young, and she clutches my hand as if she needs my attention more than anything in the world. I am certain now that this must be my sister and I love her for her tenderness.

That is when I notice him. He is sitting across the table from me, down to my right, the man with the halo hair. I cannot see his face, it is a blank slate like the others, but I can tell that he is looking at me, shyly, wanting to speak to me but perhaps it is not appropriate that he does so in this place at this time. I do not think he knows me, or I know him, yet, but I can feel that we want to know each other. I am enchanted.

CHAPTER 3

James Wentworth arrived on the campus of Salem State College a half an hour after dark. He parked his black Ford Explorer in the parking lot off Loring Avenue near the Central Campus and walked past the Admissions Office and the bookstore, stepping out of the way of a student speeding toward the bike path. After he walked into the library he paused by the door to watch the young people studying at the tables, searching the stacks, hunching over the computers, so raw and fresh they still had that new-car smell. They had so much ahead of them, James mused. The world was exciting to them, adventures waiting to be had, dreams to be discovered, loves to be found and lost and lost and found. The students in the library were naïve, yes, but that would be tempered by experience and learning. Some of them thought they already knew everything they would ever need to know, but James had compassion for them. We think we know it all, but we never do, no matter how long we live.

Class that night was lively. These students had opinions and they liked discussing and debating, which kept the energy high. There is no worse class than when there were thirty silent students who wanted nothing more than to listen to the professor speak for fifty minutes and leave. That night's class was an independent study seminar where the students chose which work of literature they would focus on. Usually, James found, the young people were predictable in their choices—Dickens, Shakespeare, Twain, Thoreau—but that term the students were more creative. One was studying Oscar Wilde's *The Picture of Dorian Gray* about the cursed man who never ages, a story James thought of often. He was amused by the choice, and curious.

"Why *The Picture of Dorian Gray*?" he asked.

"Staying young forever?" Kendall said. "How cool is that? I mean, don't you want your hair to stay blond, Professor? You want to turn old and gray?"

James shook his head. "On the outside Dorian stayed young-looking and fresh-seeming, but on the inside he became decrepit in ways no one would guess. His physical body didn't age, but the catch was, as the years passed, he grew more depraved and detached from human decency." James looked at Kendall, a Junior about twenty years of age, her sandy-brown hair slung back in a ponytail, wearing a blue and orange Salem State College t-shirt with the Viking logo. Her expression hadn't changed.

"Dorian looked young, Professor Wentworth. Isn't that all that matters?"

"A youthful appearance is certainly valued in our society, but don't you think there could be problems always looking the same while you grew in knowledge and experience?"

"But looking young forever would keep me out of the plastic surgeon's office."

"Fair enough," James said.

"I mean, my sister is twenty-five, and she's already getting Botox."

James sighed as he surveyed the classroom, admiring the bright, fresh faces, and he wondered how many others were convinced they looked old when they were oh so very young. He scanned the list in his hand and his eyes grew wide. He pressed his wire-rimmed eyeglasses against his nose as he looked at Trisha, sitting front and center, a bright student, one of his hardest workers, and he didn't know whether to laugh or cry at her choice. He wouldn't have guessed it of her.

"Why did you choose Bram Stoker's *Dracula*?" he asked.

"Because I love that genre," Trisha said. "I love the idea that there are supernatural beings so extraordinary out there walking unnoticed among us. Since we're not looking for them we don't see them, and when we do see them it might be too late."

"Do you believe in vampires?" he asked.

"Of course not. That's silly."

24

"Yes," he said. "That is very silly."

"Besides, even if there were really vampires no one would believe it. It just doesn't seem possible."

"You're right. Let's hope we never have to find out."

Levon Jackson, another bright student, an ice hockey player touted as a potential NHL draft, patted Trisha's shoulder and shouted a loud "Amen!"

James sat on the edge of the instructor's desk at the front of the room. Levon was one of his favorites that term, in two of his classes, and the young man so rarely shared without raising his hand. Though James insisted from the first day that students didn't need to raise their hands, this was college, not kindergarten, Levon was always respectful, polite, waiting for James's attention before he spoke.

"Amen to what, Levon?" James asked.

"Amen to let's hope we never have to find out. Who wants to learn there's some nasty old vamp lurking around somewhere?"

"There's nothing to find out," said Jeremy, who had aspirations of doctoral school at Harvard. "Who wants to waste time on make-believe?"

"Vampires could be real," Kendall said. As other students laughed and hissed, she turned her scrunched face to the class. "Why not? Stranger things have happened."

"How can something be dead and alive at the same time?" Jeremy asked.

"I'm not saying it's true," Kendall said. "I'm just saying it's possible."

Levon slapped his large hands over his ears, his palms flat against his head. "I don't want to hear any more about vampires!" James couldn't tell if he was joking.

Jeremy smirked. "You must cover your ears a lot, Levon. Everyone everywhere is talking about vampires. Vampire movies. Vampire television shows. Vampire books." Jeremy's fingers went to his temples and he shook his head from side to side. "I am so damn sick of vampires."

James watched his students with a mixture of amusement and caution. He didn't want to stifle the conversation, and he wouldn't quell their questioning, but he didn't like the turn the conversation had taken. Levon turned his desk so he could look Jeremy in the eye. He wasn't intimidating, James noted, only serious.

"My pastor says there are evil spirits, minions of Satan, all around us, especially at night. He says they seek innocent souls to prey on, and if we're not careful the evil will consume us." Levon looked around the room, one student at a time, without a hint of sarcasm. "I know there's evil in the world. Maybe it's ghosts. Maybe it's witches. Maybe it's vampires. Maybe it's the Devil himself. Whatever it is, I don't want any part of it, and I don't want it anywhere near me. Evil like that needs to be destroyed."

"Do you really believe that?" Jeremy asked.

"I do."

The students argued amongst each other, some louder than others. They were so caught up in their opinions they didn't notice as James moved from the desk to the window. He unhooked the latch and pushed the glass up, letting in a cool blast of air, the combined scent of the salty sea and the storm dropping soon. Suddenly the shouting voices stopped. James heard the silence, but he didn't turn around. He watched the tree leaves sigh and weave from their branches. He watched the moon hanging in wait overhead. He wasn't trying to be dramatic. He was waiting for the right words to come.

"That could be dangerous," he said finally, "making judgments and deciding where, or if, others have the right to live." He was talking to no one in particular, to the windowpane, the trees, the night breeze, his own furrowed brow. "People have lost their lives because of such judgments."

"What that is, Professor, is a loaf of bullshit," said Jeremy.

The class laughed.

"It isn't," said Levon. "I don't want anything to do with any vampires. I don't want to see anything about them. I don't want to hear anything about them. They're evil."

Silence fell over the class again. James turned from the window and saw twenty-five oh so very young faces waiting for him to make sense of it all. That was how class often went. James offered some topic of discussion based on their reading, the students would discuss, or argue, and then James would share some insight that tied the pieces together. Then the students left with some new knowledge that hopefully they'd remember, some lesson they'd carry all their lives, or at least until the next midterm. James wished they would take more responsibility for forming their own opinions, but he was the professor, after all, the one with the college degrees paid to profess his knowledge to classes of impressionable minds. But that night the class had a different feel. He didn't know if the students could sense the shift, but he could. For the first time, he didn't know what to say.

Timothy Wolfe, a dark-haired, pale-skinned student, stood up in the back of the class, a flash of anger in his black eyes. James gave Timothy a warning glance, but Timothy didn't seem to see him. Rather, James guessed from Timothy's glint, that he was being ignored.

"Why do you assume vampires are evil?" Timothy asked.

The other students turned around, surprised, as if they had never noticed Timothy before. And they probably hadn't. He was always so quiet, never answering a question or offering an opinion, staking out his usual seat in the back near the door, bolting as soon as James dismissed them. James stood back, his arms crossed over his chest, watching Timothy's every move as the boy walked toward Levon, the ice hockey goalie, looking like David challenging Goliath.

"Timothy..." James said, caution in his tone.

Timothy jabbed a frustrated finger in Levon's direction. "I mean, if vampires were real, which they're not, but if they were, everyone thinks they'd be evil. But not everyone is the same."

"There can't be any such thing as a nice vampire," Levon said. "They're bloodthirsty, angry devils who'd suck the life right out of you. Who knows how many people they'd kill. Probably one a night." Levon stood up, and his athlete's physique towered above Timothy, who looked too small, too fragile suddenly. "Vampires are the way they are, and they all belong in one category: villain."

James looked at Levon. For the first time that night he was annoyed with the young man. "You don't believe that people, human or otherwise, can overcome their violent tendencies?" he asked.

"I don't."

"No matter how much they want to change? No matter how resolved they are? Are we victims of some predetermined destiny? I knew some people who thought that way once. They weren't a pleasant group to live around."

"I think if you're mean you're mean and if you're not you're not."

"You've been watching too many horror movies," Jeremy said. He didn't try to hide his disdain. He closed his textbook and shut down his notebook computer. He looked at the time, at the door, at the window. Then he began texting on his cell phone. James didn't stop him.

"If I knew a hot vampire like Edward or Bill I'd give them as much of my blood as they wanted," Trisha said. She giggled, and so did the girls sitting next to her. "They could bite me anytime."

James looked at the clock on the wall. "Time's up," he said. "See you next week."

As the others filtered single file from the classroom, Levon turned to James. "No hard feelings, Doctor Wentworth?"

"Of course not, Levon."

Levon smiled, a flash of white brilliance, and he extended his hand. James stepped behind the instructor's desk, sliding his hands into the pockets of his khaki trousers.

"I'm sorry," James said. "I have a cold and I don't want you to get sick. You have a big game tomorrow night."

Levon pointed out his folded arm instead. "All right, elbow bump."

James laughed, and they touched elbows.

"Good luck tomorrow night," James said.

"You coming to the game?"

"I'd love to but I can't. Midterms coming up, you know. Maybe next time."

"You need to get out more. I never see you out with the other professors, and I never see you around town. You never go to the games. Are you married?"

James was startled by the suddenness of the question, and he tried to set his expression. He didn't want Levon to see how shocked he was, but the look on Levon's face told him he had not been quick enough.

"I didn't mean anything by it," Levon said. "I was just wondering if you had anyone waiting for you at home."

"Not anymore."

"Too bad. You're a youngish guy, what, about fifty?"

James shook his head. "You young people think everyone older than you is fifty. I'm thirty, Levon."

"All right, thirty, even better. From the way the girls giggle about you, you must be okay. They all have a crush on you."

"They do not."

"They do." Levon threw his backpack over one shoulder. "You should find a friend before it's too late, Doctor Wentworth, you know, a nice lady. That's all I'm saying."

James sat on the edge of a student desk, his arms crossed over his chest as he watched the young man in front of him.

"You're right," James said, laughing, like the fact that he kept so much to himself was the biggest joke in the world. "Not about finding a nice lady. I did that once. I mean about getting to a game. I'll come soon. I promise."

Levon seemed satisfied with that answer. As Levon left the classroom, James saw Timothy loitering outside. By the time James stepped over to talk to him, Timothy had disappeared. James looked down the hallway and heard the boy's quick-time steps crossing the pavement of College Drive. He knew he would have to talk to Timothy about that, again, soon. It didn't help anything to have him disappearing like a slight-of-hand trick. James went back into the classroom, packed up his book bag, and left campus, not as quickly as Timothy, but fast enough. It had been a long night.

CHAPTER 4

Sarah couldn't stop thinking about the house she saw when Jennifer drove her home. It didn't make sense that it should look familiar when it was located on a street she had never been down in a city where she was new, but she was certain it was the one she had seen in her dreams. Since the psychic reading two nights before she felt like she had restless leg syndrome, like she had to keep moving even when she didn't want to. When she slowed down, even for a moment, odd, unclear thoughts occurred to her, and she didn't want to try to make sense of them. She wanted to sweep them away, hide them in the closet, forget the reading altogether.

Walking always helped to vent her excess energy, so she decided to take a trip across town to look at the house again. It wasn't very late, the sun just setting. The gray cloth-like clouds were not in formation yet, still filtering in over the bay. It didn't look like it would rain for a few hours, so she thought she had enough time to make it there and back before the storm broke. She walked along the same tree-lined route Jennifer had driven, careful with her steps, watching for landmarks like the Hawthorne Hotel and the Salem Maritime National Historic Site. She didn't want to get lost walking home when she was still learning her way.

It was dark by the time she saw the old house waiting stoically along the road, more hidden behind oaks and shrubs than other homes in the neighborhood. Though the others were well lit outdoors, this one stayed dark. She wouldn't have known it was there if she hadn't already seen it. There were no lights on inside either, and it looked like no one was home, so she walked onto the lawn and pondered the old wooden structure, wondering what scenes it had seen and what stories it could tell. For such an old house it was well maintained. It looked like other historic buildings in the neighborhood dating from the seventeenth century, only this was no museum as the others were. This was someone's home.

She thought about the house she left behind in the Hollywood Hills, modern-looking, cookie-cutter, whitewashed stucco, one that looked light and airy on the outside but trembled inside with permanent distress from an unfortunate marriage. The morning before she left for Massachusetts she stood outside and memorized the place where she had lived for ten years, the way it peeked from a catty-corner on the curving road, the feathery bushes on either side, the waving palm trees behind, the border of blue and purple petunias lining the square front yard. As much as she loved the house itself the memories inside were too hard and it had been time to say good-bye. She moved to Salem with the certainty that she needed a fresh start, but now she was confronted with confusing thoughts about an odd psychic reading and a house she thought she knew.

At first glance the seventeenth-century wooden structure seemed dark, heavy, weighted down by an uncertain past. But the longer she studied it the more she decided that it was warmth and nostalgia she felt rather than age and decline. She still didn't see any movement or hear any sounds coming from inside, so she stepped closer to the front door, inspecting the diamond-paned windows, the wooden slats that made up the exterior walls, the ridge of the shingled roof, the two steep gables pointing upward to the moon in heaven. She walked around to the indented pendill and put her hand on the wood, listening, wondering if she could hear the house explain why it looked familiar to her. Then she stepped closer to the gnarled oak tree, touching the rasping bark, searching for some clue about why she would dream about this house. She watched the ghostly branches stretch toward the sky, each reaching for its own memory from the long history it had seen.

When the front door swung open it creaked and startled her. Though it was dark, Sarah saw a man standing skeleton-still in the shadows. He stared at her, his mouth open as if he were trying to speak though he stayed mute. She tried to make herself disappear behind the oak tree, not wishing to disturb anyone, afraid she had been trespassing. She decided she needed to say something to break the awkward silence.

"I'm sorry. I just wanted to look at the house."

She began to shiver, not from the nip of the autumn air, but from the feeling that she recognized him. But how could she know someone she hadn't seen before? What was she supposed to say to him—"Haven't I seen you somewhere before?" It was such a bad pick-up line. She couldn't explain why she thought the man or his house looked familiar, so she decided it would be best if she went home.

"Excuse me," she said. "I can see I've disturbed you. I'll leave."

As she turned toward the road she felt his hand on her arm. She didn't expect him to get to her so quickly from where he stood, and she didn't understand why he had to grip her so tightly. Finally, she could see him in the slim strings of moonlight, his blond hair, his handsome face. He was intense, needing something, wanting something, but she was afraid to guess what that might be.

He touched his hand to her cheek. "Lizzie. My Lizzie," he said. "You've come home to me." When Sarah stepped back he moved toward her, closing the space between them. "It's all right, Elizabeth. Everything is all right now. You're home."

"My name is Sarah."

He didn't seem to hear her. He kept his hand to her cheek, his skin cool, she thought, like the water at night when she walked near the shore, not cold as much as unheated. He was so taken by staring at her that she thought he must recognize his mistake, but he stayed calm, like mistaking one person for another was something he did every night. As she stared at him she noticed his eyes. In the silver moonlight he looked too pale, but his eyes were darker than a tornado in the night ocean sky. He continued staring at her, intent, desperate, as if he were hoping to see something in her that could not be there. She wanted to run away and not look back, but something kept her there, watching him, curious about him. Drawn to him.

"Are you James Wentworth?" she asked, trying to spark some recognition in him. "Jennifer Mandel said she knows you from the college. We drove past your house and I thought it was interesting so I came back to look. Please, just let me go and I'll leave."

There was a flash of light in his stormy night eyes. He let go of her arm and stepped away. "Oh my God," he said. "Yes, I am James Wentworth. I am so sorry." He dropped his face into his hands. "Oh my God," he said again. When he lifted his head he seemed as if nothing strange had passed between them, like a completely different man—rational, composed, thoughtful.

"I can see I've frightened you," James said. "Forgive me. I don't know what came over me." He walked closer to her, tentatively, as if he were afraid of scaring her again. He was inspecting her, searching her face, her hair, her hands. He leaned his face over her head, close to her hair, as if he smelled her. And then it started to rain.

"Will you come back?" he asked.

"Maybe."

That seemed to be the safest answer. Sarah turned toward the road, and when she looked back he was already by his door, watching her. Some part of her wanted to go back to him, brush his hair from his eyes, ask if he was all right, he seemed so very spent and broken. Then she felt the pull of him, as if he reached inside her and found her innermost secrets, the best and the worst of her, and yet he was still there. There was something in him, some longing, and she scolded herself for wanting to stay and discover its meaning. She needed to be far away from him so she walked, faster and faster, trying not to slip and slide in the slick, wet street, away from the old house from her dreams.

34

CHAPTER 5

Sarah avoided thinking about the beautiful strange man by the beautiful old house for most of the rest of the weekend. Monday night she was busy in the high-tech room in the library preparing for a seminar about how to access resources from off campus. Jennifer found her while she was setting up the Elmo machine.

"Need help?" Jennifer asked.

"No thanks," Sarah said. "I've got it."

Jennifer stood silently, watching Sarah fiddle with the wires connecting the Elmo to the projector. With a point, she directed Sarah's attention through the window that looked into the hallway. Sarah saw Denise, another librarian, straightening her short red dress and smoothing her hair as she walked past. Denise smiled when she saw she was being watched.

"She's leaving for her date with Wendell," Jennifer said.

"That can't be right. Wendell is a student aide."

"Exactly."

Sarah put her hand over her mouth to stop her laughter. "That isn't funny."

"I'm surprised none of the students have asked you out, Ms. Alexander."

"Please." Sarah used her hand as a stop sign like a police officer directing traffic. "No one is allowed to ask me out right now. Not for at least a year. I've decided. I can't think about another relationship right now."

"Even if you find someone great?"

Sarah flipped the switch on the Elmo and saw the logo of Salem State College, a blue sketch of the *Friendship*, on the white screen on the wall. "Not anyone," Sarah said. "Not now."

The smile slipped from Jennifer's face. "That's too bad," she said. She adjusted the lens on the projector so the logo was clearer. "So I heard you met James the other night. He teaches English here, did you know that? And he's cute too."

"Cute and scary. Maybe not scary. Intense might be a better word."

"Did he really frighten you?"

Sarah paused, watching the logo on the screen as she considered. "I wasn't sure if I was more frightened for myself or concerned for him. He seemed more upset than intimidating. He certainly is handsome." She paused because she wasn't sure if she wanted to share her next thought. But Jennifer was already her best friend in Salem, so she decided to trust her.

"I think he looks like the man in my dreams. I've never seen the man's face—it's always in the shadows—but when James first came out of his house I couldn't see his face either. I don't know. Maybe I'm losing my mind. Something about being in Witch City, I guess."

Jennifer watched Sarah with the same detective-like concentration her mother had. Then she turned her attention to the desks scattered haphazardly around the room, straightening them into five neat rows.

Sarah stared at the floor, consumed by thoughts of the other night. Her encounter with James stirred too many emotions at once: fear, concern, sympathy, attraction, but mainly disappointment in herself for finding him alluring at all.

"He was just confused," she said.

How else could she explain his sudden attachment to her? And as for her just as sudden attachment to him? It was not hard to see where her attraction came from. He was a beautiful-looking man, James Wentworth, and though he looked physically strong, there was some vulnerability there too. How else could he have shown his soul to a stranger? Even after he realized she was not who he thought she was, his soul was still out there, visible, and she felt it reach out and touch her with the aura of its warmth. She could feel it touching her even then.

When Jennifer finished pushing the desks around, she sat on a chair and gave Sarah her full attention. Sarah felt like she was supposed to say something, as if Jennifer wanted something from her. "He mistook me for someone else," Sarah said. "Elizabeth, he called her. When he realized he made a mistake he apologized."

"Did he tell you who Elizabeth was?"

Before Sarah could answer, he was there, James, standing outside the door, watching her through the window. His dark eyes were curious, wondering, though less intimidating under his wire-rimmed eyeglasses. She could feel his gaze piercing her as if he were trying to see through her, understand everything about her from the day she was born, through all her years on earth, until that very moment in the library. It was that same sense of being drawn toward him she felt in front of his house. If they hadn't been standing under the bright fluorescent lights in the library she might have been wary of him again.

He opened the door and walked into the room. "Hello, Sarah," he said. "Forgive me, I know we haven't been formally introduced. After the other night, I suppose it's hardly necessary."

Jennifer curtseyed to James, one foot behind the other, a caricature of courtesy. "Sarah Alexander, this is James Wentworth, Professor of English at our illustrious institution. Doctor Wentworth, this is Sarah Alexander, your new liaison for Humanities I studies." She winked at him. "That includes you."

"Yes, Jennifer, I know. That's why I came by. I need help locating some sources about John Keats, and I was hoping you could help me, Sarah."

"Of course," Sarah said. "Tell me what you need."

"That's right," said Jennifer. "Tell Sarah what you need. Or I can help you if Sarah doesn't want to. You weren't very nice to her the other night."

"I don't mind," Sarah said. And she didn't. Standing next to him, realizing how tall he was, noticing again how strong he seemed, she thought he was easier to be around in the light of the library than in front of his house in the dark and the rain. Jennifer nodded, smiling to herself as if she were in on her own conspiracy.

"I think Sarah has forgiven you for your transgression the other night. Isn't that right, Sarah?"

"Yes," Sarah said. "It was all just a misunderstanding."

"It was," James said, "but I frightened you and I'm sorry."

"Sarah is leaving for the night, Professor. Why don't you walk her home?"

Sarah liked the thought of being escorted by a handsome professor, a scholar of literature no less, but the memory of the other night flashed behind her eyes. She wondered which James would walk her home, the courteous, thoughtful one standing before her or the confused one who made her nervous. She looked at Jennifer, unsure what to say.

"It's okay," Jennifer said. "He doesn't bite."

James pushed his glasses back on his nose. "No," he said, "I don't bite."

Sarah knew, in her rational mind, that she shouldn't go anywhere with him after his erratic behavior, but, year or no year since her divorce, she felt drawn to him. She was curious about him more than anything, and this walk could allow her to begin to piece together the puzzle that was James Wentworth.

"All right," Sarah said.

James smiled. There was something about his smile Sarah loved instantly, as if it were her own smile, and she felt her own joy at seeing it. As they left campus they saw a black and white Salem Police car drive down Lafayette Street. On the doors it said Salem Police, The Witch City, Massachusetts, 1626, and in the center was a silhouette of a witch on a broomstick.

"I can't believe the witch is still the symbol for Salem," Sarah said. "Even *The Salem News* has a witch as its logo."

James let out a frustrated sigh. "Witches have become great commercial fodder here. Salem has become something of a gathering place for mystics, and some believe it's touched by the metaphysical and inhabited by supernatural beings." He smiled, a flash of amusement across his lips.

"My landlady insists Salem is haunted by ghosts," Sarah said. "She almost scared me out of living here, and I don't even believe in ghosts."

"Salem may change your mind."

"That's what she said."

From Lafayette Street they turned down Derby, then right on Washington Street until they were in the green expanse of Lappin Park. James pointed to a bronze statue sitting center in a paved opening surrounded by well-manicured lawns. "Have you seen that?" he asked.

They walked closer until Sarah saw a statue of Elizabeth Montgomery, who played the good witch Samantha on the television show *Bewitched*. The scene showed the show's logo, Samantha on a broomstick in front of a crescent moon. Sarah walked close enough to touch the smooth bronze.

"I should have brought my camera. I didn't know I was going sightseeing tonight."

"We can come back another night," James said. "What else would you like to see?"

Sarah felt herself blush hot along her jaw. He was already thinking about taking her walking another night, and she was embarrassed at how happy she was to hear it. She chided herself, repeating every reason she had about why she needed to be alone right now. It was too soon after her divorce. She didn't choose the right men—her marriage was proof enough of that. And this man, James, was beautiful, intelligent, a professor of her favorite subject (studying John Keats, her favorite poet, no less), and yet, as they walked in the cool Salem night, comforted by the sea breeze, he stood a distance away, as if he loved her company but didn't care much for anything else about her.

She saw him watching her, that curious expression again, so she pulled herself from her reverie and considered what else she wanted to see around town. They were close to her house at Lappin Park—she lived a few blocks down Washington Street, near Essex Street and the Salem Inn—but she wasn't ready to go home.

"I've been wanting to see the Salem Witch Museum," she said.

James stared at the half-moon in the sky. "The Salem Witch Museum," he said, as if he had never heard the name before. He stepped closer to her, inspecting her again the way he had in front of his house. She began to think she made a mistake walking home with him after all. She looked around, but there were plenty of people out that autumn night, dining at the restaurants and bars that populated the town. He must have realized he was making her nervous, she thought, because he took a step back, giving her space.

"They close at five," he said, "but I'd be happy to show you where it is."

They continued down Church Street, passing the Lyceum Bar and Grill with its brick walls and whitewashed Romanesque arches hanging over the windows, the white-potted topiaries in front. He stopped so she could get a better look.

"There are many people like your landlady who believe ghosts from the witch trials haunt Salem," he said. "Some believe that Bridget Bishop, one of the first women executed in 1692, haunts this very building."

Sarah stepped close to the brick wall and touched her hands to the rough exterior. A couple leaving the Lyceum smiled at her as they walked by, and she felt silly, as if they thought she was trying to sense any ghosts in the building. When she felt a spark of static—the same energy she felt when she touched her landlady—she pulled her hands away. She turned to James and he seemed somber, as he had in front of his house. She tried to lighten the mood.

"Do you believe ghosts from the witch trials haunt Salem?" she asked.

She meant to be light, friendly, even a little flirty with the handsome, blond, strong-looking professor. Her resolution to wait had slipped away into the static electricity in her hands. Even though she had said to Jennifer, less than an hour before, that she didn't want any man asking her out right now. Even though she had reasons not to flirt with any man. But suddenly here was James and all she could think about was how he was looking at her, as if he wanted to know her, or as if he already knew her, she couldn't tell. She had to admit, though she didn't want to, that she enjoyed his attention. She enjoyed sightseeing around Salem with him. Something, somewhere deep inside that was not logical, felt as if there were an invisible line reeling from him to her and back again, catching her and holding her to him. It wasn't a frightening sensation. This was a light, fluttery line, like silk thread.

As he watched her, his expression softened and he relaxed into an easy smile. Taking this as an invitation to come closer, she stepped near him and stood on her toes so she could see into his night-dark eyes, such a contrast to his pale complexion, like a black-white pattern in a painting. He stepped back too quickly, a man-sized jumping bean, and he turned to study the brick arches of the Lyceum as if he had never seen them.

"Yes," he said finally, "I believe that ghosts from the witch trials haunt Salem. I've never been more sure of it."

He opened his mouth to say more, but he shook his head and walked away at such a fast pace he left Sarah trailing behind. She didn't mind. She slowed her steps, hoping he'd disappear into the distance so she could slip down Washington Street and find her way home. Alone. She was being too foolish about this man, she decided. He was too unpredictable. Suddenly, he flipped the switch back to bright and slowed his long strides, waiting for her to catch up.

"There I go again," he said.

Sarah laughed, but it was a nervous laugh, tinged with low, hollow tones.

"Please," he said. He extended his arm, a courteous gesture from olden days when gentility was the norm, and again, despite her concerns, Sarah felt the invisible pull toward him. She slid her arm through his.

"There's a whole tourism industry in Salem centered around the metaphysical," he said, continuing their conversation as if they hadn't suffered an awkward moment. "There are tours guided by parapsychologists that are supposed to highlight places in the city haunted by the supernatural—ghosts, werewolves, vampires." Sarah saw that amused smile again, though it disappeared quickly. "Have you ever been to Danvers?" Sarah shook her head. "It used to be known as Salem Village, the epicenter of the witch hunt hysteria. There's a memorial there for the people executed in 1692."

"I'd like to see that. One of the reasons I came was because I was told I have an ancestor who died here during the witch trials. I wanted to find some information about her."

James stopped walking. He dropped Sarah's arm and stepped closer to her. "What was your ancestor's name?"

"I don't know."

He looked disappointed. "Perhaps you'll discover it through your research."

He extended his arm again, and again Sarah slid hers through. He slowed his pace, she quickened hers, and they shared a rhythm that matched her fluctuating heartbeat. First too fast, then too slow. It was, come to think of it, a lot like her night with James. First too hot, then too cold. Now it was heating up again. They were already at Salem Common, a nine-acre park used as public land to graze livestock in colonial times. They passed the Salem Visitor's Center, walked around Washington Square North, and there was the Salem Witch Museum, along with the imposing cloaked statue of Roger Conant, the man who first settled Salem, among America's oldest towns, in 1626.

The Salem Witch Museum was housed in a tall brick church with two castle-like protrusions on either side, a Gothic arch in the center of the building coming together at a point like two hands praying. Sarah didn't need to turn around to know James was watching her. He stepped so close she could feel him close to her hair. She kept her eyes fixed on the brick exterior of the museum.

"There are other museums around town you should visit if you want to learn about the witch hunts," he said. "The Witch Dungeon Museum on Lynde Street has actors performing scenes from the transcripts of the trials. There's a recreation of the dungeons where the accused witches were jailed—dark, horrid, illness-filled, rat-infested places. Abominations."

Sarah shuddered. She heard his words, they were simple enough, but she hardly understood him, as if he were speaking Russian suddenly, or Vietnamese. Above, the far-reaching sky was clear, no rain, and she realized that the sudden drops of water on her cheeks must have been from her eyes. The immediate emotion startled her. She didn't understand what brought it on. She brushed the wet away with the back of her hand and shook her head, trying to send the oppressiveness away. Then she felt like an ice storm had dropped and she was trapped and shivering. She crossed her arms over her chest in a poor attempt to keep the chill away. She looked around, from side to side and back again, expecting to see a monster jumping out of the shadows—a leering, laughing, pock-faced monster, grabbing her, locking her into heavy, suffocating chains, and dragging her away. She jumped in real fear. James touched her arm, and she backed away as if he were the monster. She didn't recognize him through her hallucinating eyes.

"Stop it!" she yelled. The shadows crept toward her, step by step, finding strength in the laughter of the wind. "Go away!" She held up her fists, the only weapons she had, meager though they were. She was ready to fight back if they tried to take her.

"Sarah?" James put his hands on her shoulders and shook her, gently. "Who needs to stop, Sarah? There's no one here but me." He brushed a dark curl from her mouth. He put his arms around her, pulled her close, and rested his chin on top of her head. When she didn't stop shaking, he held her tighter, whispering his sweet, strong voice into her ear, touching her skin with his words.

"It's all right, Sarah. I'm here. No one is going to hurt you."

She dropped her face into her hands, forcing herself to breathe slower, mindful of her heartbeat, staying in the fright until she could pull herself out of it. She had become good at pulling herself out of frights whenever she awoke from her nightmares.

"Sarah?"

She had yelled at James like he was the monster, but he was not the creature in the shadows. He was there helping her, the concern everywhere in the softness in his eyes. Suddenly she realized how he stood around her, his arms a circle keeping her safe inside and whatever it was that had frightened her out. She pushed herself closer to him, not wanting him to let her go. Then, as suddenly as the fear came on, it disappeared. She saw the chain-wielding monster recede with the shadows into the night, and she felt her lungs open and she could breathe again. James must have sensed that she had settled because he became business-like suddenly, dropping his arms and stepping away.

"Let me take you home," he said. He put a strong hand on the small of her back, guiding her down Washington Square.

They walked silently for some time, and after about a mile Sarah's muddled mind began to clear. She always felt like she was losing touch with reality when she had those incoherent moments, which were occurring more frequently since moving to Salem. As they walked toward Essex Street, she couldn't make up her mind about him. On the one hand he was so considerate, on the other hand prone to dark moods. She was more confused about him than she was when she left the library. And she had thought she would understand him better from this time alone.

Finally, he asked, "So how do you like living in Salem?"

It took her a moment to find her voice. "I'm getting used to it," she said. "It's so different than Los Angeles where everything is going a hundred miles an hour, the people, the cars, the lifestyle. Even Boston, where I'm from, is busier. It's an adjustment, small town life where it's quiet and slow. You can hear the birds sing here."

"Do you like to listen to the birds sing?"

"I do. Sometimes in the morning I make myself some tea and sit on the porch and listen to their songs. I've tried to whistle along, but they squawk and fly away. Wait..." Something Jennifer had said was tapping just outside her thoughts. She reached out to touch James's arm. He didn't pull away. "When you saw me the other night you called me Elizabeth."

"Yes," he said.

"Jennifer asked me if I knew who Elizabeth was." When James stared ahead, not at all forthcoming, she asked, "Who was she?"

"My wife."

"You're married."

Sarah struggled to keep her voice steady. There it was, that thing she sensed all along that must be wrong with him. Of course he didn't mean anything by his attention. He was being polite. She was new to Salem and he was showing her around. How could I be so foolish, she wondered? How could I mistake simple courtesy for attraction? She wanted to run away and hide behind the plentiful trees, taking her hot pink cheeks with her, not leaving until he was too far to see.

"Not anymore," he said, shaking his head. "Elizabeth died. It was a long time ago."

In the softness of his tone, in his stilted words, Sarah could hear his truth. Maybe that was why he was caring one moment and aloof the next. It would explain a lot, his love for his dead wife. But if he still loves Elizabeth, Sarah thought, then there's no room in his heart for me. Her first instinct had been right, she decided. She had no business being interested in any man right now.

He was going to say something, but by then they were at her house.

"This is me," she said.

She looked up at James's face and saw the longing in his eyes, such a contrast to his melancholy. With any other man, that look would have meant he wanted to kiss her. But James didn't kiss her. He stood there, looking into her house through the open door, then looking at her as if he wanted to say something but couldn't remember the words. Finally, he asked, "Would you like me to come in? I can stay awhile, just to make sure you're all right."

"I'm all right. It happens sometimes."

"What happens, Sarah?"

"Nothing. Really, I'm fine."

Though he didn't look like he wanted to leave, he nodded, said good night, and walked away. She stood outside her door, watching as he continued alone down the dark-night road. As handsome as he was, or as drawn to him as she felt, she did not know what to make of him. Once she was inside she drew a hot bath and lingered in the frothy bubbles. When she went to sleep she hoped for a happy dream. Please God, she thought as she lay her head on the pillow, tonight I need a happy dream.

I am at a wedding. It is a wedding from long ago, centuries past, a simple affair with family and a few close friends. This wedding looks nothing like the elaborate celebrations of today with the white taffeta dresses, multi-layered cakes, and lavishly decorated halls. At this ceremony the Pilgrim-looking guests are smiling, joyful even. Suddenly I realize, as my heart thuds a Baroque tune in my chest, that this must be my wedding. Everyone is beaming at me. My wedding outfit is simple, brown-colored silk, but I feel beautiful. Someone, the groom's father, is wealthy and has paid for the feast, which everyone is anxiously awaiting. They shan't be disappointed, the father of the groom says. From an imported punchbowl we shall drink spiced hard cider. We shall eat fish chowder, stewed oysters, parsley-flavored mussels, roasted game birds, red pickled eggs, succotash stew, bearberry jelly, and rye bread. There is maple syrup candy, nutmeats, and Indian pudding, too, he says, with dried plums and West Indian molasses. He smiles at me with the greatest warmth.

"The Indian pudding is always the best part of the meal, Daughter," he says. "You cannot end a meal without Indian pudding."

I also have my bride cake, a rich spice cake saturated in brandy and filled with dried fruits and nuts. I think people are happy we are getting married, but they are looking at the table with longing and I can tell by their distracted eyes that they are consumed with gluttonous thoughts of the food.

Finally, I see him, the man I am marrying. He is handsome as always, his fair hair spilling out beneath his hat, and though he is faceless I know he is smiling, happy this day has come. We are married with the beginning wispy traces of winter in the air, after the harvest months when our family and friends from the farms in the village can attend. The magistrate recites the wedding vows, and we say our part. I am wearing the ring my new husband has given me, and he is wearing mine. Rings are not a popular tradition at this time, and many where we live believe adorning oneself in any way is vain and sinful. Still, my new father-in-law has bought the thin bands for us because he wants all to see that his son and I are connected to one another forever.

"The round bands represent eternity," my new father-in-law says, "and your love will span eternity." His eyes are brimming with joy for his son and me. I think my new father-in-law is not only rich but also kind. I can see where my husband's empathy has come from.

"I shall never leave you ever," I say to my husband. He promises me the same.

I look at him and know he is generous and loving. I know that he would do anything for me, this day and always. I am blessed.

CHAPTER 6

James heard Jennifer's high-heeled footsteps tip-tap down the hall. Without knocking, she walked into his office, flipped on the lights, and closed the door behind her. He didn't look up, his pen poised over his notebook, his eyes glued to his book.

"Good evening, Professor. Haven't seen you in a few nights."

"Been busy. Midterms coming up, you know."

"You always have an excuse. You need to get out more."

He leaned his head against his chair. "People have been saying that a lot to me lately."

"It's true. You wall yourself off like you're a leper or something."

"Leper?" He mused over the word. "I never thought of it like that, though I suppose it's not far from the truth."

"You're not contagious."

"I can be."

Jennifer walked behind his chair and put her hands on his shoulders.

"Fishing for husband number three, I see." He smiled, somewhere between amused and perturbed, as he shrugged out from under her touch.

"As a matter of fact I am. Are you biting?"

"Me bite? I don't bite, remember? Besides, I'm too old for you."

"I'm thirty-four, so I'm older than you."

"That's a matter for debate."

She watched as he pulled his wire-frame eyeglasses from his shirt pocket, and she laughed when he put them on.

"Still going for the Clark Kent/Superman look, I see. I like it. It's sexy."

"Actually, I was going for the Professor Henry Jones/Indiana Jones look. I thought it was more appropriate."

James looked out the window at the heavy night sky, smelling the storm dropping from the east. The dark clouds matched his somber mood and he welcomed the rain. "Thanks for helping me find Amy," he said. "I didn't know what I was going to do after Drew moved away. It's been too long—I can't go back to doing things the old-fashioned way now."

"You and my family have known each other too long and you have done too much for us. You know we'll help you however we can."

"Your family helped me first. You always leave out that part of the story."

"We're just glad you're back in Salem. You've been away too long."

James still stared outside, lost somewhere in his thoughts. "Are you sure we can trust her?" he asked. "Amy, I mean. I know you wouldn't have asked her if you didn't think so, but you can never be too careful."

"You worry too much, James. I've known her family a long time and she's kept a lot of secrets for me. Her mother is in my coven. Everything is going to be fine."

Outside the raindrops splattered the window in a pattern of blots like a Rorschach test. He smiled when he realized the pattern he saw was long curls and full lips. Jennifer stood silently, leaning her hip against his desk, her arms crossed over her chest as she watched him.

He looked at the time on his cell phone and saw he had five minutes to get to class. He knew from his haphazard thoughts about Sarah that he would have trouble concentrating on the lecture that night. He stood from his desk and paced the ten short steps of his office, his eyes closed, his mind heavy. Since he walked Sarah home a few nights before he had been struggling to make sense of it all—what he had said, what she had said, what any of it meant, if anything. Yet no matter how hard he tried to understand, everything around him seemed confused. Even the familiar sights in his office, his desk, his computer, his books, looked foreign, like archaeological artifacts uncovered from some long-ago culture.

That beautiful dark-haired, sweet-eyed woman had managed to undo all the careful forgetting he had done. It had taken him years to get to the point where he didn't walk around feeling weighted down by the past. He had walled himself off from nearly everyone and everything, going from work to home and home to work, except for his occasional clandestine meetings with Amy, keeping busy so he wouldn't be consumed by his history. Now, since he had seen Sarah, he found himself sorting through the memories because he couldn't ignore them anymore. They were pinching him, pecking him, forcing him to pay attention. Now, he was flipping through them as though he were pasting them under their proper headings in a scrapbook—scenes he wanted to remember and others that were still too painful. If he were being honest he would admit that the memories were mostly good, only the bad were oh so very bad. He scolded himself for coming back when he should have stayed away. Forever. What was he looking for? His wife hadn't been there for a long time and she wouldn't ever be there again. He told himself he should sell the house to the Salem Historical Society and leave. Forever. But he could still feel her in the pots and pans lining the kitchen shelves, in the furnishings in the great room, in their bed. And though he knew he shouldn't come back to Salem, he did. As long as he felt connected to her there he would return whenever he could. And now there was Sarah, and he didn't know what to do about her.

He thought about the first moment he saw her. He hadn't expected anything out of the ordinary that night, but he awoke with a start, pinpointing her quick, light footsteps near his front door. Usually his neighbors stayed away since they thought his wooden gabled house was haunted. And in its way it was. He heard the dry crunch of autumn leaves, so he pulled aside the curtains, raised the blinds, and focused on the shadows outside. When he saw her he thought he was dreaming. He blinked and rubbed his eyes, expecting her specter to vanish, but she was still there. Only she was not a ghost or a phantom meant to haunt him. She was human, and she looked exactly as he remembered with her dark curls, her chocolate-brown eyes, her thoughtful expression, the full lips he wanted to kiss whenever he looked at her...

"She's so like Elizabeth," he said.

Jennifer sighed. "I know you miss her, but you need to accept the fact that she's gone. It's been a long time."

James grabbed his keys and his book bag. He stopped with his hand on the doorknob. "I know this sounds crazy, but it's her voice, her face, her hair. Everything about her is the same. Even the way she looks at me. And she became so frightened after I told her about the Witch Dungeon Museum."

"But that's just it. You keep scaring her. The last thing any girl needs is to have a hungry old fart like you jumping out from the shadows of a creepy house. Or telling scary stories while walking her home in the dark. You need to play nice if you want to get to know her."

"I'm not hungry, and my house isn't creepy."

"But you are old."

Jennifer walked to the window. She stood there awhile, not speaking, watching the watery Rorschach blots hit and slide from the glass.

"Did Sarah tell you why she wanted to see your house?" she asked.

"I don't think so."

"You should ask her."

"But you know." James put his hands on Jennifer's shoulders and turned her to face him. The sound of the rain made a quick-time tapping, matching his impatience for the information he guessed she knew. "Tell me."

"She said your house looks like the house she's been dreaming about."

"She dreams about my house?"

"And a man."

"What man?" He felt the blood under his skin quicken. "What man, Jennifer?"

"She wouldn't say."

James grunted in frustration. He locked his office door, and Jennifer followed him into the hallway. He walked to the elevator, pressed the down button, and waited.

"You should tell her," Jennifer said.

The elevator dinged, the door opened, and they stepped inside. He waited for the door to close before he spoke.

"I'm not telling her anything. She's scared enough of me as it is. I don't think I made a very good first impression. Or a good second impression, for that matter."

"I'll talk to her tomorrow," Jennifer said. "I'll tell her."

"No!" He said it with such force the steel elevator walls rattled like an earthquake had shaken Salem. He dropped his voice to a firm whisper. "It'll frighten her too much, especially after the way I treated her."

"You should give her more credit than that. I told her I was a witch a few days after I met her and she didn't mind."

"You didn't tell her everything."

"I told her enough. She needs to know, especially if you want to get to know her."

"She doesn't need to know."

When the doors opened onto the first floor, James brushed past Jennifer, out of the library, across Rainbow Terrace and College Drive to the North Campus where his classes were held in Meier Hall. Somehow, despite his internal turmoil over Sarah, he managed to talk coherently about William Wordsworth and his 1804 poem "Intimations of Immortality." He was amused by the title, and the theme, that age causes man to lose touch with the divine. He didn't tell his students how true that might really be.

CHAPTER 7

The next night James found Sarah in the library, huddled over one of the study desks, a stack of books beside her. She was so intent on her reading she didn't notice him when he pulled out a chair and sat down.

"Hello, Sarah," he said.

Her head jerked up and her mouth opened. As he looked at her lips all he could think about was how much he wanted to kiss her, but she didn't look like she wanted to be kissed just then. He pressed the idea aside, though he didn't want to.

"Jennifer can help you," she said, turning back to her book. "I'm on my break."

"I don't need help. I just wanted to say hello."

Sarah smiled. It was the same smile he remembered, full, soft, joyful. Again, those lips. She leaned back in her chair and watched him, studying him, as if she were trying to decide which James she was going to see that night, the calm, courteous one or the one who jumped out from the shadows. Her face softened and she didn't seem annoyed, so he hoped she had settled on the first possibility.

"Hello," she said.

"What are you reading?"

Her hand went to her cheek and she shook her head. "About the Salem Witch Trials. They really were dreadful, weren't they?"

He glanced at the book over her shoulder. "I know a lot about that time. Let me help you."

She looked at him, her chocolate-brown eyes taut in concentration, staring into his, as if she were trying to see his whole truth. But he didn't want her to see his whole truth. He wanted to be near her too much. He had to strike a balance, appearing available without giving everything away. He didn't want her to run from him.

"All right," she said.

He picked a book from the stack and flipped through the pages. "Why don't you start by telling me what you already know."

"I've only just started reading. I know they were about false accusations."

"Madness. The Salem Witch Trials were about madness."

His fists clenched and his jaw tightened. He made a conscious effort to relax his muscles so he wouldn't appear tense and make her nervous again. He reminded himself to breathe.

"Madness can take many forms," he said, "and each one stems from fear. Madness implies that things are abnormal, and if things are abnormal then you cannot predict what will happen no matter how hard you try. When madness consumes everyone everywhere there is nowhere to go to find sanity."

He looked at her, worried about her reaction, afraid again he had said too much, but she didn't seem concerned. Instead, he thought he saw a glimmer of something long forgotten in her dark, wondering eyes. Or perhaps he only wanted to see it there.

"But how did they start?" She leaned toward him, and he had to struggle to stay focused while enveloped in her sweet scent—strawberries and cream. He couldn't get close enough. He pulled his chair forward until it was touching hers, and he turned his head so his mouth was near her ear. He could have sat that way all night. If only they were talking about something else. But he had offered the information, and she wanted to know, so he was compelled to tell her.

"During the 1630s over fifteen thousand Puritans journeyed from England to the Massachusetts Bay Colony, a time known as the Great Migration. The Puritans who settled Salem were a stern, sober, complicated people who believed in conformity, the Bible, and God, in that order. When they brought their strict Calvinist religion to the colonies they also brought their hatred for witches. They believed in original sin, certain they were born sinful, and they were consumed with worry over the state of their souls. They believed in Predestination, where God decided if you were saved or damned before you were born. Their only hope was to live a pious life and pray that God's decision would swing their way in the end. It was troublesome for them, not knowing if they were saved. When Judgment Day came they wanted eternal salvation as a reward for their earthly toil and trouble. It was hard to live here..." He waited for the words to straighten themselves out in his mind. "It was hard for those who didn't share their strict religious views."

Sarah sat upright, her hands in her lap, her breath coming in shallow bursts. She looked like a child enthralled by a bedtime story. He was distracted by a consuming waft of strawberries and cream, and he leaned even closer.

"But the accusations." She stuttered her words, as if she couldn't articulate her thoughts. "How can people turn on each other that way?"

"The madness began the way all madness begins, with something unsettling that needs explanation. Samuel Parris's parishioners were unhappy with him as the minister of the church in Salem Village, and they refused to pay their local taxes, the funds from which he received his salary. Suddenly he was giving sermons citing how the Devil was infecting Salem, telling everyone they must pray for an end to the evil here. Around this time his nine-year-old daughter, Betty, with her cousin, Abigail Williams, and her friend, Ann Putnam, spent their days listening to mystic-filled tales told by Tituba, a slave the Parrises brought with them from Barbados. Tituba told the girls about witchery, fortune-telling, and magic spells, and afterwards the girls had convulsive fits. The only diagnosis the doctor offered was witchcraft."

"The girls must have been playing a joke," Sarah said. "Or maybe they were put up to it by Parris himself. After all, he was probably afraid of losing his job."

"The girls were coerced into naming their demonic tormentors, and they named women who were outcasts, women who didn't fit into the norms of Salem society. Women who posed a threat to the Puritan demand for conformity. They named Sarah Good, a lame, homeless woman who begged door-to-door with her children. If she were refused alms she'd leave muttering what some called a curse, and her curses were blamed for the death of some livestock one year. They named Sarah Osburn, who married her servant and didn't attend church, scandalous behaviors then. They also named Tituba herself. After Parris whipped her, a torn, bleeding Tituba confessed to being a witch."

"I read about that." Sarah took a book from the stack, flipped to the index, then turned the page and pointed to the passage. "'The Devil came to me and bid me serve him,' Tituba said."

James nodded. "Tituba spoke of demon creatures, black cats, green dogs, pewter-colored birds, and a white-haired man, a master wizard who made her sign the devil's book in her own blood. She said there were undiscovered witches lurking about whose sole goal was to destroy God-fearing people. Then the girls, Betty, Abigail, and Ann, began accusing others of being witches, and many applauded them. It was up to the good people of Salem to destroy the witches because their souls wouldn't be safe until Satan was defeated, they said. God must triumph here. After all, battles with the natives raged just miles away, and many lived in fear of an attack. There had been a smallpox epidemic a while before. God must be angry with us, they said. It's our independent spirit He's angry with. We are to be good. We are to conform and to follow. The accusations unleashed hysteria, which became fear, which became paranoia. That was the true madness, there, in the witch hunts. People began to accuse others of witchcraft because they didn't like them, because they wanted attention, because they wanted retribution for some slight they felt, because they wanted the land the accused lived on, just because..."

He couldn't go on. Speaking about it felt uncomfortable, painful, like old clothes too small to fit, but you lay on the bed, zipper up anyway, and walk around with a pinching ache. He had to shake himself back into that moment in the library with Sarah. He stood up, walked to the stacks, pulled a few random volumes off the shelves, flipped through them, put them back. He turned to Sarah, saw her waiting, her face soft, her smile easy. He could have looked at her all night.

"There you are, Sarah!"

Jennifer came around the corner, and when she saw Sarah and James together she smiled that conspiratorial grin that was becoming her trademark. "I didn't mean to disturb you two. I've been waiting to go on my break, but I couldn't go until you came back, Sarah."

"I'm sorry, Jen. James was telling me about the Salem Witch Trials and I lost track of time."

Jennifer turned to James. "Was he?"

James ignored Jennifer. He gathered Sarah's stack of books and walked her to the librarians's desk, setting the books on the shelf where she pointed. When he saw the time he realized he didn't want to leave.

"I have to go to class," he said. "Will you be here after?"

"I work until closing tonight," Sarah said.

"See you later then?"

He waited. He thought it took her longer than it should have to answer. Finally, she smiled.

"Yes. See you later."

He left the library feeling lighter than he had in oh so many years. He hoped, as they talked, that he felt Sarah softening toward him. He had to remember to keep control. Always keep control. He was determined. Sarah would not know. When you have a secret to keep, you must keep it. There is no other way.

After his first class that night he saw Timothy waiting for him. Timothy was leaning against the back wall with his arms crossed over his chest, waiting while James finished writing the assignment for his next class on the whiteboard. James didn't know what to do about the boy who looked too young to be in college. So far, Timothy had managed to avoid attention because he stayed so quiet. But that night he looked upset, and James braced himself.

"What is it, Timothy? Having problems with your paper on *Great Expectations*?"

Timothy shook his head, the frustration obvious in his close-pulled lips and flat-black eyes. He paced the room. "Silly? Is that always going to be everyone's reaction? Or evil? Or villains?"

"Are you still thinking about that?"

"I'm tired of having to hide."

James watched the students in the hallway wandering past the open door. "You have to be more careful than that," he said.

"I have another class coming in. Besides, you should be less afraid of what people are saying and more afraid of what they're doing."

"But we're real. We're more real because we last forever."

"Forever is a long time. It's a difficult concept for people who have only decades, perhaps a century at best."

"But that doesn't make us silly."

"No, it doesn't make us silly, but people aren't ready to know. Bad things happen when people are confronted with things they don't understand."

"So we have to keep hiding?"

"Yes, for the foreseeable future we have to keep hiding."

"Fine."

James had seen that sour expression before. They had had that conversation countless times.

"Timothy, the only certainly I have ever had in this existence is the need to keep moving. I look like I'm thirty so I can settle somewhere for maybe ten years since I might be able to pass for a young-looking forty, but then it's time for me to leave."

"That's my point. I like living here and I don't want to move. It's not fair to Howard to have to leave because of me."

"Howard knew what he was getting into when he became your guardian, and he loves you for who you are the way you love him for who he is no matter what night of the month it is. I've found it's best to move on before anyone notices anything odd about me and pulls together an angry mob to chase me away with torches and pitchforks."

"People don't use torches and pitchforks any more."

"I know. These days their weapons are more far-reaching and dangerous. You don't know how people can overreact when they don't understand something. You haven't lived it like I have."

"You've been shuffling from here to there and back again for so long. Aren't you sick of it?"

"Yes, but it can't be helped. That's the way it needs to be."

Timothy huffed and left at a flash, slamming the door so hard it nearly swung off its hinges. The students walking into the room hardly seemed to notice, and James taught his next class, which went by in a blur. When his last class was over he made his way back to the library, up to his office to grab a pen and some papers that needed grading, then down to the main floor. He stepped out of the elevator, smelled the air, and caught her scent. Strawberries and cream. He went around to the stacks and saw her, Sarah, pulling books from a wheelie cart, checking Dewey decimal numbers on the spines, sliding them into their slots on the shelves. Her eyes brightened when she saw him. He hoped that meant she was happy to see him.

"Hello again," she said.

"Have you read more about the witch trials?" he asked.

"I haven't had time. How was class?"

"It was...interesting." He wouldn't tell her how he hardly remembered his classes because he was too consumed by thoughts of her. He certainly wouldn't tell her about Timothy's angst. He chose a desk nearby, sat down, and spread his papers out in front of him. He picked one from the pile and began reading and making comments in the margins.

She peered over his shoulder to see what he was doing. "Wouldn't you rather work in your office?" she asked.

"I prefer working down here sometimes. During the night it can seem like everyone in Salem is sleeping, and I like that even after dark the library bustles with energy. There's life in here."

"There's life in here during the day too. You should try it some time."

"Perhaps I should."

He glanced across to the opposite end of the library where Jennifer stamped books behind the librarians's desk. As she worked, a man James didn't recognize waited to speak to her. He was a short, nervous-looking fellow in a suit and tie, uncomfortably formal among the relaxed young college crowd wearing t-shirts and blue jeans, even more formal than the professors who were also mostly the t-shirt and blue jeans type.

"Excuse me," the man said. He handed her a business card which she looked over.

"Can I help you, Mr. Hempel?" she asked.

"I'm looking for a professor named Wentworth. I was just by his office and one of his students said she saw him in here. Is he around somewhere?"

"Is there a problem?"

James looked away, not wanting Sarah, the man, or anyone else noticing that he could understand their conversation though he was too far away. He didn't know the man and couldn't guess what he might want, though he felt some foreboding at the man's sudden intrusion into his private world. James watched Sarah, who had turned back to shelving books, and he hoped she would finish soon.

"Nothing like that," the man said. "I'm writing an article for the *Salem News* and I wanted to ask him a few questions. Just looking for a source."

"That's Professor Wentworth across there," Jennifer said. "The blond man in the blue shirt wearing glasses."

James resumed writing, his gaze focused on the paper. He didn't turn around when he heard heavy, plodding footsteps behind him.

"Professor Wentworth? James Wentworth?"

James looked at the man. "Yes?" he said.

The man handed him a business card that read *Kenneth Hempel, Staff Writer, The Salem News*.

"How do you do, Professor. I wanted to ask a few questions for an article I'm writing. I hope you don't mind."

"No, not at all. Please," James gestured to an empty chair beside him, "sit down. What is your article about?"

"Supernatural happenings in Salem."

James laughed. "That's not particularly original, is it, Mr. Hempel? Supernatural happenings in Salem have been a topic of discussion for over three hundred years."

"But I have a unique angle. The stories I'm going to be telling are true."

James pushed his glasses back on his nose. "I'm sorry, but I don't know if I can help you. I teach literature. I can tell you anything you want to know about Dickens and Shakespeare, even Jane Austen or John Keats, but I'm afraid the supernatural is not my sphere. I'd be happy to help you get in touch with one of the religious studies professors here."

"It isn't specifically the supernatural I'm interested in. It's vampires."

"Vampires. Really."

James glanced at Sarah, who was whispering to a student. She didn't seem to notice them. He was grateful to the student and hoped the young man had a complicated question that would keep her busy awhile. At that moment, he wished, more than anything, that she would leave for the other side of the library, or home.

"That's right. I understand you know a lot about vampires."

"Where did you get that idea?"

"A trusted source."

James studied the reporter, his hands forming a triangle under his chin. He had to appear nonchalant, like this inquisition was the most natural conversation in the world.

"Well," he said, "I can discuss Bram Stoker's *Dracula* with you if you like. There's certainly a lot of vampire literature out there. Some of the books aren't half bad, even if it's not my favorite genre."

"I'm not interested in literary vampires, Professor. I'm interested in real vampires that walk the streets right here in Salem and probably all over the world."

James tried to see beneath the lines in the reporter's face, lines so deeply ingrained it was as if every smile the man ever had was forced across his lips. When James didn't see any clues there he wished he could read the man's mind. He pushed his glasses against his nose as he considered his reply.

"Vampires aren't real," he said. "They're legends, figments of people's dark imaginations."

"But you're wrong, Professor. Vampires are fact, not fiction. I'm sure of it."

"In that case you might want to try the Supernatural Tour here in Salem. I haven't taken it myself, too scary for me, but it's supposed to go around the creepy corners of town searching for ghosts and talking about vampire folklore, explaining how early New England settlers tried to stop the undead from haunting them. They say people run screaming from it because they're so scared. Seems to be just what you're looking for. Maybe you'll see a real vampire."

"Maybe I will. So you're new to Salem?"

James heard the rattling of the wheels as Sarah pushed the book cart to the shelf directly behind him. She didn't seem to be listening, busy as she was, but he wasn't sure. He had to fight the urge to grab Hempel by the neck with his teeth and dump him out the window. Instead, he answered the reporter's questions as quickly as he could, hoping that the nuisance would then leave him alone. Forever would be nice.

"You could say that," James said.

"Where were you before you came here?"

"Washington State."

"Were you with family?"

"I have friends there."

"How long were you there?"

"A few years."

"And you went to Harvard, is that correct?"

"Yes."

Hempel nodded as he took a pen from his briefcase, pulled out a yellow legal pad, and jotted some notes. "When did you graduate? You look rather young to be such a distinguished professor."

James looked at Sarah, who had stopped working and was now watching them through the open slot on the shelf. How much she had heard, he couldn't guess from her blank expression. From the corner of his eye he saw Hempel watching him watch Sarah, and the reporter jotted something on his notepad.

"I don't know how distinguished I am," James said. "I teach at a small state college."

"But you also have a degree from Cambridge. Didn't you teach there as well?"

"I'm hardly the only person to ever have the name James Wentworth." It wasn't the greatest comeback, but James was at a loss, concerned about what this man knew.

"But you do have a degree from Cambridge, and you have taught there."

James let out a frustrated sigh. "I've never been to England, so I've never been to Cambridge. I'm sorry, but is your article about vampires or about me?"

Hempel stood up and extended his hand. "Nice to meet you, Professor. We'll talk again."

James shook his head. "I have a cold. I don't want to get you sick."

"It's all right," Hempel said, keeping his hand out. "I have a cold too."

James didn't want to be more conspicuous, so he shook the reporter's hand as quickly as he could. But the man wouldn't let go. Hempel pulled James's fingers close to his face and inspected them as if he had never seen another man's hand before.

"You should put some gloves on, Professor. You're cold as the dead."

Kenneth Hempel smiled as he left.

When the reporter disappeared past the metal detectors, Sarah walked to James. He braced himself, concerned about what she might have overheard.

"Who was that?" she asked.

"Someone from the newspaper. He wanted some information for an article he's writing, but I wasn't able to help him."

Sarah looked in the direction Hempel had gone. "He seemed kind of creepy."

James laughed. "I thought so too."

He said good night to Sarah and went up to his office, giving Hempel time to leave campus. He didn't want to run into the reporter on his way home. As he sat at his desk he worried about what the reporter would do if he knew the truth. And he worried about how Sarah would feel if she knew. But more than Kenneth Hempel, even more than Sarah, he was troubled by the madness he knew would infect everyone everywhere if his secret went public. If make-believe suddenly became real-life. When the library was deserted and everyone else had gone home, when the campus was dark and the parking lot empty, when a hint of dawn glowed the thinnest ribbon of gold on the horizon, James made his way home alone and anxious in the darkness.

CHAPTER 8

Two weeks later it was Halloween, the most important holiday in Salem, a month-long celebration. The streets were closed to motor traffic, and James had to walk around the barriers to find his way to Pickering Wharf and the Witches Lair. When he passed The House of the Seven Gables he saw an audience watching a reenactment of Nathaniel Hawthorne's story. He passed a pumpkin festival where small children held their oddly carved treasures over their heads, and he shook his head in amusement when he saw a walking tour, a class on how to hunt for ghosts and vampires. He passed that group quickly, not wishing to be bagged as a prized game that night. The smell of sweet and salt—candied apples, sugar-spun cotton candy, popcorn, and the sea—filled the air. He enjoyed being outside in the crisp autumn night, watching the children point and laugh and eat and run while a parade of witches, ghouls, and superheroes roamed the roads. He knew the Witches Lair would be open late. It was a good time for sales, Jennifer had told him, since the tourists get bored when everything else around town closes at five. But James didn't care anything about the tourists or the costumes or the sales at the Witches Lair. He knew Sarah would be there. He was going to see Sarah.

Once at the shop he walked inside, glanced around for Jennifer, then sat behind the counter. He watched the people stream in and out, smiled at the happy children, flipped through some books on casting spells. He spotted Olivia, dressed as Raggedy Ann and moving around helping customers. Then he saw the silver crosses displayed in a basket by the cash register. He picked one up and held it close to his face. He was still studying it when Jennifer tip-tapped behind him.

"You mean the crosses don't work? I thought I could finally do away with you."

"You're thinking about werewolves. Or maybe that's silver bullets with werewolves. Most of it is such nonsense." He shook his head as he looked at Jennifer. "You're dressed as Glinda the Good Witch? I'm not sure you picked the right costume. I was thinking more like the Wicked Witch of the West for you."

Jennifer curtseyed, touching her star wand to her gold crown. Her iridescent pink dress was so wide at the waist she hardly fit behind the counter.

"Oh no, Professor. There are only good witches in Salem. And I'm at your service. I'll grant you three wishes."

"I don't think you could grant my wishes. They're beyond even your magical capacity to help."

"I wouldn't bet on that."

"Who do you think I am, Dorothy from Kansas?"

Jennifer pointed her wand at the door. "I guess that makes Timothy Toto."

James watched Timothy walk into the store. The boy looked pleased with himself as he stopped in front of the counter and threw his black cape behind his shoulders. From his tuxedo shirt to his black shoes, his brown hair run through with black dye, red streaks dripping from his lips, there was no mistaking his costume.

"You're dressed as Dracula?" James asked.

Timothy flashed his fake fangs. "What do you think?"

"I think you've lost your mind."

"It's not very original," said Jennifer.

"Not any less original than your costume," Timothy said. "Come on you two—it's the one night a year I can be proud of what I am and show the whole world. I'm a vampire, everyone! A real live vampire!"

The customers walking by, an older couple wearing orange 'This is My Costume' t-shirts, probably tourists, their cameras giving them away, looked nervously at Timothy and stepped aside to study the prayer beads. They only looked back once to see what the vampire boy was doing.

"Where's your costume, James?" Timothy gestured at James's street clothes, his gray argyle sweater, blue jeans, black Converse shoes. "It's Halloween. You're supposed to dress up."

"I'm a little old for dressing up."

Suddenly James smelled it, the fresh human blood, and he sniffed the air to center in on the source. He was afraid the temptation of oozing human blood would be too much for Timothy, who was still new to that life. Then he leaned close to the boy's face and barked in frustration. The blood was dripping from the sides of Timothy's mouth as part of his costume.

"You have human blood on your face?" James whispered.

Timothy shrugged. "It was all I had."

James grabbed the collar of Timothy's shiny black cape and pulled him close. "Go wash that off before someone sees it's human blood. Are you trying to get caught?"

"Relax, James. I'm having some fun. You should try it some time."

Timothy wiped the blood from the sides of his mouth with his hand and licked his fingers. He laughed as he left the store.

James turned to Jennifer. "You said you'd grant me three wishes. Can you make Timothy disappear?"

"Sorry. I'm only allowed to use my spells for good."

"Too bad."

James looked around at the faces, some painted, some masked, all smiling, laughing, happy with the sugar-induced candy high. He walked to the door, propped open by a black cauldron smoking from the dry ice inside, and peered up and down the wharf.

"She'll be here," Jennifer said.

He walked back into the store, heading for his place behind the counter where he had a clear view of everyone coming and going. He wanted a whiff of strawberries and cream as soon as Sarah stepped onto the wharf. He wanted to see her face as soon as she arrived at the shop. Instead, he heard the heavy, plodding footsteps he recognized from the library, and he knew Kenneth Hempel stood behind him. He tried to silently will the reporter to go away and leave him alone, forever, but Hempel still stood there. Jennifer nodded when she saw the reporter in her mother's store.

"Good evening, Mr. Hempel," she said. "Welcome to the Witches Lair. I see we have yet another Dracula here this evening. Have you come to suck my blood?"

"Good evening, Miss...?"

"Mandel. Jennifer Mandel."

"It's a pleasure to see you again, Miss Mandel. And Professor, how unexpected to see you here this evening. Not in costume I see."

James turned to face the reporter. "Not this year, I'm afraid. I like your costume though. There have certainly been a lot of Draculas here tonight."

"I'm not Dracula. I'm Van Helsing." Hempel grabbed at his belt and unsheathed a wooden cross that had been whittled into a stake. He held it an inch from James's face. "Van Helsing the Vampire Slayer."

As James stared at the wooden stake he wondered if he would have to kill Hempel right there in front of everyone in the store. If it came to a test of strength between Hempel and James, James would win. That was one of the first lessons he learned on his earliest hunts—he had the oppressive power to overwhelm his prey. After a tense moment, James realized that Hempel didn't intend to pierce him that night, at least not with the stake.

"A rather convincing costume, Professor Wentworth, don't you think?"

James kept his eyes on the stake as he spoke. "I believe you're referring to Buffy."

"Excuse me?"

"Buffy is known as a vampire slayer. Van Helsing is known as a vampire hunter. Even so..."

"But aren't they the same thing?" Hempel's brow furrowed as he considered. "Come to think of it, hunting and slaying are not the same thing. You don't need to do one to do the other. Doctor Van Helsing was very methodical in the way he hunted Count Dracula, wasn't he? He gathered the evidence and considered the facts before he made his plans to uncover his prey. He even followed the wicked vampire back to his home to capture him, though he left the actual slaying of the cursed monster to others more capable of such things. Yes, I am Van Helsing after all."

James knew Hempel wasn't entirely right about Van Helsing, but he didn't dare say so. The reporter stepped closer and smiled the same self-satisfied grin James had seen in the library. "You see," Hempel said, "you needn't fear me, Professor. I don't want to slay vampires. I want to hunt them, flush them out into the open. People need to be warned because some of them are a danger to humanity. But you're right—I am more of a hunter than a slayer. Thank you for clarifying that point."

Jennifer walked around the counter and put her arm around Hempel's shoulders.

"If you'll follow me, Doctor Van Helsing, I believe I may be able to find a vampire or two for you around the shop. You won't need to do much hunting tonight."

She led him to a group of small children, each dressed as a ghost, a witch, or a vampire, and the children laughed when they saw the man with a wooden stake at his side. Hempel seemed charmed by them.

"My children are getting into their costumes so they can go trick-or-treating tonight," he said. "I'm on my way home now to escort them around town."

He pretended to chase the children through the store as they squealed with delight, and suddenly the stake he carried looked more like a toy than a weapon capable of killing someone in the store. Push a wooden stake against a man and he'll laugh because it won't hurt. The worst a human would suffer is an annoying splinter beneath the skin. Push a wooden stake against James and witness the blood-splattered gore one expects from the special effects of a low-budget horror film. At least that's what James had been told. He had never seen it himself, and he hoped he never would.

James watched Hempel as he played with the laughing children, and he was sad that, for some reason unknown to him, the reporter had taken it upon himself to expose James's well-guarded secret. Hempel seemed like a nice enough fellow, a family man who might not be a bad person exactly but someone with a serious vendetta. James was concerned about what Hempel knew, but he didn't pursue it any further that night with the Halloween-costumed crowds streaming in and out. He wanted the problem to disappear.

He saw Jennifer watching Hempel and recognized her petulant face, the one that let everyone know she was agitated. The more she watched Hempel the more set her features became. When Hempel turned away, she snapped her fingers and the potion bottles shattered into glass and dust. The reporter glanced nervously around to see what had happened.

"I thought you had to wiggle your nose to do that," James whispered.

"That's on television."

From across the shop Olivia grunted in frustration. Unhappy at her daughter's blatant display of witchiness, her arms were crossed over her chest while her fingers tapped an agitated tune—the perfect picture of a perturbed mother. Jennifer shrugged.

Hempel, visibly upset by the exploding bottles, said good night as he walked to the door. Jennifer escorted him, her arm around his shoulders, smiling to his face.

"Good night," she said, brushing the bottle dust from his cape. "I'm so sorry. I don't know how that happened."

She stood by the smoking cauldron, watching until he was gone. When he was safely down the wharf, she joined James by the counter.

"He needs to be turned into a toad," she said, "or a rat."

"You said you could only use your spells for good."

"It would be a good thing to make that odious little man run through the sewers for the rest of his life. Are you all right?"

"I'm fine. He didn't touch me."

"So that one isn't a legend."

"That one isn't a legend."

"You can be killed by a wooden stake?"

"I can."

"But you live in a wood house."

"I live in it, Jen, I'm not being pierced by it. If I were pierced by the wood that would be a different story."

"Different how?"

"My blood would gush where the stake pierced me, and I could die from the loss of blood alone. Or it could make me too weak to fight, and if I were weak and someone decapitated me..."

"All right, James, enough." Jennifer held her hand to her mouth and squeezed her eyes.

"What are you doing?"

"I'm making the horror movie I'm seeing in my mind disappear." When she settled herself, she asked, "What do you think Hempel wants?"

"To be the one who uncovers the undead in Witch City. What recognition he would receive if he were the first to prove that such beings exist. Good enough for the Pulitzer Prize."

"I think you should talk to him," Timothy said. The boy had come back into the store without his cape, his shirtsleeves rolled up, his face still streaked with blood. "I think I should talk to him. I want to tell him the truth."

"You will do no such thing," James said. "It's too dangerous."

Timothy's dilated-black eyes widened. "I don't think it would be as bad as you think. I think people would understand."

James scoffed aloud. "You think people would understand? I can tell you a story about how little people understand."

Timothy could be a foolish boy, and the foolish are the first to act foolhardy. James knew Timothy was young, especially for their kind, but the boy was stubborn in his wish to be free of hiding and James needed to make him see the dangerous road he wanted to travel. Timothy would unleash not his own personal freedom but havoc and fear, leaving destruction and desperation behind. He had to understand.

James grabbed Timothy's collar and dragged him to the storage room. When they were alone inside, James threw the boy with more strength than he intended and Timothy crashed into the shelves of candles and incense, knocking everything to the floor with a thud that sounded like it would reverberate across Massachusetts. It took every ounce of restraint James had within him to not tear Timothy limb from limb. He was so angry he was tempted to find the Doctor Van Helsing wandering the streets of Salem and borrow his stake. That is all it would take, one push of the wood into Timothy's preternatural skin and the promise of immortality would be gone in an instant. James struggled to settle himself, to count to twenty, to think about happier days, to find compassion for the boy who only wanted to be free of hiding every night forever. Finally, James was calm enough to speak.

"People will not understand. You will start a vampire hunt if you confess to Kenneth Hempel."

"You're so old fashioned. You think it's still the seventeenth century, but things are different now. You don't know anything about people today."

James sat on an overturned shelf and wondered how to explain what he knew to the stubborn boy.

"Listen to me, Timothy. You and I and the others like us, we're not the only ones of our kind. As long as there are some who hunt we can never be out in the open. As long as there are some people need to fear, then all of us must hide. If they think one of us is evil, then they'll think all of us are evil, just like Levon said. And how can we convince them otherwise? Once people make up their minds about something it's almost impossible to make them think differently."

"That's not true."

"It is. People think in stereotypes. They don't see shades of gray. They see extremes, black or white, yes or no, right or wrong, hero or villain. And they'll do whatever they need to do to prove that they're right even if they're wrong. People don't like to be wrong. They're afraid of what they don't understand, and they won't understand us. I hardly understand us and I've been this way a long time. Far longer than you. I've seen things you cannot begin to imagine. Do you have any idea how many people have suffered because of the madness of a few? There was suffering right here in Salem."

Timothy stood up from the scattered mess. He picked the coin belts up from the floor, folded them, and put them back on the only shelf left standing. "Are you talking about the Salem Witch Trials?" he asked.

"I am."

"Your wife died then, didn't she?"

"She did."

"Was she one of the people who were hanged?"

As much as James didn't want to dwell on those memories, he felt he had no choice. Timothy needed to know the consequences of madness.

"No," James said. "She died in jail before she went to trial. They postponed her trial twice. At the time I thought the later court dates would help because there were several women from the village willing to testify against her and swear that our unborn baby was the spawn of Satan. I was naïve about human nature then. I thought if I could speak to them I could help them see the error of their lies and convince them to speak the truth about my wife. Yet even after I pleaded with them they insisted they had seen Elizabeth consorting with the Devil. I was terrified. I knew that if my wife were convicted of witchcraft she would be hung, and I took no comfort knowing that the magistrates would stay her execution until after our baby was born. They said they were forbidden to harm the innocent unborn child." James laughed a wicked laugh. "They didn't want to harm an innocent baby, but they had no qualms harming an innocent woman. After Elizabeth was arrested they kept her in irons in a rat-infested dungeon, and there she died. The last time I saw her was the day she was arrested."

"Were you turned then?"

James felt the weight of his creation story heavy on his shoulders. For each of their kind, their creation story wasn't mythic or grand. It wasn't a holiday to celebrate, like a birthday or an anniversary. James didn't eat cake and burn candles to commemorate it. It was the tale of the night he died—one of the hardest parts to remember.

"No," he said. "I wasn't turned when she was arrested. I wasn't turned until after she had been in jail a fortnight, I mean, about two weeks. She never knew me this way."

"Who turned you?"

"I don't know. I can remember his face, but I never knew his name. I haven't seen him since."

James paced the storage room, jogging himself into remembering the scene. Some memories were so difficult to see clearly, either because he couldn't or didn't want to. It was so long ago.

"After Elizabeth was arrested I'd go to the jail where she was being held. I pleaded with the magistrates in charge of the trials, self-important imbeciles who were pleased that now everyone would see the power they could wield. I tried to explain how it was all a mistake. My wife had no marks on her that would identify her as a witch. She never conjured spirits. She never sent her specter to harm anyone. I tried to find out who had accused her, but no one would answer me. They said it would all come out at her trial. They said there were even more witnesses than I knew of to corroborate the accusations. What other witnesses, I asked? But no one would say.

"They tried to confiscate everything we owned as they had done to others who were accused, but my father said it was his property so they left us our house and everything in it. People we knew signed their names to a petition stating they had never seen my wife in any act of witchcraft and we were faithful members of the church. But someone had accused her, someone weak and petty, and then others, women she considered her friends, people she trusted and loved, began corroborating the lies. Yes, they saw her use spells, they said. Yes, they saw her specter doing harm to others or consorting with Satan in the night."

"Who accused her?" Timothy asked. "Who would do such a thing?"

"I heard whisperings that it was her sister-in-law, her brother's wife, who made the first claims against her. She was an unpretty woman, her sister-in-law, bloated, spotted, and pale, with strings of black hair that flew out from under her white cap. The gray, swollen bags beneath her eyes held years of untold scorn, or an excess of ale. I knew she was jealous because Elizabeth was happy with me while she was unhappily married to Elizabeth's stubborn, overbearing brother. I suspected it was true, that she was the one who made the first claims, but I never knew for certain. Then Elizabeth was moved to the jail in Boston."

"Why?"

"Because the jail in Salem was overflowing with accused witches. I began staying in Boston and sitting outside the jail. Some nights I even fell asleep there. I just wanted to be close to her. I knew she was suffering and I wanted her to know I was there. Then people began whispering about me, saying I must be possessed since I wasn't acting like myself. But I didn't care. Every day I asked anyone I could find if he could help me. The magistrates and the reverends, the constable and the townsfolk stepped past me like I wasn't there, a specter myself, and I knew I was putting myself in more jeopardy of being accused. But I had to help my wife."

"Is that when you were turned?"

Timothy was leaning toward James, hanging on his words, as if he were fascinated hearing about the life of another of his kind, as if he had never heard another's creation story before.

"It was August 1692," James said. "One night past midnight I was sitting outside the jail, and a man in a black cloak stopped to stare at me. When I saw the amused smile on his lips I thought he recognized me from somewhere. He stared until I was unnerved, like I was being watched by the evil specter himself, the master wizard everyone in Salem was determined to find. It was an odd sensation, the prickly way your foot feels when it falls asleep, but I decided there was no reason to be concerned. He was a strong-looking figure, but he didn't seem to be carrying a weapon of any kind. He stepped even closer, still inspecting me.

"'Is your wife in there?' he asked, nodding at the jail.

"'Aye,' I said.

"'I can help you,' he said. 'Follow me.'

"I didn't know who he was, I didn't know how he might help me, but I didn't care. I would have followed him anywhere and back again if it would help me help my wife. He led me to a quiet corner of town. All the bantering noises and jostling crowds from the day had cleared away, and there was no one else around. Houses were dark. The sky was dark. I don't remember even the light of one star to help me see what was coming. The only sounds were the ripple of the wind and the exhalation of my own breath.

"'You shall thank me later,' the man said, that amused smile still lingering. He stepped so close I could smell the blood on him. I tried to run, but his claw-like grasp was too strong. His long face became a mask of gruesome evil as he gripped his teeth into my neck the way a pit bull will latch its jaws onto its victim and shake and shake and not let go. That's all I remember. I woke up later. I don't know how much later—hours, days, weeks.

"You know what it's like. Everything was nothing. When I woke up I was alone inside an abandoned house, poked awake by the streams of moonlight peering in through the mud-caked window. Once I was awake I could feel my human body dying, and I didn't understand the ultrasensory perception I suddenly had. I was crazed with hunger, and it was only instinct that told me how to feed myself. It took some time to realize that I was unnatural somehow, but I didn't know what I was and I was frightened of myself. There was no one to teach me how to live this way because whoever turned me had disappeared."

"He left you alone the way the one who turned me left me alone," Timothy said. "That's when Howard found me."

"That's right. He didn't even stay around until I woke up. I had to figure everything out for myself.

"Then a few nights after I regained consciousness I remembered Elizabeth. Can you imagine—I had to remember my wife. I tried to go out to the jail during the day and was flattened by the agony of standing in the sun and I ran back inside and hid away from the light. The next night as soon as I felt strong enough I made my way back. By then I knew I had gained extraordinary hunter's skills and I was determined to break Elizabeth free and escape with her somewhere far from Salem.

"When I arrived at the jail the first person I saw was an ornery old woman wearing rags and missing her front teeth. She recognized me when I didn't recognize her. Perhaps I had seen her before, but I was so crazed from the change that nothing I saw made any sense.

"'I want to see my wife,' I demanded. 'Bring her to me.' My voice sounded strange to my ears, as if I were growling.

"'You're late aren't you,' said the old woman. 'You haven't been here for some time. Figured you'd returned to Salem and heard the news by now.' She grinned because she knew what she had to say would crush me. She seemed to enjoy my impending heartbreak.

"'Where is my wife? Bring her to me!'"

"'You know I can't bring her to you. She's a prisoner. Besides, she's dead isn't she. Died yesterday. She was dropped in the common grave this morning.'

"My heart had already stopped beating before that night. When I woke up alone in the abandoned house I felt my heart race to an abnormally fast rate, and then like a wind-up clock whose time is up it ticked slower and slower until it stopped completely. Then, when my heartbeat was gone, I stopped breathing. For nights I sat alone, huddled with my knees to my chest, waiting to feel my consciousness slip away along with my missing heartbeat but it never did, and in my lifeless way I stayed alive. Then when that haggard old woman told me so cruelly that Elizabeth died I felt my life cease again, only this time with a painful slice of recognition that I would never see my wife again. I felt like the old woman ripped me in half with a blunt butcher's knife, and I couldn't hide my sorrow. It was the first time I cried since I was turned and I didn't realize that blood was flowing down my cheeks as freely as if someone cut a human's artery over my head and let it bleed over my face. The old woman's eyes grew wide as she watched the red stream from me, and she backed toward the wall making the sign of the cross.

"'Tis true then,' she hissed, her face flashing with false piety. 'Everyone says you're a demon and now I see 'tis true. You're bleeding from your eyes and only demons bleed from their eyes. And if you're a demon then she was too.' She made the sign of the cross again. 'I knew that one was a demon. I could see it in her couldn't I. Demon!'

"I felt myself flush with a heat-filled fury. I flew to the old woman and pressed her skull into the wall, leaving a ring of blood where her head had been. I was ready to crush her. She tried to struggle against me, but she was no match for my new strength.

"'My wife was no demon,' I said. I made no attempt to hide the thunder in my voice.

"'But you are,' she said. She spit her words in my face. 'You're bloodstained and white as a specter and cold as the dead. You are the work of the Devil. Be gone, Demon! Even God cannot help you now, son of Satan!'

"'I may be a demon,' I said, 'and God may not be able to help me now, but He cannot help you either.'

"I bent to tear her throat but I heard voices outside the jail and I didn't want to be seen. I knew I couldn't let others know what I was. I let the old woman go and left at a flash, hiding until a man arrived to relieve her from her duties. Once she was outside she glanced around and shivered as she pulled her shawl closer around her shoulders though it was August and hot even at that late hour. I don't know if she saw me jump out from the shadows as she passed me. She never screamed. I grabbed her, dragged her away, and fed from her until she was dry inside. I was more brutal than I needed to be. Even after she lay dead I broke her bones and tore her flesh and took my frenzy out on her corpse. I didn't know how else to handle my heartbreak then. To this day I wonder if I could have saved my wife. Perhaps if I had arrived at the jail sooner I could have escaped with her somewhere and helped her get the medical treatment she needed."

"Medical treatment was pretty primitive in the seventeenth century," Timothy said.

"Then maybe I could have turned her and she would still be here with me today."

"Did you know how to turn someone then? You were new to this life yourself."

"No."

"Then how could you have turned her?"

"I don't know. There must have been something I could have done."

"I don't think you should blame yourself, James. I don't see how you could have helped." Timothy thought a moment. "It must have been hell for you in those days."

"Even worse than the hell of being turned against my will was the hell of losing my wife. It's terrifying to know you're telling the truth and no one believes you. How do you convince people when they won't be convinced?"

"But didn't the accused victims have trials? Didn't they get a chance to prove their innocence?"

James laughed another wicked laugh. "The trials were a mockery of justice. Elizabeth never had her day in court, but if she had I would have tried to convince her to plead guilty. Those who were charged and still living were the ones who would plead guilty to witchcraft, while those who were executed wouldn't plead guilty to a crime they didn't commit. By the autumn of 1692, more than one hundred people were charged with witchcraft and imprisoned."

"I never knew so many people were victims of the witch trials."

"Twenty-seven people died. Some were executed, and some died in jail like Elizabeth. Our friend was crushed to death for two days under the weight of man-sized stones."

James stopped pacing. He looked at Timothy, saw the boy's folded hands, his bowed head, and thought he had shared too much. But Timothy needed to know the danger a new hunt could bring.

"I'm sorry, James. I didn't know."

"Of course, those who were hung as witches weren't witches at all while the real demons ran around turning unsuspecting victims. People were so busy pointing fingers at each other they missed what they were looking for when it was right in front of them."

"Do you think we're demons?"

James considered his answer. If he said no, we're not demons at all, he would have been lying. He didn't know how else to explain how they stayed the same despite the passing years, how they were alive when their bodies were dead, why they craved blood. Yet if James said yes, of course we're demons, Timothy would have stopped listening. So he compromised.

"I think some are demons, and others, like us, try to exist as humanly as we can. It's up to us to decide which way we're going to go."

"Humans can be demons too."

"You're right. I think humans are afraid to consider the existence of our kind because they fear the violence we might do. But I'm more afraid of humans because of the violence I've seen from them. That's why we have to stay undercover. Not everyone is ready for us."

81

"I understand," Timothy said. "You're afraid they're going to do what they did to Elizabeth, accuse innocent people. Or worse."

"I don't want to see another hunt. Living through the witch hunt was hard enough."

"Don't worry, James. I won't talk to the reporter. I won't tell anyone."

Even the little bit he had described to Timothy didn't come close to explaining the horror of it all, but he couldn't speak about it any more that night. They straightened up the mess in the storage room, pulled up the shelves, stretched out the dents, and placed the incense and candles into some semblance of order. They tried to make it look like they had never been there, but James was afraid that when Olivia looked around everything would be wrong. And then, without another word, Timothy left looking as spent as James felt.

When James walked into the hub of the store Jennifer nodded at him. He thought she heard the crash in the storage room, and he was going to tell her he would pay for any damage. She pointed at the door instead.

"I told you she'd be here," she said. "There's your girl."

James saw her through the window. Sarah. Sweet Sarah. Beautiful Sarah. The girl who looked like his Lizzie Sarah. She was shivering from the cold autumn wind, but she smiled shyly when she saw him. He greeted her at the door.

"Please," he said, extending his arm in that old-world gesture. He led her outside where it was cold, but there was a food stand a few steps away and he bought her some hot chocolate. She offered him some, which he politely declined, and they walked to the edge of the wharf where they could see the bay riding out to the Atlantic Ocean. They stood close to each other, Sarah sipping from her styrofoam cup, watching the smooth water lap like a kitten's tongue at the edge of the shore. He wanted to reach out to her, touch her dark hair, bury his nose in her sweet scent, kiss her forehead, ask her how she was feeling. Was she still frightened by the awful vision she saw when he walked her home? There was so much he wanted to ask her. But since there were so many questions he wouldn't answer about himself, he felt selfish for wanting to peel away the layers of Sarah Alexander.

But he couldn't stop his need to know her. She was so like his Lizzie.

Across the wharf James saw Jocelyn and Steve Endecott, dressed for Halloween as Sonny and Cher. As they walked to him he saw their surprise to find him there, standing next to a woman, a beautiful woman at that. When Sarah wasn't looking, Jocelyn nudged him, but he was too embarrassed to answer her unasked questions. Then Sarah saw some people she knew from the college, other professors James wasn't acquainted with, so she walked across to talk to them. Jocelyn nudged James again.

"She seems nice, James. Human too." She stroked Steve's cheek and he smiled. "There's something irresistible about humans, isn't there?"

James looked to see where Sarah was, still talking to the professors. She couldn't hear them from where she stood.

"She doesn't know," he said.

"She doesn't know?" Jocelyn couldn't hide her surprise. "You need to tell her, James. It's not going to be good if she finds out by accident."

Steve nodded in agreement. "She might be afraid at first, God knows I was, but if she's the one for you then she'll handle it. If you care about each other you'll find a way to make it work." He smiled lovingly at Jocelyn. "Like we do."

"You sound like Jennifer," James said.

"Jennifer is usually right about these things," Jocelyn said. "Here she comes."

In a moment Sarah was back beside them. Jocelyn and Steve made their excuses and continued down the wharf, Jocelyn's white go-go boots snapping on the floor, her beaded sixties-style dress swaying behind her. She flipped her long black wig over her shoulder and gave James a meaningful look as she walked away.

He looked at the sky and sighed. It was getting late for Sarah.

"May I escort you home?" he asked.

He offered his arm, which she accepted without hesitation.

"Take me to the House of the Seven Gables," she said. "It's near your house, isn't it?"

"Are you certain?" He didn't want a repeat of her terror from the night when he had only mentioned the Witch Dungeon Museum.

"I want to see it."

He tightened his arm around hers. "This way," he said.

As they continued away from the bay, down Congress Street, then Derby, he could see her watching him. He wondered if it was obvious by looking at him that he was an entirely different creature than her. Jennifer took great joy teasing him about wearing glasses when he didn't need them, but there was a reason behind the Clark Kent disguise. He had been nearsighted and wore glasses when he was alive—they called them spectacles then. After he was turned his blue eyes turned black, the pupils fully dilated, like someone had used a black marker to shade his irises. The contrast between his nighttime eyes, ghostly pallor, and fair hair was jarring. He noticed people's confusion, their eyes darting between his hair and his eyes, and he thought from their puzzled expressions that they were wondering why his eyes were so dark when the rest of him was so light. He wore the glasses to minimize the contrast, and it worked well enough. People no longer stared at him like he was a Picasso painting, his facial features too far to the right or misplaced on a diagonal somehow.

Sarah was still watching him, which made him more con-cerned about what she saw. Would she still smile when she saw me if she knew the truth, he wondered? He knew he needed to tell her, but he couldn't bring himself to say the words. He didn't want to lose the opportunity to know her because she was afraid of what he had become.

They walked in silence until she asked, "Are you feeling all right? You look pale."

"It wasn't a very good night. Until now. My night is much better now."

She blushed hot along her jaw, the pink a sharp contrast to her peach-like complexion. Just like Elizabeth. James couldn't be-lieve that the beautiful woman walking beside him was so like his wife, though everything except logic told him she was. But he would have to deal with the logistics of that mystery another night. For now, he was happy to be near her however he could.

From Derby Street they headed back toward the bay. He could hear the sleepy waves nudging the shore, whispering like close friends. When they turned down Turner Street they saw it—The House of the Seven Gables, also known as the Turner-Ingersoll Mansion. It was a grand looking home, similar to James's, only this was larger, with five more gables. Nathaniel Hawthorne, in his novel inspired by the old house, called it rusty and wooden. It didn't look very rusty, though it was very wooden. In front was a manicured lawn with precisely trimmed bushes, and on top was the clustered chimney Hawthorne described. The story reenactments had long since ended, but James and Sarah walked as close as they could.

"It's beautiful," Sarah said.

James sighed. That had been Elizabeth's reaction the first time she saw their two-gabled house after it was finished. But that must be a coincidence, he thought. Thinking the house was beautiful would be anyone's reaction upon first seeing it. He let Sarah look around, not saying anything, letting her see.

"I only see five gables," she said.

"The other two are around back. Come here."

He took her arm and walked her to the Colonial Revival Garden where the salty air mixed with the scent of lilacs. They saw the rose trellises, a border of honeysuckle shrubs, delphiniums, and sweet Williams, a splattering of pastels like a Monet garden painting with pinks, blues, white, and dashes of yellow and lavender. It was late autumn, Halloween night, but some blooms were hanging on until the winter cold shriveled them away.

"Those are many of the same flowers you would have seen here in the seventeenth century," he said. "The house was built in 1668. It's the oldest mansion around here."

"Older than your house?"

"By twenty-three years."

He pointed out the Nathaniel Hawthorne House on the grounds of the mansion. "The author Nathaniel Hawthorne was born there," he said. "They moved the house so it would be on this property. His ancestor, John Hathorne, was one of the magistrates who presided over the witch trials. Nathaniel added the w to Hawthorne because he didn't want to be too closely connected to his ancestor. I don't blame him. John Hathorne was a self-righteous, pompous imbecile who cared nothing about justice, only his own reputation."

James struggled to keep his voice even, light. He wouldn't be carried off on a tangent remembering the past and forgetting that Sarah was beside him, there in the twenty-first century, not the seventeenth. He would stay in the moment, talk about events from that time as if he were a tour guide with the privilege of showing this beautiful woman with the dark curls and full lips around Salem, and he would do his job well. Sarah wouldn't be sorry she spent this time with him. After all, he had nothing to be gloomy about. Sarah didn't seem to have an adverse reaction to the house. She had asked to see it. She was reading about the Salem Witch Trials because she had a desire to know more. And he would help her learn, just as he promised.

"You should also see Witch House, which belonged to Jonathan Corwin, another magistrate at the witch trials. There's also the New England Pirate Museum. That's not about the witch trials, but it has a recreation of a dockside village and pirate ship."

"I didn't know pirates were important here. Whenever I think of Salem all I think about are witches."

"Me too."

"Will you take me to Witch House?" she asked. She put her fist by her mouth to stifle a yawn, and they both laughed.

"Yes, but another night. Now I'm taking you home."

It was a farther walk from the House of the Seven Gables to Sarah's place. James held his hand to the small of her back and gently pressed her forward. He wanted to take her hand. They were so near his house, he could bring her home, kiss her everywhere, her lips, her hands, her neck. Everywhere. He could carry her to bed. With Sarah so near, he felt that everything would be all right again. He wouldn't be alone anymore. He thought, from her closeness as she walked, from the way she glanced shyly at him, the way she smiled at him, that she was thinking the same thing. But none of that intimacy was possible unless she knew the truth. He was weakening from his determination to keep his secret from her, caught up in whiffs of strawberries and cream. He hadn't felt alive in oh so very long. He thought perhaps he should just tell her. Would she even believe him? She might not mind. Or she might mind very much. But the more he considered it the more he decided he was not willing to take that chance. He didn't want to lose this time with her, chaste as they were forced to be. The more he knew Sarah, the more he needed to be near her however he could. If his only role was to be her tour guide around Salem, he would accept the job gladly.

He walked Sarah to her door, kissed the top of her hair, and though he wanted to stay enveloped in her sweet scent until dawn, he went home, keeping his secret safe another night.

CHAPTER 9

After Halloween James began taking Sarah home. At first they walked, but then the New England nor'easters began striking with more frequency and it became too cold, too wet, or too icy, at least for someone who had been living on the west coast in the sun for so long.

During a particularly fierce November storm, Sarah walked away from the library pulling her scarf tighter around her neck and her wool hat closer over her ears. She was shivering, and she felt her jaw tighten and her teeth click. She turned to see James slow his step so he could follow beside her.

"Still no car?"

"Not yet."

No matter how close she pulled her heavy coat around her throat she wasn't warm enough. He pointed toward the parking lot off Loring Avenue.

"Would you like a ride home?"

Sarah looked in the direction he pointed. She felt like she did that night in the library when he first offered to walk her home, unsure what to say. Since Halloween he had been very friendly, very calm. Not one melancholy moment, no jumping out from the shadows. She stopped counting the months since her divorce. She was tired of following an arbitrary rule she set up for the sole purpose of making herself more miserable. If she wanted to try things out with a nice man, then why shouldn't she? Where did she get the one year rule from anyway? If anything, James had been too gentlemanly with her, keeping his hands to himself even when she didn't want him to.

"I don't bite, remember?"

"I remember."

With his hand on her lower back, he escorted her past the library and the dining hall, around the recital hall and the bookstore to the parking lot. He opened the passenger's door to his Explorer and buckled her in.

He got into the car, started the engine, and pulled onto Lafayette Street, then left on New Derby, right onto Washington, and a final left onto Essex near the Salem Inn. Sarah was pleased with herself because she finally, after more than two months, felt she knew the ins and outs of Salem, the byways and side roads that made navigating the small town easier. When you're walking and it's cold, you want to know the quickest possible way around.

James stopped in front of Sarah's house and parked by the curb. She didn't want him to leave, so she started asking him about himself, hoping he would stay.

"How long have you been a professor?" she asked.

He laughed. "This is my first year at Salem State College."

"Have you taught anywhere else?"

"University of Washington Seattle, Northwestern University." He stopped, opened his mouth as if he wanted to say more, but didn't. Sarah stared ahead watching the rain hit the windshield in angry splats, listening to the rattling of the wind. She wanted to ask him what he was thinking, but then she thought she might not want to know. He didn't seem threatening, upset, or even melancholy. Just quiet. Then he said, "Jennifer told me you're divorced."

Sarah exhaled. She had asked him questions so she could spend more time with him. She didn't mean to have to talk about herself.

"Yes," she said, "that's true."

"I know it's none of my business, but if you don't mind telling me, what happened?"

She could have given him a superficial answer. She could have said we grew apart, or we were young, or I didn't know better. But, sitting next to him in the car, encased together against whatever was happening in the world outside, she felt close to him. She wanted to feel even closer to him, and she wanted him to feel even closer to her, so she spoke from her heart.

"The day after I graduated from Boston University I married a man I was never sure I loved, and I stayed married to him for ten years. I can remember watching him at our wedding, waiting at the end of the aisle in his black tuxedo and red carnation, and I knew even then, in the space of a hesitation, as if someone hit pause on a videotape, that he wasn't the one for me."

"But you married him anyway."

"It sounds foolish now, I guess, but the invitations had been sent out, the cake was decorated, the guests were waiting, and it seemed like the thing to do, an expected rite of passage into adulthood."

"Your intuition was right."

"Too right. I don't think my ex-husband wanted the divorce, but I had to leave. I felt stifled in my marriage, like I had been wearing my shoes on the wrong feet so long my legs became bowed. Now that I'm living here, free from the stranglehold, I feel like I'm finally stretching up straight again, like I'm standing as tall as I should."

"I understand what you mean." Again, he looked like he would say more, but he didn't.

Sarah looked at her cat sitting in the window. "I should probably go inside," she said. She didn't want to go inside. She wanted to talk to him, see him smile, listen to him laugh. She felt like she should be there beside him, and she felt the light, fairy-like thread wrapping itself around them. But James didn't ask her to stay. He opened her car door and escorted her to her door. Standing close together, she wanted him to kiss her lips, but she accepted a kiss on top of her head instead. It wasn't what she wanted, but it would do. For now.

After that night she began looking for him everywhere, on the streets, in the shops, on campus. She watched for him to come through the door past the metal detectors into the library, hoping to see him come out of the elevator from his office, giddy while she wondered when she might see him again. She felt the way she did when she had her first crush when she was thirteen, not knowing what to do with the nervous energy she felt like cham-pagne bubbles beneath her skin. She felt silly to be so infatuated with a man like that, especially so soon after her divorce. She had thought that part would stay dormant for some time. James had changed everything. She still had her concerns about him, he could be so distant at times, but she couldn't deny that he was always on her mind.

One afternoon while Sarah was on her break, Jennifer walked up from behind and saw her writing in her clothbound notebook. When she shut it suddenly, Jennifer winked at her.

"I bet you're scribbling 'Mrs. James Wentworth' in that notebook. That's why you don't want me to see it."

Sarah laughed as if that was the silliest thing she ever heard. She wouldn't admit, even to Jennifer, that she had thought about doing exactly that during dull moments in the library, something she did in high school with the name of boys she liked.

James had awakened feelings in her that she had never known before. Unlike her friends, she had never been the kind to spend her life seeking romance. She had never been one to jump from man to man trying to find it the way others did. She thought romance only gave you unrealistic expectations, and what's the point of expectations when you can't achieve them? She had never known much romance in her life, not with boyfriends, certainly not with her ex-husband. And when she looked at her friends's lives, she didn't see much romance there, either. Women love the fairy tale, she thought. They love the idea of the Romantic Hero with his unbuttoned shirt, his well-muscled chest heaving, the woman, who they imagine to be themselves, kneeling beside him, her dress this side of ravaged, revealing a bare shoulder here, a well-toned leg there, her billowy hair tossing in the breeze, her mouth an open O of ecstasy. But Sarah was too practical to retreat into imaginary worlds.

Now, here was James Wentworth. Tall, gold hair, handsome in a manly way, a smile that, when he smiled, could clear away a stubborn storm hovering over the bay. His eyes were so dark, and where at first she found them intense, now she saw his kindness, his concern. Yet, though they spent hours together, he had never said anything that made her think he wanted more from their relationship. The way it was then, with him extending his arm, sometimes kissing the top of her hair, not even holding hands, seemed to be the way it was going to stay. So it was just as she always knew: romances, where the hero sweeps the woman off her feet, carries her to bed in the heat of passion because they can't restrain themselves any longer, were a fantasy.

"Sarah?"

Sarah shook herself from the reverie that thinking of James had brought on. Jennifer smiled at her.

"I was writing about the dream I had last night," Sarah said.

Jennifer stepped closer. "I know you don't like to talk about it, but if you want to confide in someone, you can talk to me. Maybe I can help."

Sarah nodded her thanks. She was so busy the rest of the afternoon she was surprised hours later when she saw the threatening darkness outside. The wind picked up, the trees rattled, the leaves whistled, and she dreaded walking home in that weather. Maybe she would have to buy a car after all. Then she saw Jennifer looking toward the door.

"There he is. Your professor."

Sarah thought she saw James nod, but he was too far to hear. He stepped into the elevator and disappeared, a hint of a smile still lingering on his lips. Something about the way Jennifer watched him made Sarah pause.

"Jennifer..."

"Yes?"

"You can tell me the truth, I don't care, but...do you like James?"

"Of course I like James. We've been friends forever."

"No, I mean, do you *like* James?"

Jennifer shook her head, waving her hand in front of her face as if she were swatting a fly. She dropped into the swivel chair in front of the computer and clicked around in the card catalog. "Nothing like that. He's an old family friend. I mean an *old* family friend."

"He's not that old. He's about my age."

Jennifer laughed. "You like him too. Only I think you like him a little differently than I do."

"I don't think he feels the same way about me."

Jennifer spun around on her chair, startling Sarah with the suddenness. "What makes you think that?" she asked.

"We've never been on a date. He's never asked me out to dinner, a movie, even for coffee. Sometimes I think he's interested—something about the way he looks at me. When he kisses the top of my head I think there might be something more between us, but then he turns away and goes home. We've never even held hands. If he was interested he would have asked me out by now."

"He's kind of old fashioned."

"What do you mean?"

"In older days when a young man was interested in a young woman they wouldn't go out on dates like we do now. He'd visit her family, make small talk with the father, compliment the mother, have dinner with the family. Whatever time he had with his intended, the only way they could get to know each other was in front of everyone. He's just trying to get to know you without pressuring you. He's really quite a gentleman if you think about it."

"That's sweet, and odd, I think."

"It's a very old fashioned way of doing things."

"I didn't know there were still men who thought that way."

"James does."

Sarah sighed. She gathered her loose hair and lifted it off the back of her neck, waving it to fan her flushed skin. The heat in the library must be on high, she thought.

"I don't know what to think," she said. "In so many ways he's almost too perfect. No man can be so amazing without having some fatal flaw. Tell me the truth—is he really some axe-wielding homicidal maniac when no one's looking?"

Jennifer laughed. "Of course not!" she said. But there was something in the way she swung back to her work, checking the bar codes on a stack of books as if that were the most pressing thing in the world, that made Sarah wonder if he really was a homicidal maniac after all. Sarah laughed at her own paranoia, thinking she must have been watching too many scary movies on television.

Suddenly he was there, James, leaning against the librarians's desk, taking her breath away. When she saw him, the angelic smile, the gold hair, the black eyes that should have looked like voids but looked instead like darkness reaching for the light, all her worries melted away.

"Hi, Sarah," he said.

"Hello to you too, Doctor Wentworth," said Jennifer. "Isn't this your night off?"

"It is, but the weather's pretty ugly out there. I thought Sarah might like a ride home."

"I'd love a ride home," Sarah said. She glanced at the clock on the wall and saw she had another half hour on her shift.

"Go," Jennifer said. "It's a quiet night. I'll take care of closing." She pushed Sarah out from behind the desk. "See you tomorrow."

When James parked in front of Sarah's house she felt brave and invited him in. At first she was sure she made a mistake. He had such a strange expression as he looked first at her house, then at her. He looked concerned, she thought, or confused, and he took too long before answering.

"You don't have to if you don't want to." She didn't want to sound hurt by his lack of enthusiasm. "I just thought you'd like some coffee. It's getting cold in the car."

"Yes," he said finally, "I'd love to come in."

When they were in the house Sarah went into the kitchen and brewed some coffee. James went straight to the bookcase to see what books she had, and then he looked around at her furniture, simple and modern, and said hello to her cat Tillie. Tillie had quite a reaction. She spit, hissed, and leapt to her feet, and if she had a tail it would have ballooned in fear. She looked like a picture of a witch's cat on Halloween, her black fur sticking out in every direction. She ran to hide under the bed.

"I'm sorry," Sarah said. "She doesn't usually act like that."

"Cats tend to have trouble with strangers."

He picked up the book Sarah left on the glass end table. "*Persuasion* by Jane Austen," he said. "One of my favorites."

"It's one of my favorites too. I'm reading it for the fourth time." As she rinsed out the coffee grinder it occurred to her. "How funny," she said. "You have the same last name as Anne Elliot's love, Captain Wentworth."

James sat on the sofa and looked at her. "Yes, there is quite a coincidence there."

"*Persuasion* is such a romantic story, isn't it?" she said. "I love how Anne Elliot falls in love with Frederick Wentworth, but she's persuaded by her family that he isn't good enough and she breaks off her engagement from him. Years later he confesses that he still loves her, she admits she still loves him, and they come together again. It's one of my favorite endings."

She thought he was going to say something, but he stayed silent, staring at her.

"How lucky they were," she said, "to have a second chance at love. Not many people get that."

"I think everyone wishes they could have a second chance with the one they love," James said. His voice was small.

She got their coffees and hovered near the sofa. She was enjoying their time together and didn't want to scare him away. He seemed so pensive since they talked about *Persuasion*. She decided to sit on the sofa beside him, close but not so close. He sat his coffee on the glass table while she sipped from her mug.

They spent the next hour talking about Jane Austen, and James knew so much about her, even her personal life, almost, Sarah thought, as if he had known her. He knew what she liked to eat, how she spent her days when she wasn't writing, whom she visited, whom she loved. It was late and Sarah was tired, but she had that schoolgirl crush feeling overpowering her again and she didn't want him to leave. She thought she should get herself more coffee—a caffeine boost was just what she needed. She reached for James's mug and realized he hadn't touched it.

"You didn't drink your coffee."

"Actually, I don't care for coffee. I just wanted to spend more time with you. But I'll get you another cup since you look like you're about to fall asleep on me."

He went into the kitchen and she heard him rattling with the coffee pot, pouring the liquid into her cup. She was tired, it was late for her, so she put her head against the sofa and closed her eyes. She would rest until he came back. She was glad he didn't want to leave.

She must have fallen asleep. When she woke up she was in her bed, still dressed, covered with her blankets. Through the curtains she could see the pink sun peeking awake in the fading night sky. It was dark in the bedroom, but she could see James's shadow by the door.

"James?"

Instantly he was by her side.

"What is it, Sarah? Are you all right?"

"Are you leaving?"

"I have to leave. But I'll see you tonight. If you'd like that."

He kissed the top of her head, through the thickness of her hair, then left, shutting the door behind him. She thought she must have been dreaming. If only he would kiss her somewhere besides the top of her head. She didn't know if she answered him before she fell asleep again.

I am in the kitchen cooking supper, stirring a pottage in the cauldron in the hearth. My husband comes in and sits at our table, and he watches as my hands land in fists behind my hips as they try to support the weight of my aching back and bulging belly. Although I cannot see his face in the shadows I can feel the agitation in the air. He puts his arms around me and holds me to him longer than usual, as though he does not want to let go, as though he wants to keep me safe. As though he wants to make everything wrong go away so we would always be as we were at that moment, content in our lives together. As I pull away I sense something in his manner and I look at him carefully.

"What troubles you?" I ask.

He seems to wonder how to tell me. Then he says, "They've arrested Rebecca."

"Our Rebecca?"

"Aye. They've arrested her for a witch."

I am stunned, as though I have been shot by a native's poison-touched arrow. I step away from him and my mind feels muddled. I wish I had not heard what he said. I feel my hands flutter around me as though I am trying to capture some words that might make the nonsense make sense. "Of course she is no witch," I say. "Someone must speak for her. They must know she is no witch."

"They should know, but they don't. She's been accused so she's been arrested."

"Who would accuse her?" I can hear the near-hysteria in my own voice. "Who would accuse someone as good as our Rebecca of such a crime?"

"The afflicted girls," my husband says.

The sense of anguish is too much and I look at the pots and pans lining the shelves on the wall, the scrubbed vegetables on the table, the cauldron in the hearth. I can tell he is as pained by the news as I am and I wish he had not told me just so I would not have to feel the way he feels then.

"I'm certain she'll be cleared at her trial," he says. "All the evidence shall come out then."

"The false evidence," I say, "from those horrid girls. You know as well as I how rarely anyone is ever found innocent at their trials no matter how innocent they may be."

I am at a loss for what to say and my hands continue to flutter at my sides. After struggling to hold back my tears I turn back to the pottage in the cauldron and stir some more, only now my stirring is agitated, as if I am trying to vent the frustration I suddenly feel.

"I think we should go back to England." My husband says the words quickly, as if he has to say them before he changes his mind. "My father said he would pay for our voyage and give us money enough to get settled and assist me in starting a business there. Or, if we decide to go to Cambridge, he shall assist us while I continue at university."

His face is still a blank slate. I cannot tell if the idea of returning to England pleases him or not. I wipe my hands on the rag on the table and walk to him.

"I thought you were happy here," I say.

"I was. I am. But I don't understand what's happening. I don't understand how someone like Rebecca could be arrested. I don't know the facts from all the cases, and I don't know that all the people accused are innocent. Perhaps there are such things as specters and other unnatural beings. I know nothing of the super-natural world. But I know that some of the accused are innocent, and as long as innocent people are condemned then Salem is not a safe place to live."

I stare at the woven rug beneath my feet while I consider. My hands go instinctively to the bump where our baby waits.

"If we leave on the next crossing I'd give birth on the ship," I say. "Those ships are horrid enough. They're overcrowded and the food is barely edible and the air is foul. There's so much death. I saw two newborns and so many others die on my voyage here." I walk to my husband and stroke the worried crease be-tween his eyes. "Let us wait until the baby is a few months old and we know she's healthy. If things are still difficult then, we'll leave."

He takes my hand and kisses it. He seems relieved that at least we have a plan, a way away from the hysteria. Patience, our helping-girl, comes silently into the room and giggles when we kiss. Then a dawning crosses as a smile on his lips.

"She?" he asks.

"Aye. I'm hoping for a girl so I think of her as she. We'll call her Grace. Though I'm certain you wish for a son."

"I wish for a healthy child who shall not have to live in fear."

I smooth the crease that sits stubbornly in lingering concern on his forehead and he seems better. For that moment I allow myself to believe that everything will be all right, but I am anxious.

CHAPTER 10

The next night James arrived at the library with a smile. Every night he was arriving with a smile. Sarah wanted to think she was the reason for his happiness, though she wasn't sure. He hadn't said so in words. But James said a lot without words. He could be so quiet at times, content merely being there. Sometimes, when Sarah was working, checking the databases or helping students or professors, James would sit nearby and watch her. He didn't pretend to have a task at the computer. He didn't pretend to correct papers. He watched her and he didn't seem to mind if everyone saw him.

A week later at closing time he found her near the librarians's desk and presented her with a book, a well-kept older edition from days when bookbinding was an art. She turned it over in her hands, feeling the indentation of the title on the cover: *Several Poems Compiled With Great Variety of Wit and Learning* by Anne Bradstreet. Sarah was touched by his thoughtfulness. As much as she loved to read, no one had ever given her poetry before.

"Thank you," she said. "I've never read Anne Bradstreet. It seems appropriate, reading her in Salem. She lived here during colonial times, didn't she?"

"For a while, and not very well, I'm afraid. The Bradstreets lived with Anne's family, the Dudleys, in a sparse house with barely the basic necessities. In winter they all lived in one room, the only one with heat. She was the first woman published in colonial America, and it's rumored that King George III had a volume of her poetry in his collection." James looked at the book, then at Sarah. He stared at her so hard it was as if she could feel his hands on her shoulders pushing her somewhere, toward something. But where?

He opened the book to the page he tabbed with a sticky note. "She wrote one of my favorite poems—'To My Dear and Loving Husband.' He closed the book and pressed it into her hands.

"I'm not familiar with it," Sarah said. James cleared his throat before he began:

> *"If ever two were one, then surely we.*
> *If ever man were loved by wife, then thee.*
> *If ever wife was happy in a man,*
> *Compare with me, ye women, if you can..."*

Sarah clutched the thin volume close to her chest, staring at the librarians's desk, hard, as if the formica top were speaking to her, whispering the answer to a long-held question. She heard words, phrases, echoing from somewhere. She wasn't afraid. It wasn't like being haunted or chased or dragged away by chains. It was as if she suddenly remembered something she had forgotten. She said:

> *"...Thy love is such I can no way repay;*
> *The heavens reward thee manifold, I pray.*
> *Then while we live, in love let's so persever,*
> *That when we live no more, we may live ever."*

James bowed his head, looking first at the floor under his feet, then at Sarah. She had never seen such a strong-looking man seem so vulnerable, as if he held his heart out to her in his hands, as if his heart was hers for the taking.

"I thought you weren't familiar with the poem, Sarah." His voice was gentle, barely audible above the whispers in the library.

Sarah shook her head. "I'm not."

Neither Sarah nor James said much as he drove her home. They were parked in front of her house before she realized where they were. As the car clicked off, he turned to her with such need in his eyes that Sarah felt her heart stutter. She and James had shared something special in the library when she recited the lines from the seventeenth century love poem from a brilliant colonial woman to her dear and loving husband. How had she recited a poem she was sure she never read? Had she read it in college, in an early American literature class, and she had forgotten about it? Even if she did, college was so long ago, and she certainly hadn't read it since. But somehow she knew the poem. It had been stored away in her somewhere. When she looked into James's night-dark eyes she could feel that invisible, thread-thin line again, catching them up, pulling them close, not letting them go.

She had been so sure he felt the same way when their eyes locked. He smiled, as if he found something he had forgotten he needed, and the smile hadn't left his face. Until now. Instead of kissing her, grabbing her, carrying her to her bed as she wanted him to, all he said was, "Let me walk you to your door. I don't want anyone to steal you."

In front of her house, he kissed the top of her head and turned to leave. But she did not want a kiss on top of her head. She wanted more. She followed him out to the street, and when they reached his car she walked close and pointed her face up the way she pointed her face up to the man in her dreams before he kissed her. She wanted James to kiss her. She wanted him to stay all night and make love to her.

She was ready to finally feel his lips against hers, but when all she felt was air she opened her eyes and realized, with a painful punch, that he didn't feel the same way. She saw a stormy blankness in his nighttime eyes that told her he wasn't interested. He stood there, frozen, a look of real pain in his eyes as he searched her face, looking for his wife perhaps, or looking as if he had been mortally wounded by her desire for him. Without saying a word, without looking back, he jumped into his car and drove away.

Sarah walked into the house and stared, at the wall, at the blank screen of the television, at her cat, at the cream-colored wall. When the phone rang she was only half surprised to hear Olivia's motherly voice at the other end of the line.

"How have you been, dear? I haven't seen you since Halloween, and I hardly had a chance to say hello, I was so busy with the customers."

Sarah tried to be brave. She tried to keep the tears away. What did she have to cry about? James had never made any promises, never even kissed her on the lips. Just the idea of kissing her sent him speeding away, his car brakes screeching on the pavement. Yet no matter how hard she squeezed her eyes, no matter how fast she waved her open hand in front of her nose, she couldn't stop the internal thunderstorm from pouring like rain down her face.

"What is it, dear? You can tell me."

"It's James."

"James? Jennifer said you two left the library looking very happy."

Sarah wiped her face with the back of her hand. "I was hoping we had a chance, but it isn't going to happen. I tried to kiss him, but he ran like he couldn't get away fast enough. I don't think he's over his wife, and if he's not over her then he's not ready to move on. There's no room in his heart for me."

After an unsure pause, Sarah decided to share some interesting information she received via e-mail that morning. At the time, she sent a terse reply to her friend and deleted the message. Now, after James had run away, leaving her lonely and confused, she gave more importance to the news.

"I heard from my friend in L.A. She said my ex-husband misses me."

Olivia sighed. "What do you mean?"

"She said he's been asking about me. She said he's been upset since she told him I was becoming friendly with a good-looking English professor. He told her he misses me and he's thinking about coming to Salem to visit. He told her he wants me back."

"You can't go back to him, Sarah. You remember how unhappy you were."

"I know I can't go back to him."

Sarah's voice cracked as she said it, and she wondered if it were true. Could she go back to her ex-husband? Before that night she would have said there was no way she would leave Salem and James for a husband she wasn't happy with. But now, in the aftermath of a bewildered James, the thought of returning to Los Angeles wasn't as ridiculous as it might have seemed even an hour before. Sleeping had become all but impossible in Salem. Her dreams were more frequent and frightening since she moved there. In Los Angeles they had been a nuisance. In Salem they were relentless. Her hands continued shaking for hours after she was jolted awake by tremors, her anxieties fragile until morning though she turned on the lights and rationalized the fear away by telling herself that nothing she saw was real. She was awake now and everything was fine. They weren't simply haphazard, fluid scenes, these dreams, detached from reality. They were tangible, linear. Clear. Somewhere, deep in the hidden maze of her soul, she knew there was some misunderstood truth there, and she wanted to make sense of what was happening to her. The more she read about the Salem Witch Trials, the more she recognized the imagery in her dreams. It made no sense that she should dream about a woman from that time. Was she dreaming about her ancestor? She didn't know.

She was tempted to finally confide in Olivia. Maybe she had nothing to lose by bringing her clothbound notebook to the Witches Lair and letting her Wiccan friends take a look. Maybe between them they could make the disjointed pieces fit. And didn't Olivia say her friend was good at dream interpretation?

Olivia sighed. "Did you tell your ex-husband you won't be getting back together?" she asked.

"I haven't spoken to him since I left Los Angeles. I e-mailed my friend to tell her I couldn't go back to him. She said she knew, but she wanted me to know I had options."

"Things don't always happen when we want them to, but everything will come together when it's time. Trust that, Sarah."

"Thank you, Olivia."

"Anytime, dear. Call me anytime."

Sarah hung up the phone more confused than she was before.

CHAPTER 11

It was a slow night in the library since classes had stopped for winter break. There were a few lingering students, some who needed an extension on their final papers or semester exams, others lounging in the chairs by the windows reading, an instructor or two researching information. Sarah had the night off. Jennifer was seated behind the librarians's desk helping students. James was working at a computer terminal, keeping most of his attention on his work while Kenneth Hempel whispered to Jeremy, James's student, a few tables away. James had some warning that Hempel would be there since he had seen the reporter get out of his green Buick in the parking lot off Loring Avenue. He even made note of the license plate number in case he needed to recognize the car again. That night in the library Hempel wasn't hiding the fact that he was asking about James— he was doing it in front of James's face. As Jeremy answered his questions, Hempel nodded and jotted notes onto his yellow legal pad. But James was too far for human ears to hear, and they were whispering close to each other, so he had to pretend he didn't know what they were saying. It was better if he ignored them anyway. Besides, the young man sounded more annoyed by Hempel than intrigued.

"That's right," Jeremy said. "I only see Professor Wentworth at night, but that's because he teaches night classes. Why would anyone be here when they didn't have to be? I hate that I have to be here now. Asshole philosophy professor failed me and I have to retake the final exam."

James smiled to himself as he realized that Hempel couldn't have picked a less helpful source than Jeremy. Hempel spoke to

107

three other students that night, as well as a librarian James didn't know by name. She was the mathematics liaison, he thought. She couldn't have much information to share, so he wasn't concerned. Without looking, he sensed Hempel glancing at him, but he wouldn't be deterred from his work. He left the computer terminal and wandered into the stacks, searching for the book he needed. He wouldn't be run out of his own library by that daft little man. When he heard Hempel's heavy, plodding footsteps, he braced himself.

"Good evening, Professor Wentworth."

James slid the book back into its slot on the shelf. He didn't turn around.

"Hello, Mr. Hempel."

He pulled another book, checked the index, turned to the page he needed. When Hempel didn't leave, James continued to work, hoping the reporter would get the hint. Or perhaps Jennifer would snap her fingers and bring the stacks crashing down around them.

"Reading about Keats, I see. Have I told you I was an English major in college?"

"Not journalism?"

"Surprisingly, no. When I was a young man I had aspirations to write books. I wanted to be like Bram Stoker and bring the world's attention to the vengeful, violent monsters lurking unseen in the dark. Stoker did that so well, didn't he?"

"*Dracula* is a novel, Mr. Hempel."

"Perhaps. But all fiction has some element of truth."

James looked around, saw them alone in the stacks, it was close to closing, and he wondered if anyone would notice if he ripped into the reporter's throat, sucked the man dry, and discarded his corpse in the bushes beside the parking lot. Perhaps the garbage bins would be better. The bay. Yes, the bay would be perfect. Hempel's body would wash away into the Atlantic Ocean and no one would be the wiser. Would anyone notice if Kenneth Hempel was missing? He was such an innocuous little fellow. But then James remembered Hempel mentioning a family in the Witches Lair on Halloween, and he heard Jennifer speaking to a student by the librarians's desk, so they weren't alone. He knew he had to drop his idea, though he liked it very much.

"I'm actually not here to visit with you tonight, Professor, as much as I enjoy your company. I'm looking for one of the librarians. Dark hair, lovely smile. What is her name?"

James cleared his throat. "I don't know who you're talking about." He couldn't control the gruffness in his voice.

"The students seem to think you know her very well. Miss Alexander, is it?"

"If you know her name, then why are you asking me?"

Hempel smiled at James's curt response, as if that were exactly the reaction he wanted. "I just wanted to ask her a few questions. I didn't see her around tonight, and I thought you might know where she was. When you're a professional journalist you have to cover all angles of your story. I'm sure you understand."

James turned back to the book in his hand, though the sentences hardly made sense to him. The words scattered into letters and the letters spread across the pages like spilled alphabet soup.

"I don't know where she is," he said.

"I'll have to come back another time. Good night, Professor."

James tried to go back to work, but he couldn't concentrate. Now he was concerned that Hempel would involve Sarah in his quest. James remembered suddenly what it felt like to be hunted—trapped, searching frantically for a way out, hoping your captor wouldn't end you right there. The recollection of being the weaker one shocked him. He hadn't felt the torment of being the hunted since the Salem Witch Trials. His Elizabeth had died in the trap. Now, Hempel was reveling in his role as the hunter, piecing together a plot meant to ambush James into confessing his truth. The witch hunters had done something similar over three centuries before—only they tried to force their victims into confessing a truth that wasn't true. But Hempel would be disappointed. He wouldn't succeed in his quest. Not if James could help it. James considered following Hempel to his green Buick in the parking lot, but he shook his head, forcing himself to stop thinking that way. As much as he enjoyed the idea of making the reporter disappear, he knew that wasn't a practical solution to his problem. He turned his thoughts to a far more pleasant topic.

Sarah.

The rest of his nights looked pale compared to the sharp contrast of color he saw when he was with her. He knew he hurt her when he didn't kiss her. It hurt him, too, because he had been wanting to kiss those lips for oh so many years. He dreamed of it every day. But standing in front of her house that night he couldn't do it. She looked exactly as Elizabeth used to, dressed in modern clothes, perhaps, her dark curls loose and uncovered. She even stood on her toes and pointed her chin up waiting for his lips to touch hers, just as Elizabeth had. Still, in that moment he was more sad than happy to see her that way. He didn't know who he was going to kiss, Elizabeth or Sarah, and he was afraid his confusion would be too obvious. He didn't want to hurt Sarah because she thought he only wanted her because she reminded him of Lizzie. And besides, before there could be physical contact between them, lips on lips, skin on skin, she needed to know the truth. He was angry with himself for keeping his secret from her so long, and he was upset that his inability to tell her had kept them apart. He didn't want to be apart from her anymore. He would tell her.

How long he stood in the stacks, staring at the same page in the book he held forgotten in his hand, musing over Sarah, he didn't know. Suddenly he heard Jennifer say his name. He looked at her through the space between the stacks and saw her speaking into the telephone receiver as if she were talking to someone on another line.

"James, if you can hear me nod your head." He nodded, but he turned his eyes to the book as if he were reading. "Hempel left the library a while ago, but I don't want anyone to see me talking to you right now. It turns out he's been snooping around campus all day, trying to get someone in the office to give him copies of the transcripts from your degrees, trying to find where else you've taught, where else you've lived."

James walked from the stacks and sat in a chair further from the librarians's desk. He turned the pages of the book he held and waited for more.

"He's been asking your students if they know any personal information about you, who your friends are, your family, if anyone knows where you are when you're not on campus. And there's something else. My mother talked to Sarah. I know what happened." She stopped, perhaps waiting for some response, but James didn't move. "Did you know her ex-husband wants her back?"

He faced Jennifer, the surprise obvious in his wide eyes and open mouth. Anyone could have seen them communicating from too far across the library, even Kenneth Hempel, but James was stunned and his defenses were down and he was hearing too well in public.

Jennifer hissed into the phone. "Turn around!" When he looked away, his eyes unfocused on the pages of the book, she continued. "She found out her ex-husband asks about her, and he told a friend he wants her back. I thought you should know."

That was the moment when James learned about another kind of madness, the kind you feel when you've been unwilling to tell the woman you love your truth and then you lose her to someone else's waiting arms. The madness he knew centuries before belonged to others, but this time the madness was his own. He felt Sarah slipping from his grasp because of the wall he kept between them. He was making the decision to keep her in the dark regarding his secret as if she were a child, too immature to handle such sensitive information. That wouldn't do. There were no more questions in his mind—he had to tell her the truth so she could decide for herself. She had a right to know. Would she want to be with him the way he was? He couldn't say. She might think it's madness, this bizarre story he was going to tell her, which is how any reasonable person would respond. She might not mind. Or she might mind very much and run in fear, leaving him alone once more. He didn't know if he could stand the loneliness again. But he had to tell her. That night. He felt Jennifer's questioning eyes on him as he disappeared into the elevator up to the third floor. He had to consider the consequences of what he was going to do.

CHAPTER 12

At first Sarah thought Jennifer was mocking her, or maybe recording their conversation on the camera on her cell phone to post on the Internet, the video of the gullible girl talked into believing in something she shouldn't believe in.

As soon as Jennifer walked into her house, Sarah sensed something was wrong. Jennifer sat on the sofa, petting the cat, avoiding Sarah's gaze.

"What is it, Jennifer?"

"James is going to kill me. He doesn't know I'm here."

Sarah sucked in her breath. "Why doesn't he know you're here?"

"I knew you had to know and he didn't say he was going to tell you so I thought I should tell you, but I know he's going to be upset because he didn't tell me I could tell you and..."

Sarah held up her hand. "Please, Jen. What do you want?"

"I want you to believe me."

"What do you want me to believe?"

Jennifer paced to the window, pulled aside the blinds, and looked out as if she could see something lingering across the clear, cold winter night.

"Do you believe there are things out there that are real but defy any sensible explanation? Do you believe in things you can't necessarily understand, things like supernatural powers?"

"Like ghosts? I don't believe in ghosts. Why? Are we going on a ghost hunt?"

"Not exactly."

Jennifer sat back on the sofa, intent on the cat's black fur, smoothing it down the cat's back. "What do you know about vampires?" She turned to see Sarah's response.

"Vampires?" Sarah laughed. "I guess I know as much as anyone else. They come out at night. They attack people and drink their blood. People like to watch movies and read books about them. Why?"

"First of all, you can't believe everything you read. A lot of it is hearsay—folktales from centuries ago." Jennifer thought for a moment. "Do you think they could be real? Vampires, I mean."

"It doesn't seem likely that vampires are real. There's so much about them that doesn't make sense. How can something come back from the dead?"

"I know it doesn't sound logical. It even sounds silly if you think about it. But did you ever think you might actually know a vampire?"

Sarah was ready to call in the joke, but Jennifer was so serious Sarah couldn't smile about it any more.

"Are you trying to tell me you're a vampire? I thought you said you're a witch."

Sarah jumped when the banging struck her door. The thuds were awful, threatening, and Sarah thought she saw the leering, laughing, pock-faced monster leap out at her from the shadows, iron chains in hand, ready to bind her and drag her away. When she saw James through the window she relaxed, but only until she heard his frustration.

"Jennifer!" he yelled.

Sarah opened the door and he brushed past her with barely restrained fury.

"What the hell are you doing?" he demanded. "What gives you the right..."

Jennifer shrugged as if there were no problem, everything was fine. "You weren't going to tell her and she has the right to know."

"I was going to tell her! I was coming over here to tell her!"

Jennifer backed out the open door. "I'm sorry, James. I was only trying to help."

"I've been taking care of myself for over three hundred years. I don't need your help."

"Very good, then. I'll leave." She smiled at James. "Now no biting tonight, Professor, or you'll hear from me tomorrow."

"That's not funny." He slammed the door behind her.

Sarah sat on the couch, her head in her hands.

"Will someone please tell me what's going on?"

James sat next to her. She thought, as she looked into his night-dark eyes, that she had never seen anyone look so serious, not even at an unexpected funeral.

"I am a vampire."

Sarah laughed. Another joke. All right. She had a sense of humor. She would go along.

"Vampires don't exist. They're legends and nonsense."

"I'm real, Sarah. Most humans think we don't exist, yet you only have to look around during the dark night hours to discover us everywhere. We're ghost-skinned, black-eyed, and dead to the touch, but otherwise we seem the same as you. After all, we were human once. We're everywhere you are, we do everything you do—we walk, we sleep, we drink, we love. Forever."

Sarah shuddered. She realized, despite all of her reasoning and logic, that he was telling the truth. It was absurd, but she believed him.

She was afraid to look at him. "That's impossible," she said, unable to accept the fact that she believed him. "I think I would have noticed something like that about someone I've been spending so much time with."

"I decided a long time ago to integrate myself into society as well as I can. But there are differences. I can't go out during the day so I go out at night. And my human body is dead."

"You're dead?"

"No one's perfect, Sarah."

He fiddled with his eyeglasses, a curious gesture from a man who was supposed to be immortal.

"I've never heard of a near-sighted vampire before."

James laughed. He sounded relieved. He took the glasses off and waved them in the air. "They're just glass. They help me blend in better." He folded the frames and slid them into his shirt pocket.

"This is ridiculous," Sarah said.

"I know, but it's true."

He took her hand, the first time he touched her skin. She shuddered as she noticed the dead-blue undertone to his pale complexion, the flat blackness of his eyes without his glasses. Suddenly, she realized that, though he had placed her hand on his chest beneath his button-down shirt, there was nothing there. No warmth. No breath. No heartbeat. Nothing.

It wasn't a joke anymore. She leapt off the sofa, away from him. She struggled to stay calm though she wanted to hide behind silver or garlic or brandish a wooden stake.

"Don't you think that's something you should have told me sooner?" she said.

"I would never hurt anyone—I'm past all that—but I would certainly never hurt you." He smiled in a strained attempt at lightening the mood. "I'm harmless, like a trained tiger."

"Some tigers will forget their training and attack using their instincts."

"I don't forget my training."

He looked at her, through her, as if he wanted to see what she was thinking, as if he wanted to know her heart. Would she be afraid of him now that she knew the truth, his eyes seemed to ask? At that moment she didn't know. She didn't know what to say. She stayed back, away from him, watching him. She looked out the window, trying to see what Jennifer had been staring at with such intensity, but all she saw was bare-branched, snow-covered trees and the shimmer of crystalline ice reflecting on the road.

"I think you need to leave," she said.

"Sarah..."

"You need to leave."

He stood up and hesitated, as if he wanted to go to her. But Sarah held her arms tight around her chest, her hands around her neck, wondering if he was going to bare his fangs, spring on her, grab her in some preternatural lock, and drink her blood for dessert. She didn't want him anywhere near her.

He paused with his hand on the knob. "Will I see you soon?" he asked.

"I don't think so."

He opened the door and stepped into the frigid winter night. "Let me know when you're ready to talk," he said. And then he went away.

Sarah sat on the sofa, struggling to clear her head enough to have a coherent thought. Nothing made sense. Language had lost its meaning. It was all gibberish and nonsensical syllables and half-used sounds. Knowledge evaporated into useless ideas. After an hour of emptiness, she gave up. She double-checked her windows and doors, making sure they were locked, before she went to sleep.

I am standing in front of a tree. The tree is scarred, hunched, ugly, not beautiful like other trees because this tree knows its sinister purpose. There are twisted ropes swinging from the strongest branch, ropes meant to hang the five women waiting there. The women are numb and resolute, confused and terrified. They should not be here. They have committed no crime. They know this is the last sight they shall see, a riled, jeering crowd that cheers for their executions, happy to see the convicted witches go back Satan's way. But these women are innocent and they shan't confess to a crime they didn't commit because they are afraid of the damnation of their souls. They believe there shall be no peace for them in the next life if they admit to being demons in this one. They are praying for some release from this nightmare, for forgiveness for their trespasses, for eternal salvation. The one standing before the hempen skeleton rope is frail but firm in her stance. She shall not be afraid. The reverend, with his God-fearing way, asks her one last time to confess. The woman has already seen her young daughters caught up in the madness of the witch hunts and she shall not be swayed.

"I am no more a witch than you are a wizard," she says, "and if you take away my life God will give you blood to drink."

I am dumbfounded watching this horror. The accusations are foolish. Everyone must know this. But when times are hard even the most conscientious people have a life-preserving instinct. They shall point at others first so others do not point at them. One of the women waiting to die is an elderly, sickly woman I know as a neighbor and love as a friend, a good woman who should have never seen this gruesome day.

I did not mean to see this. I was out walking, trying to find some coolness somewhere, some sea breeze near the shore to settle my sweating skin because it is a sweltering, humid summer day when the air is heavy enough to hold in my hands. It is hard, doing everything for two. I walked far from the shore, and now I am here. I do not want to see this terrible scene but I cannot make myself walk away. The actions are unreal, the women unbearable to watch, but I cannot turn my head. Can no one help them, I wonder in the screaming of my mind? Can no one speak for them? I feel nauseous and do not know if it is the heat or my child or the horror.

"They're hanging her!" I say. I can hear the terror in my own voice. I see my friend praying as she waits for the realization of her own mortality. Then I feel a gentle hand on my arm.

"Come," he says.

I look up at him and though I cannot see his face I know he looks at me with great concern.

He puts his hand on the small of my back as he nudges me forward, and finally I am leaving. As I walk away I can hear the slap as the woman is pushed, the snap of her neck as she dangles—a slow, strangling, torturous death. I try to keep my weeping to myself and I hope she does not suffer long. I am crying, but he continues nudging me gently forward, ever so gently. Instinctively, my hand reaches for my stomach, bulging clearly now, and I worry what a world I am bringing this child into, a world where innocent women are hanged from the false accusations of others. Is there no reason here? Maybe my husband is right. Maybe we should leave this place. I am afraid.

CHAPTER 13

The next day Sarah could think in words again, and soon she molded those words into sentences. In the morning she did nothing but jot notes about her dream into her journal. She forgot to eat. In the afternoon she opened her door, grabbed the newspaper from her lawn, and opened to the classified section. There were some nice used cars available for not a lot of money. She could afford a nice used car. She looked at the time and sighed, dreading the library. James would be there since he had class that night, and she thought of calling in sick. But Jennifer would know why, and she didn't want them to know how upset she was. She would be brave, go to work, ignore James if he was there, ignore Jennifer as much as she could, and go home. Alone.

When she arrived at the library she realized how much she didn't want to run into James or Jennifer. Instead of working on the main floor, she switched with another librarian and spent the evening in the annex, located between the Central and North campuses. She liked it in there. Quieter than the main floor, the students in the annex were focused on their studies instead of socializing and they were a pleasure to work with. Sarah thought she would ask Jennifer to place her there permanently.

Halfway through her shift, she saw Jennifer wheeling a book cart into the room. Sarah moved behind the computer screen, hoping Jennifer wouldn't see her. She didn't hide well enough, and Jennifer stopped in front of her. Sarah nodded in greeting and returned to work. Jennifer looked around, then leaned close to Sarah and whispered.

"I've known James my whole life. My mother has known him her whole life. We're both still around to talk about it." When

Sarah didn't look up, Jennifer sighed. "He's known my family for generations. He's helped us in ways you can't begin to imagine."

Sarah still couldn't look at her. She felt like she had been played for a fool by the two people she trusted most. Here she had spent countless hours with James, and it had never once occurred to her that he was anything other than what he seemed to be. He had oddities, certainly, but everyone does. Being odd doesn't make someone unhuman. She was upset with him for hiding his secret, but she was mad at Jennifer too. Someone should have told her sooner. Someone should have given her the option to choose who, or what, she spent her time with.

"Do you need something, Jennifer?"

Sarah kept her voice pleasant. After all, Jennifer was the head librarian and her boss. She had to remain professional, but she didn't feel like chitchatting. She wanted Jennifer to go away.

Jennifer pointed to the book cart. "I need you to deliver these to Meier Hall."

Sarah recognized the books. She had ordered them herself.

"I can't bring those. They're for James."

"Exactly."

Before Sarah could protest, Jennifer was gone. Sarah fumed as she stared at the cart. There was no reason she had to be the one to bring those books to James. There were two other librarians on duty that night. Besides, his office was on the third floor of the main library building. Why did Jennifer wheel the book cart to the annex, then send her across campus to deliver books that could have been sent up in the elevator? Jennifer wanted her to see James. That was the only explanation.

Sarah stayed behind the librarians's desk, ignoring the cart, helping students, scanning barcodes. She wouldn't deliver the books. Why should she? She didn't want to see James. She had no reason to see him. But she didn't want to be weak, either. If she didn't go she would show them that she was afraid, and she wouldn't give them the satisfaction. She had fought through fear before. When she left a bad marriage that had been part of her entire adult life. When she had nightmares and pulled herself out of the frights. She wasn't going to let some vampire professor and his Wiccan friend scare her out of something as simple as a book delivery. She brought books to professors around campus all the time, she thought. This was part of her job.

The distance from the annex to Meier Hall seemed further when pushing a heavy book cart with wobbly wheels. She cursed Jennifer under her breath as she stumbled past Rainbow Terrace and the residence hall, across College Drive, around the campus center and the tennis courts, until she reached the School of Arts and Sciences. She wheeled the books into the building, checking room numbers as she went. When she turned the corner she heard James's voice coming from the classroom at the end of the corridor, the door propped open by a chair. She stopped, surprised by the warmth she felt at the sound. She didn't want to feel warmth for him. She pushed the cart down the hall slowly, trying to silence the squealing of the wheels. Then she heard laughter coming from the classroom, and she was curious. She wanted to peek around the open door, but she didn't want to be seen. She sat in a lounge chair in the hall, close enough to hear but far enough to stay hidden.

"That's not what it was called, Doctor Wentworth," she heard a young woman say.

"It is," James said. "I'm not taking any credit for it, but the name of the house was Wentworth Place. It was owned by Keats's friend Charles Armitage Brown, on the edge of Hampstead Heath. Brown said that Keats wrote 'Ode to a Nightingale' in that very house in the garden under a mulberry tree."

"That was in the 1800s," another young woman said. "It's not like Professor Wentworth could have been there."

"Of course I wasn't there." Sarah heard James's amused undertone as he continued. "The co-owner of Wentworth Place, a man named Dilke, insisted that Keats didn't write the poem at the house at all, and the story that he did was pure delusion on Brown's part."

"So who was right?" a male student asked.

"Who knows?" James said. "No one wrote Keats's biography when he was alive. After he died people tried to piece bits of his life together to form some kind of narrative, but memory is a funny thing. We remember what we want to remember and leave the rest out. Two people can experience the same event at the same time and have completely different memories of it. Which one is right?"

"I think the nightingale is right," the male student said.

James laughed with the class. "Very funny, Levon," he said.

"Seriously," Levon continued, "that was some nightingale. Keats made it seem like that bird's song could send you spinning into an acid trip or something."

"I don't think they used acid in the nineteenth century," James said. "Opium was more like it, but you're on the right track. What in the poem makes you link the nightingale's song to a drug?"

"It's right here," Levon said. "'That I might drink, and leave the world unseen, And with thee fade away into the forest dim.'"

"Very good," James said. "Yes? Crystal?"

"I don't like this poem. It seems like it's going to be a sweet tribute to the nightingale's song, but really it's about death and dying."

"It's about immortality," said another male student. "It's about removing the line between life and death."

From the hallway Sarah heard the pause in James's voice. "What makes you say that, Greg?" he asked.

"Starting on Line 61: 'Thou wast not born for death, immortal Bird! No hungry generations tread thee down...'"

"He's talking about the line between reality and fantasy," said Crystal. "He's not saying that death is a good thing. He's saying he can't tell."

"I don't get it," said another male voice.

"I know the old-time language can be confusing," James said, "but stick with it, Pete. It'll make sense soon."

Then Levon's voice: "Doctor Wentworth?"

There was a pause, then James said, "Yes, Levon, go ahead. Good luck tonight."

"Are you coming? You promised you were coming."

Another pause. "I'll do my best," James said.

Levon burst out of the room with such speed he didn't see Sarah sitting in the hallway. He tripped over the book cart and pressed his heavy hands onto Sarah's shoulders as he struggled to stay upright.

"Excuse me, Miss," he said as he sprinted down the hall and disappeared out the side exit. Sarah noticed that he was wearing his blue and orange ice hockey jersey. That's right, she thought, tonight's a big game against Bowdoin.

Back in the classroom, the conversation continued.

"Professor Wentworth, is Keats saying death is a good thing or a bad thing?"

"What do you think, Amy?"

"I think he's saying that since he's heard the bird's song and it was so beautiful he feels like he can die now. He's experienced the most beautiful thing there is. He doesn't seem afraid to die, though, almost like he welcomes it. Or like he thinks there's no difference between life and death. That's crazy."

"Is it?"

Sarah needed to see James's face. She wanted to see the man, the...man she had dismissed from her life the night before. Is this who she was afraid of, the English professor who spoke to his students with such patience, the one who gave her gifts of poetry, the one who wouldn't let her leave the library alone at night, the one who wouldn't leave her side without kissing the top of her head? She stood up, pushed the book cart forward, and stood in the open doorway. A few students noticed her, but they didn't seem concerned to see a librarian with a cartful of books. She watched James as he sat on the edge of the instructor's desk, his arms crossed casually in front of his chest, his eyes on the linoleum floor as he considered his words. An expression of such thoughtfulness. Sarah knew suddenly that her idea of a romantic hero wasn't a warrior or a superhero. He was intelligent and contemplative. Kind. Caring. Like James.

Finally, James said, "What if there isn't the line in the sand between life and death we insist on drawing there? What if what waits for us on the other side isn't better or worse than what we have now? Just different? What if we can transcend life and death to a limbo world between, and find as much joy in the next life as we can in this one...?"

"Do you really think we can find joy after we're dead, Professor?"

James saw Sarah standing in the doorway.

"I do," he said.

He stared at her until everyone in the class turned to see where he was looking. A few students snickered, snapping him from his reverie.

"All right, everyone," he said. "See you next week."

The students grabbed their laptops and their backpacks and filed out the door. A few greeted Sarah when they passed her. When the room was empty, Sarah stepped inside and waited. She wasn't afraid of him, not anymore, but she wasn't sure he wanted to see her. She had dismissed him so rudely the night before. Not that she didn't have her reasons. Though she hoped he understood, she wouldn't blame him if he never wanted to talk to her again.

James watched her, the same intense gaze he always had with her. He walked to the book cart and asked, "Are these for me?" Sarah nodded. "Thank you," he said, glancing at the titles. "These are exactly what I needed. But you didn't need to drag them across campus. You could have sent them up to my office from the main floor."

Sarah felt her cheeks blush hot. She hadn't wanted to bring James the books, and now there was nowhere else she'd rather be than in that classroom beside him.

"Jennifer told me I needed to bring them to you," she said.

He shook his head. "Jennifer. That doesn't surprise me."

"She is my boss."

"I think bossy is the word. Perhaps meddling is more like it."

He checked the time on the clock on the wall. "I have to go," he said. "I told Levon I'd try to make it to the game tonight."

Sarah had to hide her disappointment. She was hoping he'd be so glad to see her he'd sweep her into his arms and carry her back to his wooden gabled house, or at least hold her close awhile. She sighed when she realized he wasn't thinking any such thing. He was standing away from her, his hands in the pockets of his gray trousers, his eyes on the books on the cart.

"I'll bring these back to your office," she said.

"Absolutely not. You had no business bringing them out here in the first place."

He walked back to the instructor's desk, grabbed his book bag, and turned out the lights. In the hallway, he took possession of the cart and wheeled it out the door.

"Were you going to the game?" he asked.

"I was thinking about it." Actually, she had no such thought. She couldn't care less about ice hockey, but if James was going then she wanted to go too.

"I'd be happy to escort you. If you'd like that." He grimaced, a flash of concern in his night-dark eyes. "I understand if you don't want to be anywhere near me, Sarah. I don't think I would want to be anywhere near me if I were you. I know I should have told you sooner. I didn't keep it from you because I didn't trust you. I kept it from you because I knew you would be afraid. Who wouldn't be?"

Sarah put her hand over his as he wheeled the cart across College Drive. He stopped at her touch, and she didn't pull away from his lifeless skin. It didn't feel odd. It felt...like James. "I don't think anyone who talks about the Romantic poets the way you do could hurt anyone," she said. "I'm glad Jennifer sent me tonight."

As they walked they glanced shyly at each other, like teenagers with a crush. Then he stopped, stacked the books on the bottom shelf of the cart, and patted the top shelf. "Hop on," he said.

Sarah shook her head. "I could barely push the cart with just the books."

"I think I can handle it."

He picked her up as if she weighed no more than a porcelain doll, then sat her on top of the cart. He pushed her forward, onto the green near the residence hall, past the annex to the main library building. He wasn't running, but he moved quickly, and Sarah felt her heart race and her breath quicken. She felt like she did when she was a girl and she went on the roller coasters at Great Adventure, the adrenaline rushing, feeling alive. Students and professors waved and laughed as they rushed by, and they were at the library too soon. She hadn't felt such child-like glee for years. James stopped the cart, lifted her from the shelf, and placed her gently on the ground. They took the elevator to the third floor where he put the books into his office, and they left the empty cart on the main floor.

They walked hand in hand to the O'Keefe Center, to Rockett Arena where the game had already started. Sarah stopped short when she saw the "Sold Out" signs displayed in the box office windows, but James led her toward the turnstile.

"Levon gave me tickets," he said.

"Hey, Doctor Wentworth," the usher said. "Your seats are down front."

They walked into an electric atmosphere of blue and orange, and shouts of "Vikings!" or "Defense!" bounced off the walls back at the spectators like yodels down a mountain range. As she looked around, Sarah saw nearly an equal number of Bowdoin supporters in their white hoodies with their school's polar bear logo. The score was tied, 2-2, and Sarah saw Levon, the Viking goalie, set in concentration as the puck flew his way.

The game passed in a blur for Sarah. Every once in a while, if the crowd screamed loudly enough, she would check the score, but otherwise she was consumed by James. He cheered as loudly as anyone, cursed a bad call, shouted encouragement for Levon. When Levon blocked a potential Bowdoin winning goal, James stood up and shouted, "That's my boy!" Sarah smiled whenever a student recognized him and gave him the hi sign or shouted "How ya doin' Professor?" or "Hey Doctor Wentworth! Don't usually see you at the games!"

The Vikings scored again in the fourth quarter, and they won 3-2. The cheers in the arena echoed so loudly Sarah had to cover her ears to stop the ringing. Levon skated past to the locker room, and he stopped when he saw them.

"Doctor Wentworth, you made it!" He pointed his chin in Sarah's direction. "I saw you earlier. You were waiting for the professor in the hall."

Sarah felt her cheeks blush hot. "I had some books for him."

"That's right. I remember tripping over the cart." Levon grinned. "You're the Humanities librarian."

"That's right."

"She's a nice lady, Doctor Wentworth."

"Yes, she is," James said.

126

Levon looked at Sarah, still grinning. "I'm glad you're hanging out with the professor. I've been telling him he needs a friend..."

"Good night, Levon."

Levon laughed at the professor's terse dismissal as he skated away.

After the crowd cleared, James took Sarah's hand and led her back to the library. It was dark, Jennifer had closed for the night, so Sarah used her keys to let them in. She flipped on the lights of the main floor, and suddenly they were alone inside. James sat in a chair by one of the computer terminals, and he logged into his account and typed something into the keyboard. Sarah walked over to him, as close as she dared. She wanted to brush his gold hair from his eyes. She wanted to kiss him, but she wouldn't pressure him again. He took his glasses off and slid them into his shirt pocket, and she was glad he felt comfortable enough to put his disguise away, meager as it was.

"Look at this," he said. He turned the monitor so Sarah could see what he had pulled up—information about the year 1662.

"1662?"

"The year I was born."

She leaned over his shoulder so she could see the screen clearly. He leaned toward her, his hair touching her cheek.

"You're three hundred and forty-nine years old," she said. He nodded. "You look good for your age."

He laughed, though the amusement became a sigh. He took Sarah's hand and held onto it. She didn't want him to let go. He brought her around the chair and she sat on his lap. She leaned into him, her back against his chest.

"Immortality sounds like a gift, doesn't it?" He spoke softly, whispering in her ear. "Never growing old or feeble. Never ailing, never dying. But my nights became monotonous. I had to find a way to give meaning to my time, so I began teaching. It's an odd job for me, I suppose, but then any job besides Grim Reaper might seem odd for one of my kind. I enjoy sharing the knowledge I've gained, and since so few people know what I am, no one questions me. I'm virtually undetectable in this world."

"Where were you born?"

"London. I moved to the Massachusetts Bay Colony with my father, John, who made his fortune as a merchant. We both wanted a fresh start after my mother died, and we were intrigued by the untapped opportunities in the New World. We knew of the seaport here and the possibilities of making more money in the merchant trade, so we immigrated."

"Did you meet your wife here or in London?"

James paused, and she turned her head so she could see his face. His brow was furrowed, his eyes closed as he rested his head against the chair. He seemed to wonder how to say what he needed to say.

"I met my wife here, through friends of the family, over supper one evening. She died too young. Many people died young in the seventeenth century, but she didn't die from illness or childbirth as so many did then. She died for all the wrong reasons."

Something James said made Sarah pause, something tugged at the edges of her memory, but she didn't try to make sense of it then. She was just happy to be near him.

"You must have had a fascinating life," she said.

He looked sad as he nodded. As Sarah sat on his lap, feeling his strength envelop her, part of her, her logical mind, began to balk against the supernatural hocus pocus. Though she had felt his unbeating chest, he was so human in every other way. How could this young-looking man have been born during colonial times? How could he be dead but alive, talking to her, stroking her hair? She touched her hand to his cheek, felt the lifelessness there, and she was reminded that the hocus pocus was true. Silently to herself, she tried to list all the changes that had happened over the last three hundred years.

"It must be jarring to you, the passage of time," she said. "Like that old saying, the more things change, the more they stay the same."

"It can be quite a shock sometimes to remember it's the twenty-first century and not the seventeenth, though human nature hasn't changed much in all that time. Apart from the new-fangled technology, what people want from their lives has remained essentially the same. They want their basic needs met. They want security. They want to know they matter."

Again, Sarah thought of James's wife. She remembered his reaction the first time he saw her the night she went to look at his house.

"When you saw me the first time, you thought I was your wife even though she died over three hundred years ago?"

"Yes."

"Do you still think I look like her?"

"Yes."

He spoke quickly, as if he needed to change the subject. "I'm sure it's hard for a human to accept the fact that my kind exists. There are probably around a million in all, more in Salem as well. Timothy, for example."

Sarah had seen the pale-faced, dark-eyed, dark-haired boy following James around the library like a faithful puppy with his tongue out and his tail wagging. Whenever she saw the boy she thought he seemed too young to be in college.

"And Jocelyn. You met her on Halloween. She was dressed as Cher."

"Jocelyn and Steve are vampires?"

"Not Steve. Just Jocelyn."

"A vampire married to a human?"

James shrugged but he smiled. "It happens," he said.

"It must be hard for a human to be married to a vampire."

"Jocelyn and Steve seem to manage. They're one of the happiest couples I know."

James paused and his face softened as he watched her. She wanted to love the way he was looking at her, but she couldn't help wondering who it was he looked at with such tenderness, the memory of his wife Elizabeth or her. She wanted to believe he saw her since she was the one sitting on his lap, but then she remembered what happened the other night, the coldness between them when all she wanted was to be closer to him. She shuddered at the memory of the way he jumped into his car and sped away.

"I suppose it depends on how different the human is willing for her life to be," he said, his voice trailing away with the thought.

"I didn't know about you until last night. You don't seem that different."

"But I am. I've become better at hiding it over the years. For one thing, we're on different schedules. Most of life happens during the day while I'm sleeping. And I drink blood, Sarah. I need blood to survive."

"That is different."

"There's also the fear factor. Some people might be too nervous about the fact that their significant other drinks blood. She might be afraid her vampire would suddenly decide he's hungry one night and start feeding on the closest human he can find."

"And you're dead?"

"You remembered."

He shook his head again. Of everything Sarah had learned about him, that fact amazed her the most. How can a body function without a heartbeat? Even a vampire body. Especially a vampire body. Looking at him as he held himself so still, she wanted to reach out, pull him even closer, run her fingers through his hair. He was the bigger, stronger one by far, yet something about him looked so vulnerable then. But instead of grabbing him, she reached out her hand and touched his chest where his heart should be. The nothing that had frightened her so much the night before, no rise and fall of air, no pounding life rhythm, now seemed merely an interesting fact about James. She looked into his night-dark eyes and saw a faint smile, maybe one he didn't intend for her to see. With a little more courage brought on by his smile, she pressed her ear where her hand had been. She could have stayed that way all night. Then she felt his chin on top of her head. His head felt heavy, but the pressure felt right. She stayed there longer than it took to hear the hollow silence inside his chest.

"Still nothing," she said.

"Yes."

"How does the blood you drink flow through your body if your heart doesn't pump?"

"I don't know."

She raised her head from his chest and looked him in the eye.

"Tell me about Elizabeth."

He shook his head. "Another time."

"Tell me anything. Tell me about the day you met."

James closed his eyes again. He stayed that way so long Sarah thought he fell asleep. When he opened his eyes to look at her, she thought he seemed far away, as if he had traveled back in time. When he spoke his voice sounded different, like an actor in a Shakespearean play. He smiled as he thought of that long-ago day.

"I remember how my heart danced dizzying circles the first time I saw her over the supper table where my father and I were gathered with friends. Her family was new to the Massachusetts Bay Colony having just arrived from England."

"What year was it?"

He thought a moment. "1691. From the moment I saw her I knew I had never seen anyone as beautiful. She was talking to her younger sister in a sweet, motherly way, and I might not have been there at all for all that she noticed me. When she finally looked around the table and saw me gazing at her, our eyes met and I knew instantly she was the one for me. It came as no surprise that other young men had noticed her. I didn't think I had a chance to win her hand. Surely she could find someone better than me, I thought, but she was always on my mind.

"My father, ever my friend and protector, noticed how distracted I was and how gammy, how clumsy, I had become. I was tripping all over myself, knocking everything over, unable to concentrate at my work. There was a particularly embarrassing incident one afternoon when I spilled hot coffee over a potential buyer. My father had found a new supplier for the beans and he was hoping this man, Mr. Smithers, would purchase most, if not all, of our product.

"'James,' my father called, 'bring Mr. Smithers some of that coffee I brewed this morn. He should taste how warming and delicious the drink is for himself.' Though I was standing but a foot away I hardly heard him.

"'James?'

"'Aye?' I said.

"'The coffee, Son.'

"'Coffee?' I answered.

"'Aye, James. Coffee.'

"I rushed to the tea service, an expensive set my father had imported from somewhere exotic, and I clanged around until I fit the right top onto the right pot. My father and Mr. Smithers watched with amused grins. I tripped over I-didn't-know-what as I brought the tea service to the table, and I knocked into a chair and the pot fell over, spilling hot liquid all over Mr. Smithers, down his white linen shirt and white stockings. Mr. Smithers, as if nothing strange had happened, touched his fingertips to the puddle on his breeches and put his hand to his mouth.

"'Quite good,' Mr. Smithers said, nodding in appreciation.

"'The finest you'll find anywhere,' my father said."

Sarah laughed at the image of James spilling hot liquid over the poor, unsuspecting man.

"Was your father very angry?"

"Not at all. After the man made his purchase and left—fortunately he was a good-humored fellow who didn't hold my ungraceful maneuver against us—my father prodded my feelings from me.

"'Are you well, Son?' he asked. He smiled as I sat behind my desk, a feather quill listless in my hand. 'You're wearing your spectacles so I reckon you can see well enough. What ails you?'

"I hardly heard his questions while I stared with confused eyes out the window at the passing horse-drawn carts. I knew I was supposed to be doing something, but I couldn't remember what that might be. Then I remembered my task, calculating figures from our latest importing venture. I attempted to work, but I couldn't remember anything about how to add or subtract numbers. Did three come before or after four?

"My father crossed his arms in front of his chest as he watched me, his knowing smile relaxing into an impish grin.

"'Your distraction wouldn't have anything to do with a certain Miss Elizabeth Jones, now, would it?'

"I sighed as I looked at him. ''Tis that obvious?' I asked.

"'Tis obvious in certain ways. I've seen how you go out of your way to cross paths with her, how you gaze at her in church when your head should be bowed in prayer, how you've been slack with your duties here. And, well, at the moment your garters are undone.'

"I saw that my garters were indeed undone and my white cotton stockings were hanging uselessly down my legs. My father laughed as I bent to fasten my straps.

"'Now when should I go?' he asked.

"'Go? Where?'

"'To speak to Mr. Jones. You want Elizabeth's hand, do you not?'

"'Aye!' I spoke with such excitement my face flushed.

"My father laughed again. 'Then you shall have it. I'll speak to Mr. Jones directly.'

"'You'll go this day?'

"'This moment. And you needn't thank me since 'tis for me as well as you. I can tell by the folly in your manner you're not likely to complete your tasks here lest I secure her hand for you.'

"'What if she won't have me?' I asked.

"'Won't have you? Of course she'll have you. You're a good boy, James, patient, kind, even-tempered. And handsome too. Thank God you took after your mother. Besides, I believe the feeling is mutual. I've seen her on the other side of the aisle in church staring back at you when she should have been praying as well.' My father tapped the desk in front of me with his hand. 'Don't worry, Son. I shan't take no for an answer.'

"My father told me afterwards that he talked me up as the heir to his prosperous merchant trade, a business that often took him to exotic ports around the world. He explained how I knew all manners of the business, and I was indispensable as a son and friend.

"'There is no better young man than my James,' my father told Mr. Jones. 'My son was educated at Cambridge. I had no choice but to send him to university, you see. He seems to have been born with his nose sewn into bookbinding. Always reading. Always learning. He wishes to be a professor at university, but he's a fine son, biding his time helping his old father with business now.'"

"You knew even then you wanted to teach," Sarah said. "You haven't changed."

"In some ways I haven't changed at all. In other ways I hardly recognize myself."

"I haven't had the same transformation as you," Sarah said, "but I understand what you mean. I feel so different now than I did when I was living in Los Angeles. I feel like the light has been switched on."

James smiled, and she felt the heat lick her cheeks pink.

"So Mr. Jones accepted your offer?" she asked.

"It didn't take much persuasion. My father said Mr. Jones seemed inclined to accept me right away. After all, my father was one of the wealthiest men in England, let alone the colonies. He explained to Mr. Jones that I had some savings of my own, and he assured him that, should it be agreed Elizabeth and I were to be betrothed, he would gladly buy us some land and build us one of the grandest houses in Salem Town."

"Salem Town?"

"It was divided into Salem Town and Salem Village then. Mr. Jones said it was the best offer he had had for Elizabeth all year. He even told my father he had been worried since she was heading past marriageable age, at twenty-two. He was afraid she would never marry because she was a stubborn girl who had refused two previous offers.

"'If your boy wants her, and she's agreeable, then 'tis all well enough by me,' Mr. Jones said. He told my father that he had promised his wife that he would never force his daughters to marry someone they were not inclined toward. Fortunately for me the feeling was mutual, as my father predicted. I remember the day I told him to hire the sawyers and the carpenters to build our new house. I knew Elizabeth would be my wife, and I wanted to get our home ready for our life together.

"I didn't tell Elizabeth the house was being built, and the carpenters worked quickly. The day the last peg was hammered into the wood my father and I brought her to see it for the first time. She gasped out loud when she saw it.

"'Tis beautiful, James,' she said. 'Tis the grandest house in Salem Town.' She walked to the front door, touched the latchkey, and looked through the diamond-paned window to the furnished room inside. 'Whose is it?'

"'Tis yours,' I said, 'if you want it to be.'

"There we were, standing in front of the house while my father waited inside, and I asked her to be my wife. I knew it had all been agreed upon before, but I wanted to hear her response with my own ears."

"Were you very happy together?"

"Happier than I thought I had any right to be."

James looked at Sarah. He leaned so close their heads touched. His dark eyes penetrated her, reached inside her, as if he were grasping for something. She felt the way she did the night she first saw him when he had mistaken her for his wife—disjointed and confused. The more he looked into her, though, the more there was something there, some semblance of a dream, or was it a memory, she couldn't tell. The feeling disappeared as soon as it came on, and then she became fidgety, her fingernails tapping a worried rhythm against the side of the chair. He must have sensed her discomfort because he turned away.

"We were married in late 1691," he said. "I don't remember much about our wedding ceremony except a yearning impatience to be alone with her. I remember the feast my father paid for, set out for our guests like a king's ransom waiting to be plundered. I remember the magistrate mumbling something. After the ceremony was over and our guests were well satiated, my father walked my bride and me to our new home. He came into the house with us, which surprised me, and he took great pleasure showing Elizabeth how he completed the home for us with the finest furniture the best carpenters in Salem Town could build. He even had a few pieces, including the blue and white hand-painted Delft dishware, imported from Holland. When he finally left (it took a few pointed stares from me before he understood) I was alone with my wife for the first time."

Sarah felt his body curving around hers, and she leaned into him. She couldn't get close enough. She felt his hands in her hair, his lips on the back of her neck. She wanted him, there was no denying that, but he had just been talking about being alone with Elizabeth for the first time. Sarah knew she looked like Elizabeth, and her desire for him was tempered by the fact that, if they did make love that night, who would James really be with? Her? Elizabeth? Sarah sighed. Here they were, finally close, and he had been speaking about being alone with his wife. She began to wonder if they had a chance after all.

James brought her home. He was distracted with his own thoughts and didn't speak at all on the drive. She thought she saw concern in his eyes, and she wondered if he was thinking the same thing she was—maybe the fact that she looked like his wife was going to keep them apart.

As she got ready for bed she had her moments when it seemed like a trick, the idea that James was anything other than human. There are yogis who can stop their breath or slow their heartbeats for a dangerous amount of time. Maybe James had learned to do that. But what would be the point of such a trick? He was pale, but being pale doesn't mean you're dead, so she tried to be logical about it. Had she ever seen anyone else with skin like the light of the moon, so white it looked vein blue or translucent gray? Whenever he touched her she noticed that he felt cooler than she did, but did he feel as cold as a dead body? She had never touched a dead body before so she didn't know. His hair was gold but his eyes were night-sky black, an unnerving contrast to the blue she still expected them to be. Aren't vampires walking corpses with pointed ears, hideous leers, and sharp fangs that pierce you until you die? Don't they flutter as bats outside your window and drink your blood while you sleep? But she had felt his still chest, twice, heard the silence inside, and in the end that was all the proof she needed. She fell asleep dreaming about when she would see him again, hoping that his dead wife would stop being a barrier between them. She only had one nightmare that night that woke her up cold and afraid, and it wasn't a nightmare about vampires but a terror about a prison that looked and sounded too real.

Though I am too weak to see clearly I know I am locked in a dank, gloomy dungeon infested with rats. I can hear the faint cries of the other women in the cages around me. The dim candlelight is flickering demons, there are the real demons I want to cry, not us, there they are in the shadows on the walls. I am so ill I am delirious, barely conscious or alive. I feel the blood on my legs from the scraping of the iron chains around my ankles, an extra precaution, they said, to prevent my specter from vanishing through the walls. As if chains could prevent a real specter from doing anything it wanted. The women surrounding me are groaning, or scratching their itching skin, or reading the Bible, or praying softly, hoping God could hear them even there.

I am in hell. I am waiting for someone, anyone, to realize this mistake. I should be home with my husband. We shall have our baby soon. I try to speak but only spittle escapes my cracked lips. I close my eyes and know I am dying, my baby dying with me. I let the tears flow freely because I think I shall never see my beloved again, and I know how devastated he shall be when he learns that I left him though I promised I would never leave him ever. I know he has been outside the jail doing everything he can to get me out. I feel his agony. I know his body shudders in pain like a knife blade ripping his skin. With my last strength I press my hands against the wall and whisper "I love you" to my husband. And then nothing. I am gone...

CHAPTER 14

When James arrived home he locked himself into his house, lit a single candle, sat at the table, and stared at the cauldron in the hearth. So much about that house hadn't changed in over three hundred years. He looked at the seventeenth-century furniture, his vast collection of books, the peaked roof ending in two points overhead. He shut his eyes so tightly it hurt. He was trying to summon Elizabeth, begging to see her, wanting to feel her in his arms again. Sarah was so like Elizabeth, and yet she was also her own woman. Again, the problem of wanting to be with Sarah and feeling Elizabeth so strongly the two became confused. He could sense that Sarah felt it that night too. He had wanted her, and she had wanted him. He knew it from the softness in her eyes, from the way she pressed her warm curves against him, yet the ghost of his wife stood squarely between them, arms out like a boxing referee, separating them and keeping them apart. He was mad with desire for Sarah, but he didn't know what to do about Elizabeth.

His thoughts turned back to his wedding night. After his father had left, Elizabeth was standing by the wall along the back of the great room staring at that very cauldron in the hearth. Though he had been dreaming of being alone with her from the first time he saw her, he was shy and tongue-tied suddenly and didn't know what to say. He stood mutely, waiting for her to speak, but she was feeling shy, too, and she pretended not to notice him standing there. Then he felt the absurdity of the situation—they were husband and wife now, he thought, there's no reason to be shy with each other. He laughed, and she did too, smiling that smile he loved so much. All of a sudden his life made sense to him. This was where he was supposed to be, and there was no one else in the world for him to be with.

He removed his hat and cloak, walked to her, and stood as close as he dared. She looked up at him but shyness overcame her again and she turned away. He tilted her chin with his hand and caressed her cheek until they both exhaled. When she looked at him with the same longing he had felt for her he couldn't hold back any more. He kissed her, first gently on her temple, then her cheek, then her lips. When she kissed him back with as much yearning as he felt the passion overtook them and he carried her to bed. He thought she would be self-conscious when he undressed her, but she wasn't, which was good because it took some time. He left her coif, the white cap she wore tied over her hair, and her brown silk outer gown to her to remove. Then he had to make his way through her underpants, stockings, petticoat, chemise, bolster—a padded roll she wore tied around her hips under her gathered skirt—and her bodice. They were easy about it and laughed because it was funny, an erotic comedy of manners as he fumbled with the ties and fastenings of his wife's clothing and tried not to appear too greedy to get to her bare flesh beneath. But she wanted him as much as he wanted her and she waited patiently, often with amusement, and finally she was free from the constraints. The first time he made love to Elizabeth had none of the awkwardness of two virgins fumbling their way through a blind, impetuous maze. His hands knew where to caress her. She knew where to stroke him. Somehow, he knew that she loved to be kissed on the nape of her neck and he lingered there. Instinctively, they understood each other and knew how to be together.

They had found their own little bubble of joy in a harsh colonial world. He was happy whenever he awoke in the morning and saw his wife standing over him, already dressed, her apron on, her white cap tied over her hair, pulling the blankets from him.

"James?" she'd say. "Jamie? You're dallying again. The sun has been risen this hour past. 'Tis time to awaken."

With a frustrated sigh she'd start tugging on his arm as she tried to pull him out of bed.

"James Wentworth," she'd say, "you are the most slothful man yet born!" Then he'd pull her into bed and try to run his hand under her skirts before she slapped him away. "Slothful and lustful," she'd say, pretending she was annoyed. "You've already committed two of the seven deadly sins and you're not yet clothed."

""Tis difficult to commit some of the sins when clothed," he'd say.

She began every morning by standing outside near the trees, listening to the birds sing, trying to whistle along. Back inside, she brushed his clothes and set them out, his cotton stockings, garters, breeches, doublet, shoes, and hat. After he was dressed she'd fasten his points, the strings which tied his breeches and doublet together. He'd wash his face and hands in the basin, then say a blessing before they broke their fast with either white pot, custard made of baked eggs and milk, or samp, cracked corn mush. Every day but Sunday he would walk to his father's where he would help with whatever business tasks necessary.

There was no time they loved more than their nights together when he would read to her while she sewed. She didn't care what he read—the Bible, poetry, literature, pamphlets, news—she loved it all. Her favorite was Anne Bradstreet. Every night he would read "To My Dear and Loving Husband" before they blew out the candles and went to bed, a ritual they both looked forward to. As much as she wanted to hear James read was as much as he wanted to hear her voice. He didn't care what she was saying as long as she was speaking to him. There were times when they talked late into the night, about what he did at his father's that day, who visited, what they talked about, what his father said, what the other person said in return. She found the Puritans too stoic, as he did, but at least they had reprieve from the pious eyes in the sanctuary of their home.

After the witch trials began to suffocate everyone in Salem, everything he knew to be true became false. Frightening. There was so much more he could have told Timothy about the witch trials. He still shuddered whenever he thought of that time. There was so much sadness then. In 1692, nineteen "witches" were hung on Gallows Hill, but there were other fatalities as well,

141

including their friend Giles Corey, a respected farmer in his eighties who was tortured to death, suffocated under the weight of heavy stones because he refused to enter a plea at his trial after he was falsely accused of wizardry. Six others, including his wife, died in prison. Seven if you counted their unborn child, which he did.

James looked out the window at the lightless sky. The nightmarish memories had been unleashed in him, and it was hours until dawn when he could find reprieve in his daily death. He had no choice but to dwell on them.

CHAPTER 15

To the casual observer looking at the brick house in the center of town, seeing the snow on the roof, the white swing on the porch, the Christmas decorations on the front lawn, the lighted tree in the window, there was no evidence a different kind of family lived there. The wife was a dentist who kept her office open at night to handle after-hours emergencies. The husband was a high school science teacher. They were a nice young couple, friendly with their neighbors, and they seemed very much in love. No one suspected that the wife was a nonhuman married to a human husband, and they probably wouldn't have believed it if someone had told them, even someone like Kenneth Hempel who wrote for their local paper. Jocelyn Endecott, not human? She might be a bit pale, but flesh-colored foundation and cream blush helped to make the death-like pallor look more rosy and alive. She kept night hours, odd for a dentist, certainly, but hadn't she seen their children at midnight when they woke up screaming with a toothache? And how could she possibly handle being a dentist when *they* love blood so much? Her neighbors would scoff at such foolishness as someone calling their friend anything other than what she seemed to be, a lovely young woman, and they would turn away, snickering, telling everyone that the reporter from *The Salem News* had lost his mind. Jocelyn Endecott could not possibly be *that*.

When James and Sarah arrived at the brick house, Jocelyn and Steve welcomed them with open arms. Jocelyn embraced Sarah and took her hand.

"I'm so glad you're here," Jocelyn said. She led Sarah to the dining room table, which was set out with food and drink for the humans, eggplant parmesan, garlic bread, meant as a joke, red wine, and discrete, covered coffee mugs for Jocelyn and James. After dinner, Sarah helped Steve clear off the table and put the plates in the sink. When they were in the kitchen, James heard Sarah ask Steve about the one thing that had her curious.

"So how did you and Jocelyn meet? You're not the likeliest of couples."

"No," said Steve, "I guess not, but then neither are you and James. You don't need to do that, you know. You're the guest." Steve was washing the dishes while Sarah dried them.

"I don't mind. So how did you meet?"

"She was my dentist."

"Are you kidding?"

"Not at all. I came in from Boston one night to visit my mother and I had the worst toothache ever. I called around and Jocelyn was the only dentist who had late hours so I went to see her. I knew she was the one for me as soon as she walked into the exam room. I took one look at her and thought, 'Now that is one hunk of a woman.' I asked her out that night. She refused. Then I called her the next night, and the next, and the next. I called her every night for a month. It took some persistence, but I finally wore her down. She said, 'If I go out on one date with you, will you leave me alone?' So I agreed. We went out on one date and we've been together ever since."

"Good for you," Sarah said. "Persistence usually gets you what you want." She stacked the plates and Steve put them into the cupboard. "So Jocelyn didn't want to date you because you're human?"

"That had nothing to do with it. She didn't want to date me because I was her patient."

Jocelyn walked into the kitchen and put her arm around Steve. "I have a very strict policy against dating patients," she said.

"Had," said Steve. "You had a very strict policy."

"That's right—I had a very strict policy against dating patients. But he was too cute to resist."

"And you didn't care that she was a...?" Sarah asked.

"Why would I care? It took some getting used to at first, and I might have been a little nervous until we worked through some of the logistical problems, you know, like where she was going to find blood to drink. There's also the night hours, but she's the girl of my dreams and I wasn't going to let her get away. And younger guys with older women is all the rage these days, isn't it?"

Jocelyn whacked Steve with the dishtowel. "You know better than to say anything about my age," she said. "That is not a topic for discussion."

Steve and Sarah stayed in the kitchen while James and Jocelyn went outside to the backyard. Jocelyn closed the glass door behind her. James sat on a snow-dusted lawn chair and watched the twinkling Christmas lights glisten like stars on the ice.

"She's nice," Jocelyn said. "And all it took was finding a girl who looks exactly like your dead wife."

"I don't ask for much," James said.

Jocelyn sat on a folding chair. "What is it, James? You sounded serious on the phone."

He walked to the edge of the yard, gripping the picket fence, staring out at the empty street. "What happens to us when we go out in the sun?" he asked. "I've only been out once since I was turned, over three hundred years ago, but I didn't last a minute before I went running back inside."

"I don't know what happens to us in the sun. It never occurred to me to try. It isn't so bad living only at night. The moon and the stars can be beautiful too. Why are you asking? You're not thinking about going outside during the day, are you?"

James shrugged without meeting Jocelyn's gaze. He wasn't prepared to share his half-formed plan.

Jocelyn brushed an icicle from her chair. "I've heard that the sun makes us weak. I've heard we can be killed more easily in the light, or it burns our eyes out, or it kills us instantly and we melt away like the wicked witch. I suppose there must be some of our kind somewhere who know the truth."

She looked at the moon and smiled. "Wouldn't it be funny if it turned out to be a legend—about the sunlight? Like silver and garlic? Those don't harm us at all yet they're considered the perfect weapon. Maybe there's no reason we can't go outside during the day, but we're all so convinced into believing it we never tried. Maybe it's just a story passed down through the centuries, like cautionary tales meant to teach children lessons?"

"There must be some truth to it. I went out during the day once, and it was...hard."

"Then you know there's some danger. You didn't tell me why you're asking."

"Just curious."

James watched the rainbow lights reflect off the windows of the house. He saw Sarah though the glass, laughing at something Steve said, and he was happy at the sound. He had to remind himself what that feeling was whenever he was caught by an irrepressible grin or a warmth in his dead-cold body. He was getting used to it again—joy. It had been oh so very long.

Sarah and Steve came out into the yard though the winter weather was too harsh for them without coats and mittens.

"Go back inside, Sarah," James said. "It's too cold."

"Not without you."

Shivering, she walked to him and took his hand. He was overcome with emotion. He wanted her to understand the irony of it all. When they first met all he could think about was how much she was like Elizabeth, and now he was fine with her being Sarah, just Sarah. Only Sarah. He hoped when the time came he would find the right words to help her understand.

CHAPTER 16

James didn't have class the next night, but he went to his office anyway. The memories of the seventeenth century were ceaseless now and he wanted the distraction of work. As he put a coffee mug into the microwave on the bookcase he heard a knock on his door. I must be distracted, he thought. I didn't hear the footsteps. Worried about who might be waiting outside, he sat back and didn't answer. Then he caught the familiar scents, sandalwood for one, rosewater for the other.

"James? It's Olivia. Can I come in?"

He opened the door and in came Olivia waving a newspaper. Jennifer stepped in, too, shutting the door behind her.

"Have you seen this?" Olivia asked.

James shook his head. "I'm afraid to look. A present from our friend Mr. Hempel?"

"I wouldn't call it a present exactly," said Jennifer. "More of a trick than a treat."

He took the paper and read aloud: "Do Vampires Live in Salem? By Kenneth Hempel, Staff Writer." He tried an unconvincing smile. "The demon tales from long ago Salem may not be as fictional as many have come to believe. Do you know any demons? Or, perhaps a better question is, do you know any vampires? Before you laugh you may want to consider the facts. Vampires may be prowling as close as your hospitals, your favorite clothing stores, your dentists's offices, even lurking in Salem State College."

He crumpled the paper and threw it into the trashcan. "Lurking in Salem State College?" He took his glasses off and rubbed his eyes. "Did he name me?"

"He didn't name anyone," Olivia said, "but he mentioned dentists so he might know about Jocelyn too. I think he's building suspense before the big reveal. He has enough information to be titillating, but not enough to prove anything. Seeing someone only at night doesn't mean he's a vampire. Some people are just night owls."

"I want to know who's been talking to him," Jennifer said. "As soon as I find out I'm going to cast a spell that will make him wish he was never born."

"Jennifer, you know we can only use our spells for good."

James shook his head. "It hardly matters now, knowing who's been talking. Hempel is going to keep searching until he gets the proof he needs to go public."

"Sounds to me like he has suspicions but no real evidence," Olivia said.

"You don't need real evidence to convince someone something is true. You need to speak with authority, sound like you know what you're talking about, and manipulate enough people into believing you."

"What will you do if it comes out?" Olivia asked.

"I don't know. This is one problem I've never had to deal with. There were times when people grew suspicious of me, especially when I stayed somewhere too long, but even then I don't think they suspected the truth. When I thought people were beginning to wonder about me I moved on."

"It won't be easy to move on this time, will it?" Olivia asked.

"No." He realized that for the first time since he was turned it wouldn't be easy to start somewhere new. He didn't want to leave Salem without Sarah, and he didn't think she would be willing to drop everything in this new life she was trying to create to go somewhere new with him, especially with all the tension between them.

The microwave beeped and he slid back on his wheelie chair, took the mug out, and dipped his finger in the warmed fluid. Jennifer leaned over him and frowned.

"Ugh," she said.

"You know what I drink."

"I know, but in all the years I've known you I've never actually seen you do it. That's disgusting." She shook her head as if she were trying to get the acrid smell out of her nose. "And I would give Sarah a while longer before you let her see you do that. That might be the one thing that will scare her away from you for good. I've known you my whole life and I'm scared of you right now."

James held the mug out to her face. "Would you like to try some?"

"No, thank you. It's all for you."

He smiled at Olivia. "Would you like to try some?"

"Oh, no thank you, dear. It's bitter, isn't it?"

He took a sip and paused while the heavy liquid flowed through his body. "Right now Hempel doesn't have enough information to name names," he said. "We can't give him any more proof than he already has, whatever that is. It all seems pretty circumstantial to me..." He grimaced. "That's right. I forgot we were in Salem. Circumstantial evidence works here. Even spectral evidence will do."

"From the article it seems like he's fixated on the fact that he's never seen you during the day," Jennifer said.

James looked out the window at the night sky as he considered. "I don't know how long I would last in the sun," he mused, "or what it would ultimately do to me." He stood up, paced the ten steps of his office, his plan coming into focus for the first time. He thought he might finally know how to handle Kenneth Hempel.

"The sun?" Jennifer couldn't hide her shock. "Why are you talking about the sun?"

"If Hempel saw me during the day, he might stop."

"Stop what?"

"Hunting me. If he keeps searching he might uncover some real evidence against me, or against Jocelyn or Timothy or any of us. Or he'll find another way to convince people we're real. How many innocent people will suffer if a new hunt breaks loose here? And I can't risk him hurting Sarah. He might find some way to implicate her."

"Why would anyone implicate Sarah?" Jennifer asked.

"Why would anyone implicate Elizabeth? I couldn't protect my wife from the witch hunts, but I will protect Sarah."

"But you can't go in the sun, dear."

James sat back at his desk and took another sip from his mug. "After I was turned I went out during the day, once, and felt such excruciating pain behind my eyes I never went out in the light again. But that doesn't mean I can't go out at all during the day. It doesn't mean I'll die from the exposure."

"Don't you know what will happen?" Olivia asked.

"No one of my kind has ever seen another in the sun."

"Jocelyn?" Olivia asked.

"She doesn't know," James said.

Olivia shook her head. "It sounds dangerous. You should find another way. You don't want to do anything to put yourself in danger. Not now."

Jennifer looked James in the eye. "If you need help dealing with this Hempel, then I will help you. He's not just after you. He's after Jocelyn and Timothy and the others. Then he'll move onto us." She gestured at her mother. "Next it'll be Howard and his family. He can't do this. I'll do whatever I can to help."

"And you have my help as well, James," Olivia said.

"Thank you both, but I need to do this on my own. Hempel seems to have taken a particular attachment to me for some reason."

"What about Sarah?" Jennifer asked.

James sighed. He didn't want to think about Sarah and Kenneth Hempel at the same time. "I haven't told her about him yet. I keep hoping the problem will go away. Perhaps Hempel will get bored hunting for something that isn't supposed to exist and give up. It does sound ridiculous when you think about it—hunting for vampires in the twenty-first century. Perhaps people will scoff at his article. If no one believes him he'll have to let it go."

"Maybe," Jennifer said.

James paced to the window, pulled open the blinds, and looked at the moon. It was big that night, full, bright, and yellow. It was jarring sometimes when he remembered that the moon was the largest object he had seen in the sky for over three hundred years. He remembered sometimes that he missed the sun. When he was alive he loved spring and summer. He loved the warmth, the way the world would spring back to life when the light made its appearance again after the bleak winter months. He laughed

150

when he remembered how much he hated the cold then and the irony that now cold was all he knew. What would it be like to see the sun again after so long? How would it feel to have the heat on his dead-cold skin and stand in the day glow of sunbeams? Would it be as brilliant as he remembered?

"Have you spoken to Sarah today?" Jennifer asked.

"No," James said, "I haven't seen her yet."

"Maybe I should cast a love spell."

Olivia nodded. "That would be using a spell for a good reason. Though we're not supposed to interfere in people's lives without their consent."

"Yes, Mother, I know. You've told me so about a thousand times."

James wondered if a love spell could help him break through the barriers that still kept him and Sarah apart. His logical mind told him no, but then he reminded himself what he was and he decided he was in no position to judge the truth of magic spells. He came this close to giving Jennifer his consent—it couldn't hurt, after all. Then he caught a whiff of strawberries and cream coming down the hall. He opened the door for her and she smiled when she saw him, though she seemed surprised to see Olivia and Jennifer there.

"Wonderful to see you, Sarah," Olivia said. "We were just leaving." Mother and daughter slipped down the hall, whispering to each other as they disappeared into the elevator. James watched Sarah standing there, her dark curls pulled back into a loose ponytail, her rose-colored dress revealing her curves. He wanted to take her into his arms.

"How do you drink?"

Her terse tone startled him from his other thoughts.

"What?"

"How do you drink? I never thought about it until Steve said something last night. He said he was nervous until he knew where Jocelyn was going to get blood to drink. Where do you get blood from?"

"Does it matter?"

"That depends on where you find it."

She tried to smile, but he could see the strain she was hiding behind her upturned lips. It pained him that she still worried about whether or not he would spring on her and drink her dry.

"Are you sure you want to know?" he asked.

"Yes. I think so."

He sent a quick text on his cell phone, then grabbed his keys, locked his office, took her hand, and walked her to his car. They drove to Highland Avenue and parked. Sarah gasped aloud when she realized where they were. Her hand went to her throat as if she were afraid James was going to attack her right there.

"This is Salem Hospital," she said.

"It's all right. I think you can handle it."

He opened the car door for her and led her to a bench near the emergency entrance of the North Shore Medical Center. He held her hand while they waited. She shivered in the winter air. It had snowed the day before, and the ice sparkled under the streetlights like scattered crystals on the pavement. James was wearing a scarf he didn't need, so he wrapped it around her neck. She moved so she was sitting closer to him, then she turned her gaze to the starless sky and sighed.

"I love the sunlight so much," she said. "I don't think I could live only at night."

"After I realized it was painful for me to go out during the day I thought it would always be darkness for me, but over time I became accustomed to the night. I missed the sunlight for one hundred years before I reconciled myself to living only under a pale moon and far away stars. I had to accept that the full light of the sun was forbidden to me forever and a day and a day and a day..."

He looked toward the hospital and saw a young couple holding hands, and he couldn't turn away when he saw the glowing warmth between them. For someone with only human eyes it might have been hard to see their faces in the dim night sky, but even their body language seemed very much in love. When they passed beneath the street lamp their enamorous expressions were illuminated. James smiled because he knew what it was like to feel that way. The girl who lit him up from the inside out was sitting there beside him. He looked at her, saw her watching him, and at that moment he wanted to kiss her more than anything in the world. He leaned toward her, she leaned toward him. Then, just before their lips touched, like a rude tease, he heard his name.

"Doctor Wentworth?"

He grinned when Sarah sighed in frustration. He turned to the young woman in green scrubs standing a few feet away. "It's all right," he said, nodding toward Sarah. "She's in on it."

The young woman held out her hand and showed him four red-filled medical bags. He looked around to be sure no one was watching, then took the bags and slid them into his black backpack.

"Thank you," he said. "Though I think we're past your calling me Doctor Wentworth. How about just James?"

"But you're my professor. I'm in your Romantic Poets class."

"Yes, Amy, I know."

Sarah was fascinated by the young woman standing there. "You know why James needs that?" she asked, pointing at the black backpack.

"Sure," Amy said. "Jennifer told me."

"And you don't mind?"

"Why would I mind? Everyone is different in their own way, and he seems harmless enough. Anyone who can talk about Wordsworth and Keats the way he does won't hurt anybody."

"That's what I thought," Sarah said.

"Amy knows she can't tell anyone," James said. "For any reason. Bad things happen when people are confronted with things they don't understand. This is Salem after all."

"The witch trials were a long time ago," Amy said.

"It's not that long ago to me."

"Things are different now. People are more accepting these days."

"People haven't really changed. Not in any meaningful way. Maybe there are some who are more enlightened, but there are still narrow-minded people to be concerned about."

When Amy left, James took Sarah's hand and walked her back to the car.

"Not too gory, right?" He winked at her. "More like a drug deal than anything you'd see in a horror film."

Sarah slipped on some black ice in the parking lot, and as James caught her she fell into him. He held her a long time, longer than it took to help her upright. As he kept her close in his arms he saw her watching him, as if she were trying to x-ray through the flat blackness of his eyes to see what was there beneath his dead-cold exterior. Did she see him as he was then, a mild-mannered college professor who only wanted to live and let live? Or did she see only what he might have been in the past, savage and bloodthirsty? She wasn't pulling away. If anything, she pressed herself into him. As he looked into her, as deeply as she looked into him, he thought he saw Elizabeth staring back at him, the way her jaw blushed hot, the way her eyes crinkled when she smiled. Yet he also realized, looking into her chocolate-brown eyes, brushing a stray curl from her cheek, that he loved her just as she was. Sarah. Not the idea of some ghost from his past. He loved the beautiful woman there in his arms. The one who accepted him as he was, turned, when few others would. The one who watched him with such longing in her eyes. The one who startled his long-dormant heart into feeling like it was pumping again. An odd thought popped into his mind as they stood pressed against each other in the hospital parking lot, but it was too outlandish, even for someone as familiar with the paranormal world as he was. Sarah was a dead ringer for Elizabeth. So much about her was the same. She knew the words to Elizabeth's favorite poem though she said she hadn't read it. She had this need to know about the Salem Witch Trials. He had lost Elizabeth during those brutal hunts—she had been snatched from him because of weaker people's accusations, politics and prattle. The situation might have been entertaining if it were only the plot of a prize-winning play, but the Salem Witch Trials were not just a figment from a playwright's imagination. His wife died miserable and frightened because of them. Then the questions began:

Why was Sarah so compelled to learn about the witch hunts?

Who was that nameless ancestor she thought died here then?

What was that horrible vision that accosted her at the mere mention of the Witch Dungeon Museum?

And then, when he allowed himself to dwell on the thought...

Was his instinct the first night he saw her correct after all? Could she be his wife, come home to him after all this time?

After their moment of bonding in the parking lot, he helped her into the car, buckled her in, and drove her home. While they were in the car he pressed the foolish questions aside, wondering if it really mattered. As much as he mourned the loss of his wife, now he loved Sarah. I'm not lonely anymore because of you, Sarah, he thought.

He parked in front of her house, leaving the car running so he could keep the heat on her. She didn't seem too eager to get inside, which pleased him. He didn't want her to leave.

Sarah sat in the car, looking at James. She wanted to invite him inside, but memories of other nights, the one when she wanted him to stay and he ran away, the one when she learned that the man who had awakened such human feelings in her was not a man at all, kept her quiet. As much as she could see the longing in his eyes, and she felt her own longing for him, she was still convinced that when he looked at her he saw his wife, and that wasn't enough for her. She wanted all of his heart, just as he had all of hers. But something kept her in the car, beside him, not wanting to leave. She needed to see his face, hear his voice, feel his hands on hers, his lips on her hair. That thread-like bind she felt the first night she saw him outside his house still held her. As she had on other nights, she started talking so he wouldn't leave.

"I didn't make the connection until tonight at the hospital, but you were here during the witch trials. That's why you know so much about them."

"Yes."

"Will you tell me what you saw?"

James sighed. A burst of icy air slipped through the car window, and the steam from Sarah's breath made clouds on the glass. She shivered, and he turned all the vents in her direction. He closed his eyes as he spoke.

"I remember the day I walked the dirt-road lanes of Salem Town with my father, past the wooden houses with their thatched roofs and vegetable gardens, past the artisans at work in their shops, past the horses and cows grazing languidly on the common, around the meetinghouse where we held church and town meetings. The witch hysteria was in full swing that spring day, and many believed the Devil had been unleashed in Salem. There was a lingering worry humming in the air, a blank-eyed terseness that covered everything we saw. I hardly noticed as we passed Ezekiel Davies languishing in a stockade. People, mostly children, were throwing small rocks and spitting on him, and my father fumed as we walked past. We pretended not to notice that our friend was being humiliated in front of the town.

"'What has he done?' my father asked, his face red, his fists clenched. He was always angry at any public display of punishment, though he had seen plenty of it in England as well.

"'He missed a fortnight of church,' I said.

"'A whole fortnight. We can't have that now, can we?'

"My father's lips were pulled and thin. The grimace in his eyes made him look like a stubborn old man, and the expression looked wrong on his easy features. He scoffed aloud when we saw George Pemberley, the elderly man's frail legs struggling beneath him as he stretched his head and arms through another termite-infested stockade.

"'And Old Man Pemberley too!'

"'He fell asleep in church,' I said.

"'Fell asleep in church! Don't they tickle the old men with feathers when they fall asleep in church? I know church attendance is mandatory, but I haven't read a thing in Scripture that says we must stay awake.'

"'Silence, Father,' I said. I glanced at the people walking past on their way to somewhere else, paying little attention to us. 'Someone will overhear you and you'll end up in the stockade yourself. Or someone will accuse you of witchery and they'll hang you as a wizard.'

"'Nonsense,' he said, 'I'm an important man in Salem Town. I cannot be touched by their folly.'

"'We are all vulnerable,' I said. 'That is what frightens me.'

"The further we walked the angrier my father grew. 'These Puritans think they know everything about God, yet they know no more than anyone,' he said. 'They proclaim that they are God's chosen people and only they understand God's will. Anyone who disagrees with them is not only wrong but damned, they say, but we're mere humans, James, even the Puritans, and none can know Our Lord's will but He. Worse, they believe they can punish people as though they were doing Our Lord's work for Him, but I believe 'tis not our place to judge. Let he who is without sin cast the first stone, that is what Our Lord says, but the Puritans cast stones aplenty.'"

"Was there a lot of public punishment then?" Sarah asked.

"There were stockades and whippings, even hangings meant to show the good citizens of Salem the wages of sin. The Puritans believed firmly in the wrathful, vengeful Old Testament God, the God who would send you to Heaven or Hell based not on your beliefs or actions but because He is God and knows best. They believed it was their duty to keep the sinful people obedient to God's will, at least God's will as they defined it. After all, they thought, whatever physical punishments they might administer would be less horrible than any hellish punishments God Himself would give.

"In those days there was feuding between Salem Town and Salem Village because, while the Puritan farmers in Salem Village could do little better than subsistence farming, Salem Town grew into a prosperous seaport. The people in the village disapproved of us in the town because we hadn't come with the intention of purifying the Catholic influences out of the Protestant Church of England. We had come with the intention of creating our own way in the world, expanding our opportunities, and making profits. The Puritans thought we were not pious enough with our Christianity so they formed a church separate from ours.

"If you disagreed with their views they banished you from the colony, sometimes in winter with little hope of survival. Sometimes they were kinder and put you to a quick death. They infuriated my father to no end. 'I say let them have their own church,' he said. 'Let them teach their own children to be seen and not heard, and let them forbid their own children from playing as children should. Let them show their long, humorless faces to each other. I cannot stand to look upon them.'

"Many were unhappy with Samuel Parris, and they wanted him to give up the parish. ''Tis their own folly for allowing someone as insufferable as Parris to head their church,' my father said. 'What an unlikable, selfish man. Fool!' He said that last word as though he were spitting a foul taste from his mouth, slapping his hand in the air as though he were swatting at Parris himself. 'I'm tired of their talk about Predestination. They think what we do in our daily lives doesn't matter because God already knows who will be damned and who will be saved. I think what we do matters. Give unto Caesar what is Caesar's and give unto God what is God's!'"

"But didn't they leave England to escape religious oppression?" Sarah asked.

"They left persecution and became the persecutors." James shook his head, his eyes tight. "When the witch hunts started it became clear that no one was safe. When Rebecca Nurse was arrested, that was when I began to think that it might be time to leave Salem. Telling my father and my wife that Rebecca had been arrested was one of the hardest things I ever had to do."

"Why?"

"Because it meant that the madness was inescapable. When we arrived back at my father's house I finally told him what had happened to Rebecca. When I finished he said nothing. For the longest time, not a word, and my father was never short for words. He stared at his work desk as if he didn't recognize it. He stood up and paced the room, there and back, there and back. 'These people are superstitious and they frighten me,' he said. 'They believe everything bad that happens in their lives is the Devil's work, and they look at everything as if it contains some hidden message from God that must be deciphered through the Bible. Yet I believe we must be more afraid of human nature than any supernatural being. The Devil himself cannot do more harm to us than we do to ourselves.'

"My father fell silent again. Then he asked, 'Are you still considering returning to England?'

"'Aye,' I said. 'After this now I think we must be on our leave as soon as possible.'

"'What says Elizabeth?'

"I shrugged. 'I haven't yet asked her,' I said.

"'As the husband you don't have to ask. You have to decide. She must do your bidding. 'Tis your right as the head of the family.'

"'I won't force her to go somewhere she doesn't want to go. Besides, I don't recollect your making any decisions without first asking Mother.'

"My father laughed. 'Too true, Son. We have both been swayed from reason by the love of a beautiful woman. Just remember my offer to you and know it still stands. If you choose to return to England I shall assist you however I can.'

"When I told Elizabeth about Rebecca she was devastated, as I knew she would be. She was stirring supper in the cauldron when I arrived home, and she knew as soon as I walked in that something was wrong. We discussed leaving Salem and returning to England, but nothing was settled. She had a hard time on her journey here, and she wasn't ready to leave."

"Why?" Sarah asked. "She must have been frightened by what was happening here."

James shook his head. "It hardly matters now. A few days later she begged me to go to Rebecca's pre-trial, and I agreed. I couldn't believe the stories I heard about the trials because they were too absurd, and I wanted to see what was happening for myself."

Suddenly, in the back of her throat, slivering up her spine to the base of her skull, Sarah felt a torment, a throb of a scream unlike anything she had ever known. Her hands went to her head, pushing her temples, thinking she could stop the ache with more pressure. James caressed her cheek, smoothed her hair. He had such compassion in his eyes.

"That's enough for tonight," he said gently. "Let me walk you inside."

"Tell me the rest."

As distressing as it was, though she felt the chains slithering behind her as if they meant to catch her by surprise, she needed to hear the story.

"Sarah..."

"Tell me."

He shook his head, but she wouldn't be swayed. The determination in her eyes must have softened him. "All right," he said. "But let me take you inside. I can see you're cold."

Inside Sarah's house, James went into the kitchen, scanned her cupboards, and found a box of hot chocolate. He poured water into the kettle he found on the stove and pulled a mug from the shelf. Sarah said nothing, watching him from the sofa in the living room. When the kettle whistled he poured the water into the mug, added two tablespoons of cocoa powder, stirred it together, and brought it to her. While she sipped her drink he found a throw blanket on the recliner and set it around her shoulders. He sat next to her and took her hands.

"Perhaps I should go," he said. "You look tired."

"Please, James. I don't know why, but I have to hear the rest of the story."

She put the mug on the coffee table. He put his arms around her shoulders and pulled her close, his cheek resting on top of her head.

"On March 24, 1692 my father and I went to the meetinghouse in Salem Village to see Rebecca's pre-trial examination. Before I left the house that day, Elizabeth told me that if I could get close enough I should tell our friend that we were praying for her and keeping her close in our hearts. I told Elizabeth I didn't think I could get close enough since Rebecca was being held as a prisoner, but I would try. I knew that people speaking out on behalf of the accused were often accused themselves, but I was afraid of the man I would be if I allowed such fears to prevent me from offering comfort to my friend.

"It was settled in the meetinghouse when my father and I walked in, the normal hum of conversation. The afflicted girls sat calmly, waiting. The judge, John Hathorne, was accompanied on either side by two assistants, making five imposing figures seated like royalty at the front of the room. Samuel Parris, who encouraged his daughter and her friends in their accusations, was ready to record the events of the day. How I loathed that man. Then seventy-year-old Rebecca, bound in chains, was dragged in by the pock-faced constable."

"She was chained?"

Sarah's hand went to her throat and she felt a stutter in her chest. For a moment, until she could breathe easily again, she thought she was having a heart attack. She looked around, searching again for the chains she felt slithering everywhere behind her, but all she saw was James, the worry in his eyes, the stillness in his features. He took her hands, stroked her fingers, brushed her curls from her face, soothing her fears away with the gentleness of his touch.

"Yes," he said. He waited, his concern for her everywhere on his face.

"I'm all right," Sarah said. "Tell me the rest."

"As soon as Rebecca appeared the afflicted girls began to flail and scream and bark and moan and cry, setting the scene with the flair of master actresses. Judge Hathorne glared like a reigning king across the courtroom, scanning his loyal subjects. Then he asked twelve-year-old Abigail to explain her accusations.

"'Just this morning she accosted me,' Abigail said. 'She's tormenting me.'

"'Who,' asked the magistrate, 'is tormenting you, Abigail?'

"'She is,' said Abigail. She pointed at Rebecca.

"Several men from the village were called as witnesses, and each of them claimed to have seen Rebecca engaged in some form of witchery. 'I saw her specter try to strangle someone,' one man said. 'I know her specter bedded several men from the village,' said another. One elderly farmer said, 'I saw her turn into a bird the color of the sky during a storm.' When the judge asked the fifth man what he had witnessed concerning Rebecca he responded by saying, 'What is that you say? Her specter is putting her fingers into my ears and I cannot hear you.'

"Suddenly others were yelling that Rebecca had accosted them as well. I looked at my father, wanting to say something that would help the absurd scene make sense, but I was mute. My father was speechless as well. By the end all Rebecca said was that she did think the writing girls were possessed and she couldn't help it if the Devil appeared in her shape. It was enough of a confession for Hathorne to order her held for a trial. I never did get close enough to speak to her."

"What happened next?" Sarah asked.

"The verdict from the jury came back Not Guilty, but after the decision was announced the girls threw fits and the decision was reversed. Rebecca was convicted. She was excommunicated from the church and executed on Gallows Hill. Elizabeth and I accidentally stumbled upon that horrible scene, and afterwards I had this throbbing in my skull telling me that I must get my family out of Salem, I must. I felt a stricken panic settle at the base of my throat as a tightening in my airway. I tried to rationalize the fear away, and I decided I was being paranoid and foolish. Of course the madness of the witch trials wouldn't touch us, I thought. There was no reason it should. I must have switched a dozen times from deciding that we should stay in Salem where we had built a comfortable life to thinking that we must flee for England immediately. After Rebecca's pre-trial I decided I should take Elizabeth and leave Salem behind forever. I begged her to leave, but she insisted on staying until..."

Sarah was startled when James stopped. He looked tired, which was unusual for him. It was still a few hours until dawn.

"What happened next?" she asked.

James shook his head. "I'll tell you another time."

"But..."

He kissed her forehead, letting his lips linger.

"I promise, Sarah. Another time."

He didn't leave. He pressed her close to him, resting her head on his shoulder, her cheek on his chest. He pushed her dark curls from her face and stroked her face from her temple to her chin. She had a flicker of a reminder that the chains were still there, always there, but she felt comforted because James had his strong arms around her, keeping her safe. With the exhalation of her breath she released her fear and fell asleep in his arms. When she awoke in the morning he was gone.

CHAPTER 17

The puddle-colored sky threatened rain as Sarah walked to Pickering Wharf. A nor'easter would drop soon, the news said, and residents along the coast should prepare for flooding. But the winter weather didn't keep her from her mission. Clutching her clothbound journal, the angry wind whipping her lips and cheeks raw, she walked to Wharf Street, alongside the gray-blue buildings with the white trim. She walked past the coffee shop and the florist, around the crafter's market and the Rockmore Drydock. She felt the water sprinkle around her, but she wouldn't turn back. When she finally reached the Witches Lair, she froze. She couldn't bring herself to go inside. She turned from the store and walked toward the antique dealer, but she chided herself for weakening. She knew what she had to do. There was no turning back now. When she arrived again at the Witches Lair Olivia was waiting by the door.

"What are you doing out in this weather, dear? I was about to close for the day. Come in."

Sarah couldn't control herself and the tears dripped down her cheeks like the rain that had broken through, washing Salem clean. She watched the floor, certain the heavy iron chains had followed her. She expected them to reach out like tentacles, grab her, and drag her away to somewhere she would never escape. She searched the store's shadows frantically for the leering, pock-faced monster who wanted to make her disappear. She couldn't see him, though she felt him everywhere around her.

"Oh no." Olivia put her arms around Sarah. "What's wrong?"

"Nothing makes sense. Who is this woman? Why is she haunting me?" She waved the clothbound notebook around her face, her eyes frantic, nearly hysterical. "How is it possible?"

Olivia took the notebook from Sarah's hands and helped her sit in the chair behind the counter. "How is what possible, dear?"

"How can I be dreaming through James's life?"

Olivia stopped cold. She stood so still Sarah thought she lost her motor movement. Olivia exhaled, then leaned over Sarah, brushing her matted curls from her eyes.

"Tell me everything."

Sarah sighed. She would have cried more, but she was exhausted suddenly and didn't have the strength.

"James has been telling me about his life with his wife. They lived here in Salem during the witch trials. Last night he told me how he knew Rebecca Nurse—he went to her pre-trial examination. When I woke up this morning something kept nagging at me...something he said. Then I remembered my dreams." Sarah's eyes grew wide, and she had to choke out the words because her throat was dry. She leaned close to Olivia and whispered, paranoid that the chain-wielding pock-faced monster might overhear. "I've been dreaming about his life. It's all right there in the notebook."

"Haven't you been reading about the witch trials? Perhaps that's where your dreams are coming from."

"Maybe. I don't know. I haven't even made it to the museums yet. I've been busy with the library, and..."

"And James."

Sarah blushed. "Yes, and James."

"Are all your dreams about the witch trials?"

"No. I don't think so. They're about some other woman's life, but I don't know who she is. I thought she might be the ancestor my great-aunt told me about, but how can I dream about some woman when I don't even know her name? And now James is telling me about his life..."

Sarah grasped her head with her hands, trying to still the same frantic pounding she felt the night before in the car. Olivia nodded, looking as she always did, warm and motherly, as though Sarah's meandering thoughts didn't surprise her at all. She gestured to the clothbound notebook on the counter. "This is where you write your dreams?" Sarah nodded. "May I see it?"

Sarah handed her the journal. Olivia read aloud:

I am looking lovingly into the eyes of a man, though I cannot see his face because it is featureless, like a blank slate...

I am sitting at a table surrounded by people who look like they should be part of a Thanksgiving Feast tableau with their modest Pilgrim-style clothing, old-fashioned manners, and antiquated way of speaking...

I am at a wedding. It is a wedding from long ago, centuries past, a simple affair with family and a few close friends...

I am in the kitchen cooking supper, stirring a pottage in the cauldron in the hearth...

I am standing in front of a tree. The tree is scarred, hunched, ugly, not beautiful like other trees because this tree knows its sinister purpose...

Though I am too weak to see clearly I know I am locked and chained in a dank, gloomy cage in a dungeon infested with rats...

When Olivia stopped reading it was silent in the store, the only noise coming from the rain pellets striking the store with barely restrained fury. Sarah walked to the window and looked out at the wharf. She saw the murky black sky, the water crashing down, the bay cracking in harsh waves under the nor'easter's strength. She stayed by the window, watching, finding comfort in the acerbic weather. The disturbance she felt locked inside was there as a winter storm for all of Salem to see. When she felt Olivia watching her, she turned and saw concern in her friend's steel-gray eyes.

"The one about her husband telling her that Rebecca had been arrested—that's the story James told me last night. He had done the same thing, gone home to tell Elizabeth that Rebecca had been taken away. Elizabeth was cooking in the cauldron, and they talked about returning to England..."

Olivia handed Sarah the clothbound notebook. "What do you think it means?" she asked.

"I don't know," Sarah said.

Olivia closed her eyes and nodded her head the way she did the night of Sarah's psychic reading, a rhythmic meditation. Suddenly she was still and she stayed that way a long moment. When she opened her eyes she smiled. She clutched Sarah's hands so tightly Sarah flinched.

"I think I know what to do. Will you meet me at Jennifer's tonight, Sarah? And bring James. He should be there as well."

Sarah agreed. She would agree to anything that would help her make sense of her dreams.

CHAPTER 18

Jennifer's house was silent, the nervous, impatient kind of silence you feel when something unwanted is about to happen. Along with Jennifer, Sarah and James were there, as well as Olivia and her friend Martha, a heavy-set woman with her black hair cut into a flapper's bob. Martha lingered near the window on the fringe of the scene, silent, listening, watching. Sarah stood with her back to the wall, her arms crossed in front of her, her body a tight standing board, her muscles stiff, her joints heavy. She felt like she needed to shield herself from something, only she didn't know what. Everyone darted their eyes around the room, looking at each other, away from each other, but no one was speaking. Somehow she knew she wasn't going to like what they had to say.

"James," Jennifer said, "why don't you tell Sarah how your wife died."

James didn't look at Sarah. He spoke to the polished wood floor beneath his feet.

"My wife died during the Salem Witch Trials. She was accused of being a witch, arrested, and she died in jail before she was tried."

He looked at Sarah with the same searching stare he had since he first saw her outside his house. But all Sarah could think to say was, "I'm sorry. That must have been horrible."

"It was."

Olivia put her hand on Sarah's shoulder. "You've been dreaming about the witch trials, haven't you? Don't you dream about watching some of the convicted witches die as they're hung from a tree?"

"Yes, I dream about that."

Sarah looked at everyone in the room, and she could tell by their drawn, worried faces that they were trying to tell her something she might not want to know.

"Think about this," Jennifer said. "The first time we drove by James's house you thought it looked familiar. Then you went back to get a better look. What happened when he saw you?"

"He was confused. He called me Elizabeth. He thought I was Elizabeth." She closed her eyes as she remembered that night. Then she looked at James. "Elizabeth was your wife." He nodded. "And she died during the witch trials? She died in jail?" He nodded again.

"And didn't you tell me once that you thought James seemed like the man in your dreams?" Jennifer asked. "You can't see his face, but the silhouette is the same?"

Sarah pressed her hand to her chest, pushing on her ribs because her heart felt ready to implode through her bones. She sat in the chair next to Olivia, darting her eyes around the blank canvas of the white wall, afraid to look at anyone.

"Who you are is not yourself," Sarah said, recalling Olivia's cryptic words from her reading at the Witches Lair five months before. "He will find you. He is here and he will find you. Who you are is not yourself." Her hands went to her head. James rushed to her side.

"Sarah? What's wrong?"

"Nothing makes sense," she said. The words felt scattered in her mind, like disconnected letters on a crossword puzzle. She shook her head, pushing the unnerving thoughts away. Olivia took Sarah's hand, then gestured toward Martha, standing silently in the background.

"Martha is here to help you, dear. If you learned the truth about what your dreams are telling you then it might make the nightmares go away. You could sleep again."

Sarah sighed with stilted breath. Her eyes brimmed with saltwater, the terror barely tucked beneath the edges of her mind. "What are you trying to tell me?" she asked. But she already knew. The pained look on their faces verified what she already knew.

"We think you might be the reincarnation of James's wife," Martha said. She spoke with a southern accent, her voice soft and easy. "We think Elizabeth's spirit has been reborn in you, and I'd like to lead you through a past-life regression to see if it's true."

Sarah jumped out of her chair. "How can you say that to me! How gullible do you think I am? What other metaphysical powers do you want me to believe in next? Now I have to believe in vampires because James is a vampire." It was the first time she spit the word out with disgust, as if it left a bitter taste in her mouth. She stared at Jennifer, pointing an accusing finger. "Now you're going to tell me you're not just a Wiccan but a witch with real magic?"

Jennifer held her hands out, palms up, a gesture of surrender. "Yes, Sarah, I'm a witch with real magic."

Olivia squeezed Sarah's hand. "Don't worry, dear, we're not wicked witches. It's part of the Wiccan Rede that we can't use our spells for evil, and the Covenant of the Goddess says we can't interfere in people's lives unless we have their permission. People need to acknowledge the power our magic contains before we can cast a spell for them. Harm none, Sarah, that's our motto. We harm none."

"Black arts is a terrible term for what we do," Jennifer said. "We're good witches, Sarah. You have nothing to fear from us."

Sarah slumped in her chair. "Great," she said, the sarcasm grating her voice. "Next you're going to tell me werewolves are real and Frankenstein lives down the street."

The others shook their heads. Sarah was so visibly disturbed they were afraid to say anything that might upset her more. She looked at them, one at a time, but they stayed silent.

"James?"

He didn't look at her. "There's no such thing as Frankenstein," he said.

"There's no such thing as Frankenstein," Sarah repeated, a manic hysteria creeping into her voice. "There's no such thing as Frankenstein! So there are vampires, witches, and werewolves in the world, walking around among us while most people think they're make-believe. And now you're trying to tell me that someone else's spirit is living inside my body? What does that make me, a ghost? Doesn't that make us one great big happy haunted family. We should join the Halloween festival next year."

She began pacing the kitchen, around and around the granite island. She couldn't face the others, and she couldn't hold back the despair she felt creeping inside her fragile, sleep-deprived mind.

"Sarah," James said, "you don't have to do anything you don't want to do. If you don't want to do the past-life regression then don't. It's your decision."

Sarah dropped her head into her hands and wept. She was too overwhelmed. James walked to her, put his arms around her, pulled her close.

"Everything is going to be all right," he said.

"Don't you touch me!"

Sarah tried to push him away, but he was too strong. She turned away from him instead.

"This is all your idea," she said, spitting the words like wooden stakes aimed at his heart. "All you ever cared about was finding your wife. You want me to be your wife so you won't have to miss her anymore."

"Sarah, no," James said. "That's not true."

"You don't care that I look like Elizabeth? That's not why you want to spend time with me?"

"It was at first, but not now."

Sarah didn't want to hear anything he had to say. It didn't matter. It was all nonsense. She pushed her way out the front door, weeping and unable to see in front of her, her vision blurred with salt and bitterness. She was determined to make it home where she could lock herself inside, safe from the superstitious madness she was sure they were trying to feed her. James reached the street first and frightened her.

"Sarah, please, listen to me."

He grabbed her arm and turned her toward him. When he wouldn't let go she tried to wriggle away.

"Stop it! You're hurting me!"

He dropped her arm and stepped back. "I'm so sorry—I just want you to listen. Sarah!"

But she was already running away.

"Sarah!" he called. But she kept running away.

She wanted to escape Salem and go back to Los Angeles, back to the husband she never loved but who wouldn't let her give in weakly to the dreams, the man who wouldn't expect her to believe such ludicrous superstitions. Back to a life where she could be like everyone else, going to work, coming home, reading books, watching television, listening to music, going out with friends. Normal things normal people do every day. Since she moved to Salem she had been asked to believe things no sane person should be expected to believe. She began to feel foolish for ever going along with any of it. Vampires, witches, and werewolves, oh my. Where was normal here?

If the others hadn't been so serious she would have laughed in their faces. She couldn't believe what she heard, and worse, they seemed to expect her to believe them. There she goes again, she thought, silly Sarah too gullible to be rational, too out of touch with reality. She felt paranoid suddenly, as if they were trying to push her over the edge of sanity where she would stay, sitting forever in the corner of the mental hospital, a modern-day Renfield waiting for the call of her demon master. She would spend the rest of her life babbling about vampires and witches and how she had known some once. Then she would tell the doctors that who she was was not herself because she was really someone who died over three hundred years before. The doctors would nod with grim faces as they scribbled notes onto their legal pads, upped the dosage of her medication, and ordered a straight jacket to bind her arms to stop her from rubbing away the horror movie of evil witches and bloodthirsty vampires playing on a continuous reel behind her eyes. The thought of being bound by the straight jacket terrified her as much as the tentacle-like chains that followed her everywhere in her nightmares.

Her mind was muddled, and she was too angry to say what she was really thinking. She was afraid they were right. She was afraid that what they said made sense because she saw the connections between her dreams and James's life, and yet the thought of it, of being possessed by a specter, of something separate from her living inside her body, mind, and soul terrified her. She wondered if she even had a soul, and if she did, whose was it, Elizabeth's or hers? At that moment she was too afraid to wonder. Her terror bubbled its way up from agitation in her heart to fear in her throat. She had learned about specters she didn't want to know could exist, and worse, that she might be one herself. She was out of her mind with an emotion somewhere between fury and panic, so she lashed out at them, trying to make her fear disappear by making them disappear. If she didn't have to look at them then none of this would be real.

Running home she watched the shadows, expecting to see the hideously disfigured Nosferatu jumping out at her, catching her with his quick arms and claw-like fingernails, strangling her with his wicked bite, drinking her blood until she became the corpse and he was healthy and fed. In the lights of the windows she saw green-faced witches casting evil spells, standing over bubbling cauldrons, watching her in haunted crystal balls the way the wicked witch watched Dorothy's every move. When she escaped into her house she turned on the lights, looked inside the closets, and checked the door three times to be sure it was locked. Only then could she exhale, though she was still afraid there was something she couldn't see lurking somewhere she didn't look. She imagined she saw the binding chains slink like snakes toward her ankles.

She woke up screaming that night, though screaming in the night had become normal for her. She couldn't remember what it felt like to sleep through the darkness, to feel the stress of the day melt away, to drift and dream and awaken refreshed. She was tired of being tired. She had tried sleeping pills, more than one pill some nights, more than two pills other nights, but nothing helped.

She didn't try to go back to sleep, so she went into the living room and turned on the television. She knew from other sleepless nights that there was nothing worth watching after midnight, nothing but infomercials for exercise routines and kitchen gadgets. She flipped to the movie channel and began watching a familiar scene though she had never seen the movie before. The setting was familiar—wooden houses, horse-drawn carts, farmers, reverends, and magistrates wearing Pilgrim-looking clothes. Then she realized she was watching the film based on Arthur Miller's play, set in Salem during the time of the witch trials. As she watched she kept her hand on her chest to remind herself to breathe. She was keeping the air trapped in her lungs. There was seventeenth century Salem in its gritty Hollywood recreation, the manic accusations from the girls, the possessed, horrible faces, the disgust of those who thought it was all nonsense, the terror of the accused, the arrogance of the magistrates. When she watched the arrested women as they were wheeled away to a dungeon and death unless they confessed to being witches, she cried.

When the movie was over she looked out the window at the moon, the stars, the void beyond. She wondered what else was out there she couldn't see or understand, and she realized she needed to face her fear. She had to learn the truth about her dreams and understand why they were recklessly haunting her.

She remembered the look on James's face the first time he saw her. "Lizzie. My Lizzie," he said, with such sweet gratitude, "you've come home to me."

She considered the possibilities. Maybe she was Elizabeth come home to him. Why did she choose to move to Salem? She could have gone anywhere. Why did she think James's house looked familiar? She had never seen it before. Why did James's silhouette, though ghost-skinned and dark-eyed, look familiar, like it was the man in her dreams? Learning that James's wife died in jail during the witch trials was the final stroke of the panoramic painting. There was only one answer that made it all make sense. But what would that answer mean for her? Would Sarah Alexander cease to exist if Elizabeth Wentworth appeared from the past?

She sat on the couch, looked out the window, and watched the stars dance and twirl in the distance. She meditated on the brightest star, mindful of her breath, struggling to still her mind. Soon the answer came. She had to see James. Right now. She needed to apologize, beg his forgiveness, hope that he loved her, not because she might be the reincarnation of his wife but because she was Sarah, plain Sarah. Everything needed to be all right between them. Whether she was Sarah or Elizabeth or someone else she didn't know, whether he was a supernatural phenomenon or a gentle demon, he would always be her James. She knew that so clearly now she didn't know how she couldn't see it before.

She looked at the clock and saw it was 3:20 a.m. Outside her window weighted darkness covered everything everywhere, not even a faint light peeking from beneath a cloud to say dawn would come soon. If she left then, she decided, she would still have some time with him before sunrise. She pulled her black hoodie sweater over her t-shirt and pajama bottoms, slid her feet into her slippers, grabbed her keys, and left at a sprint. She ran down one road, then another, and one more, until she stood across the street from the wooden gabled house. It was quiet in the neighborhood, all the houses dark, all but one, the one that creaked old-time tales with two gables pointing at the napping night sky. Standing across the street, she saw the soft glow of candlelight flickering through the diamond-paned window, and she thought she heard the house whispering her name. But was it Elizabeth or Sarah she heard? She wasn't sure. She watched her steps as she walked across the street. It might not be a good idea to sneak up on someone like James no matter how friendly he seemed, but she couldn't bring herself to leave.

Before she crossed the yard to knock on his door he was there, James, standing in the open doorway. She was startled when he appeared so suddenly.

"I'm sorry," he said. "I heard your footsteps and hoped you might want to come in." He opened the door wider and stepped aside so she could walk past. He smiled when he saw her pajamas.

"I couldn't sleep," she said.

Standing by the door, she hesitated when she realized she had never been inside his house before, at least not as Sarah, if she had ever really been anyone else. She walked in and stopped. She saw the high, gabled ceiling and the wood beams. She saw a large open great room lit only by candlelight, the kitchen to the left, and another smaller room to the right. The kitchen made her smile. It was old-fashioned, right out of the seventeenth century, with pots and pans and blue and white dishes lined up in shelves along the wall while a cauldron hung in the hearth. But there was also a modern sink, refrigerator, and a microwave oven. The eclectic coupling of the past and the present fit well in this house. Everything in the great room, the walls and most of the furniture, was simple and wood. The only modern furniture was a flat-screen television, a long reading chair, and a laptop computer on the seventeenth-century desk. Then she noticed the English professor's book collection. There is nothing more lovely to a librarian than a roomful of books, and she marveled at the sight. She recited one of her favorite quotes: "I who always imagined Paradise to be a sort of library."

"Jorge Luis Borges," James said.

She nodded, pleased that he knew the quote. As she stood there she wondered if the inside of the house was as familiar as the outside. She wasn't sure. Maybe it was the addition of the modern amenities, or maybe the idea that she was the reincarnation of James's wife was nonsense. James stood beside her, his arm brushing against hers.

"What do you think?" he asked.

"It's more modern than I thought it would be."

He flipped the electric lights on and off overhead. "I had to keep up with the times. I have to admit, though, I still prefer candlelight. Electricity can be so jarring." He reached into a drawer in the wood desk and pulled out a feather quill with a sharp tip. "Believe it or not, sometimes I still use this. It gives me time to think while I'm writing."

Sarah walked to the bookshelves. "If anything ever happens to the library at Salem State College you can send your students here to do their research," she said.

"I've wanted to organize the books into a real library, you know, with categories and bar codes. I was going to ask Jennifer, but maybe you could help. If you want to."

"I'd love to work with these books. How did you collect so many of them?"

"I've had a lot of time to read." He laughed at the thought. "Some people collect postcards from their travels. I collect books. Look at this." He pulled a Dickens novel from a shelf and handed it to her, watching her face while she flipped the pages and saw the date.

"Is this a first edition *Oliver Twist*?" she asked.

"It is. And here."

He gestured to a whole shelf of first edition Dickens. Sarah laughed as she pulled them off the shelf and turned the pages. This was even better than any librarian's dream of Paradise.

"How did you get so many first editions? These must be worth a fortune."

"I was there."

"You were where?"

"In London, on and off during the nineteenth century." He paused to let her grasp what he was saying. "Dickens's novels were serialized in magazines, and I got them hot off the press as soon as they were published into book form. But that one," he gestured back to *Oliver Twist*, "is special because Dickens himself gave it to me."

"You knew Charles Dickens?"

"I met him several times. I was a tutor at Cambridge then."

"What was he like?"

James considered her question. "He was still a young man, a dandy, already a successful author before *Oliver Twist* was published. He was very changeable, Dickens. One minute he'd be laughing and dancing a sailor's jig, and the next he'd be so dark and gloomy you hardly knew what to say to bring him out of his mood. Manic-depressive I guess we'd call it today. Perhaps he was a bit obsessive-compulsive as well."

"And you knew Jane Austen? It sounded like you knew her."

"Yes, I did. But that was before Dickens."

"Did you know Shakespeare?"

James laughed. "Believe it or not, there were things that happened before my time. I was born forty-six years after Shakespeare died." He took her hands and held them to his chest. "That's enough for now. I'm glad you're here, and I don't want to scare you away again with too much information. It's a lot for you to adjust to."

"I'm beginning to understand."

He nodded as he pulled another book for her to see. "Look at this one."

She flipped the book over in her hands and saw the title, *Persuasion* by Jane Austen. Without opening the book she guessed, "It's a first edition, too, isn't it?"

"Yes." He pressed it into her hands. "I want you to have it. Please accept it as a gift from me."

She loved the gesture, but she tried to hand him back the book. "James, you know how much I love that story, but I can't. It's a first edition Jane Austen. It's too much."

"It is not too much, it is too little, and as you can see I have many books here. I want you to have it. I like the thought that every time you look at it you think about second chances. They can happen."

Sarah clutched the book close to her heart. "I love it. And I will think about second chances whenever I look at it, Professor Wentworth. I promise."

He gestured to the sofa in the middle of the room. "Would you like to sit down?" he asked.

They sat close to each other, their shoulders touching, their eyes darting to and from each other. Then they spoke the same words at same time: "There's something I want to tell you..."

Sarah held up her hand. "Please, James, let me go first. I've been thinking about what I want to say to you."

"Very well then."

She closed her eyes as she gathered her thoughts. She had rehearsed it so carefully on her way over.

"I'm sorry for the way I acted earlier tonight." James started to speak, but she pressed her fingers to his lips. "Let me finish. Before I moved here I was a divorced librarian who tried to get through her day like everyone else. I thought I understood about what was real and possible, what was fiction or nonfiction, but since I moved here all that has changed. I don't know what's true anymore, what's legend, what's folktale, what's pretend. And the thought that I might be touched by the supernatural myself is more frightening than any nightmare I've ever had. But what if I am Elizabeth? It would explain a lot."

177

James took her hands in his, pulling her close to him, trying to soothe her fears away. She gripped his fingers and looked into his night-dark eyes.

"Yet as frightened as I am about knowing the truth, I know I have to. I'm afraid of falling asleep because of the terrible scenes I might see when I dream. So I've decided to go through with the past-life regression. I have to know."

Sarah thought James looked more worried than she felt. She began rubbing his hand, stroking his fingers. She brought his hand to her lips and kissed it. Then she pulled herself away and walked to the diamond-paned window. When she looked outside she realized they didn't have much more time. The sun would rise soon. The fact that James was different became more real the closer it came to dawn.

"Does it matter to you? If I'm Elizabeth? You want me to be Elizabeth, don't you? I don't know which truth you want to hear. That worries me more than anything."

"When we first met all I could think about was how spending time with you was like being with Lizzie again. But now that I know you, it doesn't matter anymore. After all these years of wishing for Lizzie, I'm happy I found Sarah. If Lizzie is in you somewhere, then I'm glad she's here. But more than anything, I'm glad you're Sarah."

Sarah was surprised she didn't feel more joy at his words. It was exactly what she wanted to hear. But while almost all of her believed him, she felt that one fraction of self-doubt that still thought he only cared for her because she reminded him of his wife.

"But if I am Elizabeth, if I do have the soul of some long-gone woman living inside me, are you sure you won't want only Elizabeth and toss away the parts that are Sarah, like trash along the side of the road?"

"That will never happen. You are my Sarah. My Sarah."

She sat next to him, not wanting to miss anything about the way he looked then, his eyes serious, his hands gentle, trying to share without words what was in his heart. Finally, he melted his lips into hers. Finally, they kissed. Why had it taken so long? He kissed her gently at first, and when she didn't pull away he kissed her more deeply. She felt welded to him, as though this was how it was supposed to be between them all along, and she forgot why she had been so upset just moments before. After he kissed her darkness away, they sat huddled together, intertwined, until iridescent rays flashed pink along the bottom of the sky. She counted the hours until she could see him again.

CHAPTER 19

Three weeks later, the night of the past-life regression, it was nearly silent outside the old gabled house. The only sounds in the neighborhood were the chirping of love-calling crickets and the wheezing of the New England wind rustling the new-smelling leaves and the fresh-growing grass. Spring in New England is tawny as the skeleton barrenness of winter is magically, as if overnight, transformed into scented color and budding life. Darkness becomes light. The sun, for those fortunate enough to see it, makes life vigorous again. But at night everything became nearly silent. The old gabled house was used to silence. In over three hundred years it was left empty more than it was occupied while James was off living somewhere else and somewhere else again, hiding himself among people, trying to stay inconspicuous, going about his nights and moving on again when he felt prying eyes watching too closely. Even when he was home it was silent inside except for the scratching of quill and ink against paper, the turning of book pages, an occasional sigh from breathless lungs. The house was not haunted by a ghostly specter, though it seemed that way to passers-by who saw the candlelight flickering through the window even after electricity became the norm. Those who looked closely enough could see the phantasmal man illuminated in the shadows, and he was always alone. But more than a specter, as the neighbors suspected, the house was haunted by memories. There was no happy laughter in that house. There were no stolen kisses, no passion. Not anymore. There was, once, a long time ago, but the house had been in mourning since. The silence was fitting since it spoke to the mute longing of the sadness left behind in the walls, the rugs, the cauldron in the hearth. The house, even with its modern amenities, was set firmly in a frame from the past like a painting that captured another era.

But that night was different. That night there were people inside. Maybe there would be life in the house again. It would never be exactly the way it was before since time, for all its incessant rolling toward tomorrow, cannot go backwards. Yet new laughter, new kisses, new passion seemed possible. Maybe there really were second chances. Maybe it could happen again.

The hearth in the great room was lit despite the warmer weather, sending heat and cinders into the air, and the house glowed shadows and gold. There were thirty candles set out around the hearth, on the tables, in the sconces on the walls. Martha, dressed in flowing white, waved a lace fan, then a candle, then incense around the four corners of the room, blessing the space and showing the good spirits the way in and the bad spirits the door. She waved her hands to the heavens, the east, west, north, and south, praying, her voice a whisper, beckoning the spirits to bring them safely on their journey. Jennifer and Olivia sat at the table holding hands, their eyes closed, their mouths whispering Wiccan prayers only witches would know. There was a tangible turn in the energy in the room as it shifted from being just James's house to something else entirely, a calming haven where the mystical was possible. The air felt static, as if there were sparks of electricity, like fireflies in the air.

Sarah struggled to maintain her outward composure. She didn't want anyone to know how agitated she felt, as if someone were pricking her skin with the point of a pin. The sharpness stopped when James knelt beside her and took her hands in his. He kissed her lips.

"No matter what happens, it'll be all right," he said. "Look at everything that had to come together for us to be here now. I had to come back to Salem at the right time after being away, and you had to move here at the right time. You felt compelled to learn about the witch trials, and your dreams have been bothering you enough for you to need to understand them."

"You had to be—turned—or you wouldn't be here now."

"That's right. Tonight is the final piece of the puzzle, but the whole picture has been there all along."

"And if I'm not Elizabeth?"

"It doesn't matter. You are my Sarah. My Sarah."

Martha stepped beside them. "We're ready to begin," she said.

Sarah sat alone in the center of the sofa, her hands folded in her lap, her eyes wide and worried as she stared at the weaved rug beneath her feet. She felt like a schoolgirl waiting to see the principal for something she didn't do. Martha knelt next to her and took her hand.

"There's something I need you to understand before we begin," Martha said. "I'm sure you're worried about what's going to happen to Sarah if we find that Elizabeth has been reborn in you. You don't need to be afraid. You'll always have your own memories. You'll always have your own personality, your own sense of humor, your own emotions. You'll always love who you love." Martha looked at James. "It's not like being possessed by an evil spirit, or even a kindly spirit. It simply means that Elizabeth's memories are inside you."

Martha sat close to Sarah as she tried to explain. She spoke slowly, natural for her southern accent, enunciating her words. Sarah thought Martha was being careful because the concepts she took for granted in her mystic-filled life were too out there, too hocus pocus, for average people who believed in nothing more than their five senses could tell them. Sarah realized suddenly that those people lived in a small box in a big universe.

"Not everything about us dies when our bodies die," Martha said. "Humans are composed of body, mind, and spirit, and though our bodies will one day cease to exist in any earthly way, our spirits go on. They can't be harmed. Even with the destruction at the end of the world, our spirits will go on. Sometimes spirits exist close to the ones they loved in life and help guide them through the perilous journey we face here on earth. Sometimes spirits help creation. Sometimes they change energy. Sometimes spirits are reborn in new life. No one knows for sure why a spirit may choose to be reborn. Some speculate a spirit will continue being reborn until it learns some lesson it's supposed to learn. Or righted some wrong. Or reconnected with someone it loved." Again, Martha looked at James. "So you see, Sarah, there's nothing to be afraid of. I've been doing this a long time and I've helped many people find new peace by understanding their past lives. Are you ready?"

Sarah nodded. "Yes," she said, "I think so." She looked at James, and he nodded in encouragement. He knelt beside her, took her hands, and kissed them.

"Don't be afraid," he said. "I'll be right here. The whole time. Right here."

Martha stood up and walked across the room. "Now, Sarah, lay back. Close your eyes and relax. I promise you everything will be fine." Martha raised her hands in a sweeping gesture toward the ceiling. When she spoke her voice was controlled, calming.

"Sarah, as you hear me you will fall into the deepest sleep you have ever known. You will be conscious and unconscious. You are relaxed and comfortable because you know I will lead you safely on your journey. Can you hear me, Sarah?"

"Yes," Sarah said, "I can hear you." Her own voice startled her because she thought she sounded as if a ventriloquist were working her mouth, making her words come from somewhere else, from across the room, or somewhere farther away. Her eyes closed and her body fell limp. She didn't feel like she was sleeping, only like she wasn't quite connected to herself.

"Now I want you to picture yourself falling backward, spiraling through a long line of yesterdays. You aren't afraid while you're falling because you know your landing will be as soft as a feather bed. Are you falling, Sarah?"

"Yes, I'm falling."

"Have you landed?"

"Yes, I've landed."

"Take a moment to look around. Notice your surroundings. Tell me where you are."

Under her closed lids Sarah felt her eyes move from side to side as if she were in REM sleep. "I'm in Salem, I think, but it's a long time ago."

"How do you know it's Salem?"

"A lot of it looks the same, the houses, the seaport, the bay. The people are in Pilgrim clothing and everything looks sparse and rural."

"Where are you now? What are you doing?"

"I'm kneeling by the shore, splashing water on my face. It's very hot."

"And then what?"

"He helps me to my feet."

"Who helps you?"

Sarah's brow furrowed. "I don't know. A man."

"What man?"

"I think he's my husband."

"What does he look like?"

"I can't see his face. I can never see his face."

"What else can you describe about him?"

"He's tall, and his hair is gold, like an angel's halo. I still can't see his face, but I think his eyes are blue."

"What is his name?"

"His name?" Sarah had to think. "I don't know his name."

"Take your time. You'll remember. What is his name?"

Sarah shook her head. "I don't know."

"All right. Now what are you doing?"

"We're out walking, and we walked far. We pass a rocky hill with ropes hanging from an ugly tree and a crowd of people jeering. I wanted to leave as soon as I realized where we were. I didn't want to see it."

"What did you see?"

Sarah shook her head. "They're hanging her but she's innocent. She's not a witch. She's a good, kind woman. How can they hang her for a witch? They're hanging her!"

Martha brushed Sarah's hair back from her forehead. "It's all right. You're not by the rocky hill any more. You've moved onto somewhere else. Look around. Where are you now?"

Sarah's face softened. She was somewhere more pleasant than the gallows on the hill.

"I'm in my house."

"Which house?"

"This house."

"The one we're in right now?"

"Yes."

"What are you doing?"

"I'm over there," she gestured toward the kitchen, "cooking Indian pudding for my father-in-law. He's coming over for supper and he loves Indian pudding more than anything. Suddenly he comes in the door."

"Who comes in the door?"

"My husband."

"The same man who was by the seaside with you?"

"Yes."

"What does he do when he comes in?"

"The same thing he always does. He lifts me, kisses me, and tells me how seeing me is the best part of his day. He tells me how much he misses me when he's gone."

"And then?"

"He sits at the table there next to the hearth." She gestured toward the table where Olivia and Jennifer sat. "He pulls me close and kisses me more, but I'm blushing because our helping-girl is watching, and I need to keep stirring the pudding or it will scald. Indian pudding tastes terrible if the cornmeal or the molasses burn. But even as I'm pulling away he's pulling me closer, and we're laughing because it's funny that he can't let me go long enough to finish cooking for his father. And then..."

She stopped, her body tense, her face troubled. Her head turned as she listened for something.

"And then what?" Martha asked.

"And then there was angry banging on the door, like the walls would buckle and the gables would crash down. I knew immediately something was wrong. We were expecting my father-in-law, but that was not his knock."

"Who was at the door?"

Sarah cringed in terror, and she saw it all again, being accused and arrested. Being in jail and dying. Knowing all along that no matter how much her husband loved her this chain of events was beyond his control. There was no helping her. No matter how many kisses he gave her he couldn't stop the madness from consuming her as it consumed so many in Salem then.

"He was," Sarah said, her hand over her eyes so she wouldn't have to see him. "The man who arrested me." Sarah's mouth

HER DEAR & LOVING HUSBAND

opened in a circle of fear, her body rigid, trying to disappear into empty space so no one could grab her and drag her away to hell.

"No!" James yelled. "Stop it! It's hurting her too much."

"James," said Martha, "I know this is hard for you, but she needs to do this. She needs to remember."

"She can't do this," he said. "It's too hard."

Jennifer spoke softly. "Is it too hard for her, or is it too hard for you?"

Sarah heard James groan, but he didn't say anything more. After a moment, Martha said, "Tell me what happened when the man came to arrest you. Tell me everything you remember."

Sarah shook her head, her hand on her cheek. "My husband and I gasped in horror when we saw the man we despised for arresting the charged witches standing in front of our home. He grimaced at me with his pockmarked face as though he were wearing a skeleton mask."

"'Are you a witch?' he asked me.

"My husband laughed. I laughed. It had to be a joke. Dear God, please, I begged silently, this has to be a joke. Surely no one would speak out evil lies against me. I had no enemies, only friends. But I felt the impending doom in my gut and thought I would vomit.

"'Did you sign a pact with the Devil in your own blood?' the constable asked. 'How long have you been a witch?' The man's eyes blazed with haughty fire. My husband and I weren't laughing any more. I don't think I ever laughed again.

"'I am no witch, sir,' I said.

"'I can assure you,' my husband said, 'my wife is no witch. What proof have you for such groundless accusations against my wife?'

"'We know she's a witch because witnesses have spoken against her.' Then, to me, 'Why don't you confess?'

"'I am no witch, sir,' I said again.

"Though I tried to be brave for my husband's sake, I couldn't hide my fear. It was in my quivering voice. It was in my wide eyes. I held myself still, pressing into my husband, praying that somehow he could protect me. I had seen my friends and neighbors taken away, and now it was happening to me. The pock-faced man wouldn't be swayed. He showed us the arrest warrant where I was named.

"'I have a warrant for your arrest, Goody Wentworth, and you must come with me.'

"My husband tried to stop him from taking me, but the man was already well practiced at getting his prisoners away. Then my father-in-law arrived. My husband ran to him, shaking him. My father-in-law was an important man, I thought. Surely he must have the influence to do something.

"'Father, please,' my husband said, 'we have to help Lizzie.'

"'What is it, Son?' he asked.

"But I could see the torment in my father-in-law's eyes, and as he looked at me he knew the worst had already happened. I didn't want to seem weak, but I couldn't stop the tears from spilling down my cheeks. The constable bound me in chains. Horrible, hard, heavy chains, as if I were a dangerous criminal, as if I had done anything to deserve this. I felt suffocated by them, as if the leaden links were reaching around my neck and strangling me, slowly taking my breath, and my life away. Somehow I knew I would never escape the chains.

"My father-in-law was not only kind but brave. He could have been named as a wizard himself for speaking out, but he walked to the constable and roared in the man's face.

"'What business have you with Goody Wentworth?' he yelled.

"'I have a warrant for her.'

"My father-in-law grabbed the paper and read it, and in that moment I knew there was nothing he could do. My husband became enraged.

"'You dare take an innocent woman away on false charges?' he yelled. 'Ask her to recite the Lord's Prayer. Ask her to recite the Ten Commandments. You think witches can't speak them because the devil won't allow it. Test her! If you knew the Commandments yourself you'd know the ninth—thou shalt not bear false witness!'

"The constable smiled in a self-important way. 'If you know the Bible so well then you also know First Peter 5:8,' he said. He continued smiling as he waited for my husband's response. My husband said nothing. My father-in-law put his hand on my husband's shoulder.

"'Be sober, be vigilant,' my father-in-law quoted, 'because your adversary the devil, as a roaring lion, walketh about, seeking whom he may devour.'

"'And from Exodus?' asked the constable.

"My father-in-law winced. 'Thou shalt not suffer a witch to live,' he said.

"'My wife is no witch,' my husband said. 'She's an innocent woman. Please, let her go and we shall leave here and never return.'

"'If she's innocent then it shall come out at her trial,' the constable said.

"That's when I knew all was lost. I would receive the same kind of trial Rebecca had, which was no real trial at all. Then I was driven away and left to rot in a dungeon, still in chains. Always in chains. I never did escape them. Suddenly, I was gone..."

Without warning, everything, the loss, the helplessness, the terror, the unfairness of it all, jumped like tremors inside her. Sarah shuddered and she wept and she wept and she shuddered, alternating between the two chasms for some time, cleansing herself out from the inside of every lamentable thing that happened then. Without opening her eyes she knew that James knelt close to her. He wiped her tears away with his fingertips and stroked the sweat-soaked hair from her eyes.

"It's all right, Elizabeth," he whispered in her ear. "I'm here now. No one will ever hurt you again."

"Very good," Martha said. "Now Sarah, you are ready to come back. You will remember everything that happened here, and you will know that the spirit of Elizabeth Wentworth has been reborn in you. Are you ready?"

"Yes," Sarah said. She felt herself there but not all together, lingering on the cusp of consciousness. She felt her eyes darting from side to side, seeing something, some image teasing her like a connect the dots puzzle, but she couldn't make it out no matter how hard she tried.

"Sarah?" said Martha. "You're awake now, Sarah."

But Sarah couldn't respond. The words were trapped inside.

"What's wrong with her?" James asked, the panic cracking his voice.

"I don't know," Martha said. "I've never seen this before." She patted Sarah's face. "Sarah? It's time to wake up."

Martha called to Jennifer for some water, but Sarah couldn't drink. James stayed close to Sarah, stroking her hair, rubbing her hand, trying to spark some movement in her somewhere.

"Sarah," he said, "please wake up. Everything is all right now. I'm here."

Then, like a paint-by-numbers drawing where colors were layered one-by-one, the blurred image Sarah had been struggling to see fell into focus, as if someone adjusted the lens on a projector. She was looking at a man. A faceless man. He was tall, strong looking. With gold hair, blue eyes, and a smile that could wipe away the most hefty nor'easter storm. He was walking up to her as she stood outside that very house, puttting his arms around her, and she gasped aloud as he hovered just a breath above her lips and his features became clear. Finally, she saw his face. And he was beautiful. As soon as she knew who she was looking at she came back to herself. She turned her head and saw James sitting next to her, stroking her hair, his face still beautiful but now very worried, and she smiled. She couldn't take her eyes from him.

"Jamie," she said. "I never saw his face until now, it was always in the shadows, but he stepped into the light and I saw him and it's you. You're the man I've been dreaming about. You're my dear and loving husband. That's how I knew the poem. You used to read it to me."

He took her into his arms, cradling her head against his shoulder. "That's right, Sarah. I was your dear and loving husband then, and I love you now."

How long they stayed like that, with Sarah pressed against his chest, her tears soaking them through, his lips touching the top of her hair, she didn't know. He could have held her there forever and it still wouldn't have been enough. She didn't pull back until she heard Martha, Jennifer, and Olivia slipping away.

"Thank you," she said.

"I was happy to do it," said Martha. "Now listen to me, Sarah, because this is important. There's going to be a period of adjustment. It could be hard, getting used to having Elizabeth's memories as well as your own. Call me if you need anything."

"Yes," Sarah said. "I will."

"There's still one thing I don't understand," James said. "She's Elizabeth reborn as Sarah, yet I knew her the moment I saw her. How can she look the same?"

Martha shrugged as if the answer were obvious. "We look like what we look like, James, whether it's today, three hundred years ago, or six hundred years from now. Souls are drawn to bodies that resemble themselves. It makes perfect sense that you would recognize her when you saw her again."

James laughed. "A vampire recognizing his long-dead wife. Perfect sense."

"Your souls are intertwined, James. You and Sarah will always be together, whenever, wherever. It's your destiny."

He looked back at Sarah.

"I know," he said.

James stood by the side of the road, waving once as the ladies drove away. He lingered outside and thought he should have been more eager to join Sarah, but he was nervous at the thought of facing her again. He had been married to Elizabeth years ago, but he didn't know what Sarah's reaction would be to him now. There were no guarantees that she would want to be with him, perhaps for no other reason than he was not the same as he was when he was married to Elizabeth. He wondered how well Elizabeth would recognize the man she loved in his preternatural body. He looked through the window, and when he saw Sarah in the trembling candlelight all time stopped. There were no days, months, or years. No decades or centuries. There was only now, as in the seventeenth century, before the witch trials brought madness to Salem, and now as in now, in the twenty-first century when everything was different.

Time had passed. Things had changed. The woman sitting there was not entirely Elizabeth, but she was entirely Sarah. Where would the past end and the present begin, he wondered?

He didn't know. At that moment all he knew was that he was willing. No matter what the sacrifice, no matter what the cost, he was willing. As he looked at Sarah huddled with her knees pulled to her chin, her eyes gazing, perhaps not quite seeing, the fire that had dwindled to an occasional spark in the hearth, he knew the decision about their future was in her hands.

He hadn't offered a prayer since before he was turned, but looking at Sarah, spent and unmoving, he thought it couldn't hurt to try. Please, God, he thought, let her want me again. Even as I am, let her want me again.

And he walked inside.

Sarah didn't seem to notice him as he came into the great room. He saw her shiver so he took the patchwork quilt from the back of the sofa, tucked it around her shoulders, and sat next to her. As soon as he was close enough she leaned against his side. They sat silent for some time, and for a while Sarah looked like she was sleeping. Then, when her eyes were open and she was looking at him, he knew he should say something.

"How do you feel?" he asked.

"I feel better than I have in a long time. All of a sudden everything makes sense." She laughed a beautiful, relieved laugh that sounded like joyful chimes to his ears.

They lapsed again into an easy silence between people who have secrets together. Then she sat up and looked at him, her eyes troubled.

"Was I pregnant when I died?" she asked. "I feel so detached from myself referring to Elizabeth as 'I,' but that seems to be the only way to speak of her now."

"Yes," he said sadly, "you were."

Sarah nodded. He saw her cringe as if the memories were coming back, her bulging belly, the trials of working for two, feeling the life inside her dwindling as her own life ebbed away.

"What happened after I died?" She laughed. "What an odd question."

"A few weeks later the executions stopped. Increase Mather gave a sermon called *Cases of Conscience Concerning Spirits* that brought the trials to an end. He said it would be better to set some witches free than to condemn even one innocent person.

Then in 1697, the Massachusetts Bay Colony observed a day of atonement, as if one day of fasting and prayer could repent for what they did. One of the judges asked for forgiveness, but I didn't forgive him."

"They were trying to make amends, James. That's more than most people do when they've been wrong."

"They were more than wrong, they were cruel. Some of the girls who perpetuated the false accusations confessed on their deathbeds, but their apologies sounded false to me. I thought the only reason they apologized was to appease their own guilt and save their own souls."

"Who apologized?"

"Ann Putnam was one."

"I remember Ann Putnam."

"'It was a great delusion of Satan that deceived me in that sad time,' she said. 'I did it not out of any anger, malice, or ill will. I desire to lie in the dust and earnestly beg forgiveness of all those I have given just cause of sorrow and offense.' I would have spat in her face if I could have. Then in 1711, the Massachusetts legislature passed a bill restoring the property and good names of the victims. But none of it meant anything to me. It was too late to bring you back."

"Three hundred and nineteen years is a long time. Maybe it's time you forgave them."

"I will never forgive them. They took so much from so many."

Sarah sighed. After more time to reflect, she asked, "What happens now?"

"You have to decide. I made my decision about you the night I saw you standing in front of this house. I love you as Elizabeth, and I love you as Sarah. My heart has always been yours, and I'm here now, if you want me. If you want me the way I am. I'm not the same as I was then."

Sarah grasped her head suddenly, pushing on her temples, as if she were trying to stop her skull from imploding. James took her face between his hands.

"What's wrong?" he asked.

"It's...I don't know. I can feel Elizabeth's memories very strongly right now."

193

When Sarah spoke it was as though her voice echoed from far away, as if Elizabeth's words were channeled through her, telling her what to say. At first she seemed to struggle against them, but finally she let Elizabeth have her way.

"You're wrong," Sarah said. "You are the same as you were then. Your thoughtfulness, your kindness, that incessant need you have to analyze every thought you've ever had until you think you understand it. Your love. It's all the same."

"Do you really see me that way?"

"When I look at you, I see the man who has always loved me, even as you are now, turned, as you say. And I love you even as I am now, a ghost from the past come back to find the man I love."

"But how can you love me if I let them take you away?"

"How could you have stopped them? If you had spoken out about my innocence any more than you did you could have been arrested yourself. There was nothing more you could have done. Have you been carrying this around all these years? Guilt that somehow you were responsible for my death?"

He couldn't speak. She leaned into him, pressing her head against his shoulder. He put his arms around her and pulled her close, but it wasn't close enough.

"Oh James." She began to stroke the stray gold hair from his eyes. "My poor Jamie. I knew you were outside the jail, there in Boston, trying to set me free. You did as much as you could. Don't blame yourself."

"I've been blaming myself so long I don't know if I can flip a switch and stop the guilt. But you still need to decide what this means for us." He kneeled in front of her and took her face between his hands. "If you want me, if you can be with me the way I am, then I'm here Sarah. And I'll never leave you ever."

"I don't want you to leave."

"What about your ex-husband?"

"Who?"

Sarah smiled the most beautiful smile James had ever seen.

They had kissed before. He had kissed the top of her head many times, her forehead once as she drifted off to sleep. They had even kissed on the lips before, the night Sarah decided she needed to do the past-life regression after all. Then he had kissed

194

her to soothe her, and it worked. She melted into him and seemed to forget whatever it was that worried her in the moment before their lips touched.

But they had never kissed like this before. Certainly not since 1692. Again, he felt the seconds stop while the time warp settled around them, keeping them close. Now it was the twenty-first century, not the seventeenth, and they were in the home they had shared when they were married then. But now their home had electric lights and cable television. Now she was not only Elizabeth but she was Sarah too, sweet Sarah, beautiful Sarah, the woman he loved Sarah. In that moment Elizabeth and Sarah melded into one woman in his mind and there was no longer any difference between them. He was kissing the woman he loved just as he had all those years before, shyly at first, and then he remembered how it was the first time he made love to Elizabeth on their wedding night. He tilted Sarah's chin with his hand and caressed her cheek until she smiled with the memory. He was slow with her, savoring this time with her, kissing her, sliding her sweater off her arms, pulling her tank top over her head. Then he stopped tugging on her clothing and laughed.

"What is it?" she asked.

"I was just thinking how much easier it is to undress you now."

Sarah leaned back, her head against the sofa cushion, her eyes closed as she remembered.

"You were very clumsy as you struggled with the complicated clothing. But you tried very hard to seem nonchalant about the whole thing."

"You were rather amused by my awkwardness."

"You were so very adorable."

Sarah opened her eyes and looked at him. He recognized the heat-filled passion, and he couldn't wait any longer. She wasn't waiting for him as Elizabeth had. She undressed him quickly, impatiently, as if she had wanted him for over three hundred years, as long as he had waited for her. James was overcome knowing they would finally be together again. When he saw the longing in Sarah's eyes he kissed her the way he remembered kissing Elizabeth, first on her temple, then her cheek, then her lips. But

Sarah wasn't content waiting for him to replay a love scene from ages past.

"Make love to me, James," she said.

He kissed her, and she kissed him back with so much feverishness he felt warm-blooded for the first time in over three hundred years. With a sweeping gesture he lifted her from the sofa and carried her to the bed they had shared all those years ago. Just the way they had melded together before, the first time Sarah and James made love had none of the awkwardness of two people being intimate for the first time. Instinctively, they understood each other and remembered how to be together.

CHAPTER 20

When Sarah opened her eyes the next morning the day had already started its early consciousness, the sun sending shivers of color in a long, thin arc along the bottom of the night. As she looked around the bedroom she felt disoriented, not quite sure of her surroundings until she remembered where she was and why she was there. James was in the bed next to her, sleeping on his back, his head turned to the side, his arm covering his face, looking exactly the way he had looked over three hundred years before when he slept, and she smiled at the memory. Already by that morning, the day after the past-life regression, she couldn't find the metaphysical line separating her from Elizabeth. It wasn't a frightening sensation. Instead, it felt right to have this other knowledge from this past life whispering memories in her ear. Looking at James, flushed by a lightheaded swell of love, she felt like she was the one who had been married to him in another time, and in a way she guessed she was. She smiled more when she realized she slept well the night before. No haunted dreams had scared her, and she was no longer afraid of the slithering chains. She knew what they were now—the chains the constable wrapped around Elizabeth before he dragged her away to jail—and now that she knew what they were they no longer held any power over her. She let them go.

She stretched her arms to the gabled ceiling, sending shivers down her sides. She wanted to wake James with kisses. She wanted to shake him until he felt her passion rising and he made love to her again, and again, the way he had the night before. All that frustration, over all those months when she didn't know if they would ever be together, was all worth it. They were still right for each other. They still fit. It was their destiny.

As she leaned over him, ready to kiss his lips, she stopped when she realized that his dawn was her dusk. When he was first falling asleep she would first be waking up. That would take some getting used to, she thought. She saw a streak of iridescent sun brushing his arm and she jumped out of bed to the window, dropping the blinds and pulling the blackout curtains closed. The spots of sunlight didn't seem to harm him, but she wasn't taking any chances. With the curtains drawn the room was cave dark, not even a glimpse of light, but she knew he needed it that way.

She sat on the edge of the bed, careful not to wake him. She wasn't sure how soundly he slept, but one of the few things she could recall hearing about his kind was that they slept like corpses, or they were corpses, dead, until the sun dropped in the west and they were reanimated with life again. She sat there, listening, since she couldn't see him in the lightless room, but all she heard was the sound of her own breath. She touched his chest and felt his still body, and she guessed that must be where the legend that they were corpses came from—they didn't pretend to breathe while they slept. She already knew that James made a pretense of breathing when he was around people. He said it was like blowing air through a straw. You can blow air through a straw as much as you want, he said, though the straw doesn't need the air and doesn't care if you blow through it or not. She realized she had a lot to learn.

She stood up and stepped toward the door. It was so dark she couldn't see, but she knew where the door was. In her way, she had lived there before. As she walked away James grabbed her arm and pulled her toward him.

"Are you leaving?" he asked.

"I'm hungry. I'm going home to get something to eat."

"This is your home. This has always been your home."

"Olivia told me I would find my way home again, and I have."

"Yes, you're home again."

She kissed his forehead, tucked the covers around him, and brushed the stray gold hair from his face. "Go back to sleep," she said. "I'll see you tonight." He was already sleeping again.

From the moment James saw Sarah standing in front of their house he knew he loved her. The past-life regression only proved that his suspicions were correct: his Elizabeth had come home to him in the form of his Sarah. He couldn't describe the simple contentment of holding her, kissing her, knowing her again. Together James and Sarah learned what it meant to be a reincarnation. Together they learned how to straddle the line between then and now. Together became the most beautiful word to him.

One night, a week after the past-life regression, James woke up and heard Sarah park the Explorer in front of their house. He walked out to the great room, looked through the window, and saw her dragging her suitcases, a few grocery bags, and her cat, meowing from her carrier, from the back of the car. He went out, grabbed the suitcases and the bags, and set them down inside. After Sarah unlatched the pet carrier, the cat spit and hissed as she raced out and hid under the sofa. After he helped Sarah fill the refrigerator with the groceries, he took her into his arms and kissed her.

"I'm glad you're here," he said.

Sarah looked around like a contractor surveying a job. "We need to make this place more human friendly," she said. "A new kitchen would be nice."

"What's wrong with the kitchen? It's a perfectly fine seventeenth century kitchen."

Sarah laughed. "For one thing, I need something to cook in besides a microwave. I have a lot of good memories of that cauldron, but I could use an oven with a stovetop, a larger sink, and a garbage disposal. And a dishwasher."

James stroked her cheek. He lifted her chin with his hand. "Whatever you want, Sarah. If I can give it to you, it's yours."

"I'll do the same for you."

"I already have everything I want. Everything."

And he kissed her.

Later, after Sarah had gone to bed, James was sitting at his desk writing lecture notes when he heard a faint rustling. He looked toward the bedroom where Sarah slept, then at the diamond-paned casement window. He didn't hear anything more, so he turned back to his work. When he heard the noise again, this time near the front of the house, he opened the door and saw the shadowy figure standing there, smiling that smile he remembered from all those years before. Seeing that long face again brought back too many emotions at once: surprise, concern, even a seething anger that had been repressed for over three centuries.

"You," James said.

"Yes. Me."

"You're the one who turned me."

"Yes. Or should I say aye."

The shadowy figure looked unapologetic as he stood outside the door, as though turning unsuspecting men was something he did every night. And as far as James knew, perhaps it was. He was dressed in modern clothing, a black button-down shirt over a white t-shirt with blue jeans, but otherwise he looked the same: spikes of gray in his red-brown hair, black almond-shaped eyes that seemed to see through everything, dead-pale skin, long face. He leaned toward the doorway and sniffed.

"Well done," he said. "You've made friends with a human." He sniffed the air again. "A girl too. Even better. Their blood smells so much sweeter, doesn't it? What is that, strawberries?"

James blocked the doorway. "What do you want with her? Leave her alone!"

"I'm not going to hurt her. I'm glad you've found a playmate. How long can one mourn his life? By God, James, I think you've set a record."

"How do you know my name? How do you know anything about me? I haven't seen you since that night."

"I've been keeping track. I like to know what becomes of my vamplings after they're turned."

"You left me alone!"

"Boo bloody hoo. I left you alone. As if that's the worst one can do to our kind." He smiled that amused smile as he looked around James to the great room. "Aren't you going to invite me in?"

James stepped forward, closing the door behind him. "Why would I do that?" he asked.

"Come now, young fellow. I told you I wouldn't hurt your little strawberry friend. I just want to say hello, catch up on old times, ask a few questions."

As he looked the shadowy figure up and down, James decided that he was the faster of the two. He could protect Sarah from this intruder if need be. And perhaps the sooner he heard what the visitor had to say, the sooner he would be gone. James stepped aside and he walked in, nodding, easy about it all. He flashed to the bookcases and looked at the titles, pulling out a few volumes, flipping through them, putting them back. James heard Sarah stir in the bedroom and hoped she wouldn't come out. He didn't want her to be afraid of this stranger in their home when he didn't know himself why he was there.

"Nice house you have. Wood. Interesting choice, I reckon, but still very nice. What is all that?" He gestured to the desk where James's work was spread out.

"My notes," James said.

"Notes? For what?"

"My job."

"You have a job?" He guffawed at the thought. "I heard you had a job but I didn't believe it. What do you need a job for? We don't have jobs."

"I teach at the college." James struggled to maintain his calm though the visitor irritated him to no end. "I have a job because I want to feel useful since I'm going to be alive every night forever thanks to you."

"Useful. That's a human word." He smiled that smile again. "I told you you'd thank me later." He looked smug. James wanted to run a stake through him.

James heard Sarah's footsteps and he braced himself. He didn't know how he would explain this presence in a way that wouldn't frighten her. Until that night, the only others she knew were Timothy and Jocelyn, who, like him, were harmless enough. She hadn't yet met any of these more earthy creatures, and he didn't want her first experience with one to be in their home after midnight under uncertain circumstances. She pulled her robe around her as she came out of the bedroom, and she stopped when she saw them.

"James?" she said.

"It's all right. He's just visiting."

"Who is he?"

James saw the stranger studying Sarah, admiring her too eagerly for his comfort. James took her hand and pulled her toward him so he could protect her if he needed to.

"I don't even know your name," James said.

"I am Geoffrey." He bowed in a courtly manner in Sarah's direction.

"This is Geoffrey, the one who turned me."

"The one who left you alone?"

"Yes, the one who left me alone."

Geoffrey threw his hands into the air, confounded. "Is that all you vamplings ever have to say when I come round to say hello? All the whinging I've had to listen to for hundreds of years, you left me, I was all alone, I didn't know what to do, wah wah wah. How come no one ever speaks of my rugged good looks or my charming wit?" He looked at Sarah. "Has he ever mentioned my rugged good looks or my charming wit to you?"

Sarah laughed. "No," she said.

"Just as I said. Very vexing, I assure you."

Suddenly, all the terror from those nights in 1692 revived in James's mind, and he remembered when he had to learn how to live this unnatural way on his own. As he recalled those nights, he felt the high-beam flashes of fury leave hot spots on his cold skin. The smug visitor standing in his home, disturbing Sarah in the middle of the night, maddened him.

"I didn't ask to be this way," James said.

"Who asks to be this way?"

"I didn't know what I was! A stranger had to tell me what I was! I didn't know anything about living this way."

"You figured it out."

"I didn't have a choice!"

"That's right, and when one doesn't have a choice one either rises to the challenge or one doesn't. It's survival of the fittest, even for our kind."

As James raged the thought of decapitating the insufferable Geoffrey crossed his mind. Sarah backed away from them. James saw her tense stance behind the sofa so he closed his eyes, concentrating until he visualized the red-faced outrage melting into a white wonderland of peace-filled snow. He wouldn't allow her to see him that way.

"What do you want?" he asked Geoffrey. "Why are you here?" He wanted this unwelcome presence gone, never to see him again.

"Come now," said Geoffrey, "let's be friends, shall we? I didn't come round to rehash tales from olden times to upset you. You're hardly suffering. Really, you're doing quite well for yourself. You have this nice wooden house. You have that nice job at the college. And you've made friends with this perfectly nice little human person. What is your name, little human person?"

"Sarah," she said.

"That's right, Sarah. You've made friends with Sarah. And I am intrigued."

Geoffrey studied her again, and James saw a lightning spark in the black eyes. Geoffrey flashed to Sarah, but James reached her first. James pushed her back, away from the ridiculous vampire, ready to fight to the death to protect her.

"Don't you dare get that close to her. You will not touch her!"

"I told you I wasn't going to hurt her. I just wanted a closer look. When I found you outside the jail that night you were upset about your wife. I saw her after she died, did you know that?"

"I don't know anything. I never saw you again until tonight."

"Let's not start that again. I only meant that a few nights after I turned you I heard your wife was gravely ill so I went round to see her, this woman you loved so much you made yourself vampire bait over her. I was going to turn her, but by the time I arrived at the jail there was nothing left to turn. I remember her because even dead she was quite lovely to look at, and it's only this moment it dawned on me. This is her, isn't it. This Sarah is your wife."

James didn't know what to say. How could he explain to this stranger the journey he and Sarah had traveled to make that discovery for themselves? Sarah took his hand, watching him with wide eyes.

"You don't have to say anything," Geoffrey said. "I can see it's true." For once he didn't have that smirk on his face. "I'm certain there are others of our kind who would like to find their loved ones again."

"What do you want, Geoffrey?" James asked again.

Geoffrey became serious. "I want to know what you know about Kenneth Hempel. I know you know him."

James was shocked to hear the reporter's name. Hempel had not been seen or heard around campus for a few weeks. James thought the reporter must have been laying low since his tease of an article appeared in the *News*. There were enough negative comments on the newspaper's blog from people certain Hempel had lost his mind, some even calling for his immediate dismissal. And James had been so caught up in the joy of starting his life with Sarah that he had actually forgotten about the annoying little man and his insistent pursuit.

"How do you know I know him?" James asked.

"We live in a small world and we like to talk."

James looked at Sarah, concerned because she didn't know anything about how Hempel was hunting him.

"Who is Kenneth Hempel?" she asked.

"A mutual acquaintance," James said. He took her hand and stroked her fingers. "You look tired," he said. "Why don't you go back to bed. Everything is fine. Geoffrey and I will be finished talking in a few minutes."

She looked at James, then Geoffrey, then back at James. "All right," she said. She looked at Geoffrey once more before she went into to the bedroom. James closed the door behind her.

"The human doesn't know," Geoffrey said.

"No." James closed his eyes as he considered what to say. "I don't know much about him. He's a reporter for *The Salem News*, and he's taken it upon himself to expose the truth about us."

"I've heard he's been harassing you. Is this true?"

"Yes."

"Why you?"

"I don't know. He must have seen or heard something. Why do you want to know?"

"Because he's been snooping, and humans should never snoop when they don't know what they're dealing with. There are many of our kind who are upset with this person, some who are eager to do away with him before he goes public with some real information. Humans cannot know about us. It will cause too many problems."

"That's what I've always said," James said.

"See, there's something we agree on. We're not so different after all."

James laughed at the thought. "Tempting as it is, you can't just do away with him. He has young children. Besides, people will become suspicious if something violent suddenly happens to him after that article he wrote."

"That's been my argument as well, but I'm afraid the angry ones aren't listening. Some of our kind are more instinct than reason, but you know what that's like. Many never find their self-control again as you did. You must talk this Hempel person out of his hunt straight away. It's for his safety as well as ours."

"I don't need you to show up after three hundred years to tell me what to do," James said. "I have it under control. I know how to handle him."

"Do tell."

"It would be best if I didn't."

Geoffrey nodded as he opened the door. "You're proactive. I like that in a vampling." He smiled that smile again. "It's been good seeing you again, James. Really, you're doing quite well for yourself." He stepped outside and turned back. "I'll be in touch."

As the visitor disappeared at a flash James wondered if it would be another three hundred years before he saw him again.

CHAPTER 21

James walked quickly to the library, nearly springing up the steps ten at a time. He knew he had to settle down so he wouldn't draw attention to himself. He didn't want any problems that night. Everything, after so long, was falling into place. Sarah had been the missing piece, and now she was there, the picture complete. He knew she was inside the library, waiting, as anxious to see him as he was to see her. He knew she would smile when she saw him, and how he loved to see her smile, a sweet, beautiful smile that hadn't changed at all in over three hundred years. He wanted everyone to feel, at least once, the openhearted happiness, the looking-forward joy he felt then. When he was alive, until close to the end of his life, he was an optimistic person, a man looking forward to something new every day. He looked for challenge. He looked for adventure. He abandoned everything and everyone he knew in London for a precarious journey across a dangerous ocean to an undiscovered country. He wasn't afraid. He was thrilled by the potential. And he had been lucky. His father's merchant business thrived in Massachusetts. He married for love, and everything he did he did for that love. Now he was feeling the return of his former optimism.

So this is what it's like to look forward to seeing the woman I love, he thought. I had forgotten. It's been oh so very long.

He stopped short at the front entrance, his senses alert, when he heard the heavy, plodding footsteps approach from the parking lot. He wouldn't let on that he knew anyone was behind him. If this hunter wanted to catch him acting as anything other than human he would be disappointed. James pushed on the library door and stepped one foot inside.

"Professor Wentworth. Good evening."

James turned around, his face a pleasant mask. "Mr. Hempel, my own personal stalker. I don't know if I should be flattered or call the authorities and take out a restraining order against you."

"I don't think that's necessary, Professor. I hardly think there's much I could do to harm you. Do you mind?" Hempel gestured toward a stone bench behind some shrubs near the parking lot. "I'd like to speak to you somewhere more secluded. Just a moment of your time."

James followed the reporter to the bench, his fingers clenched in his pockets. What if Hempel knew the truth? What if he had some convincing proof? Or what if he didn't, but he named names anyway? James wondered if the news would start a new hunt in Salem, only this time the target was really there.

And, more importantly, would he expose himself by going outside in the sun? He still couldn't piece together one cohesive story about the extent of the risk. Just as Jocelyn said, some believed the sun liquidated them as soon as they stepped into the light. Some believed they disintegrated into dust. Others believed it was painfully uncomfortable because of their dilated eyes but not necessarily deadly. They might become weak. A rare few, like him, tried to go out during the day but they were turned away by the blinding pain.

James's hope that the problem would disappear vanished into the intensity in the reporter's eyes, which blazed with the same self-righteous fire James saw in the magistrates in 1692. He recalled the similarities between then and now. But there were differences too. Kenneth Hempel was not a magistrate but a staff reporter for a local newspaper. Hempel didn't have the law on his side, but he had the ability to sway the court of public opinion, which could prove more deadly in the end. Before, James wouldn't have hesitated taking the risk. But now he had Sarah. Was his newly found optimism finished already? After their years apart, was this all the time they had together again?

He touched the tree trunk, the bark scratchy and hard. He wouldn't look at the reporter. He thought his eyes would give his heart away.

"What can I do for you, Mr. Hempel?"

Hempel sat on the stone bench, hidden from view of passers-by by the bushes. "Just a few more questions. I hope you don't mind."

"I do mind. I'm tired of being asked about a subject I know nothing about and getting the third degree for my answers. I'm tired of hearing that you're snooping around campus asking about me." He faced the reporter. "If you have something to say to me, Mr. Hempel, if you have some accusation to make, I think it would be best if you told me what it is so I know what I have to defend myself against."

"Very well, then. I know you're a vampire."

James held Hempel's gaze as he spoke. "That is the most outlandish thing anyone has ever said to me. What could you have seen that would convince you of something so preposterous? I'd hate to think being out at night gets you labeled a vampire. There are a lot of people out at night, Mr. Hempel. You have your work cut out for you."

"It doesn't mean you're a vampire if you're always out at night, but it might mean you're a vampire if you're never out during the day. I know this must be hard for you, learning that some human has discovered your secret. You've obviously kept it well hidden. But the right answer is always there if you're willing to look for it. The truth always prevails."

"Does it? Because I can think of a few times when the truth didn't matter at all."

"I'm sure you've witnessed a lot over the years."

James turned away. He felt a blind heat bubbling up from his feet to his legs to his chest, radiating out to his arms, and he let the breeze floating through the branches of the tree cool his frustration.

Hempel held out his hands. "Look, Professor, it seems we've ended on the wrong foot and that was not my intention. People scoff at the idea of vampires and toss them carelessly into the category of myths and legends, but they need to be warned if there are threats to their lives lurking unseen in the darkness. They have a right to know you exist. After all, not everyone of your kind has the self-control you do. Some are savage, intent on wreaking havoc and murdering innocent people."

James let out a frustrated sigh. "You seem to be an intelligent man, Mr. Hempel. Do you really believe in vampires?"

"I've known the truth since I was fifteen years old. You see, my father was killed by a vampire. I was there and I saw it. I was lucky I wasn't killed myself."

James sat on the bench. In one glance he saw that the reporter spoke the truth. But James needed to convince him that the truth was false.

"Are you sure it was a vampire you saw? You must have been terrified when you saw your father being attacked, and our minds tend to play tricks to protect us from trauma like that. It was probably a wild animal you saw, and in your fear you thought..."

"Do not mock me!"

Hempel leapt from the stone bench and glowered, his eyes large and reaching, the purple veins in his neck bulging. He was too close for James's comfort, and James stepped back. Hempel seemed to expand upward in his anger.

"I was there! I saw it!" The reporter leaned forward, his hands on his knees. "I'm sorry," he said. "This always happens whenever I think about that night." When he was calm enough to breathe easily he looked at James. "My father grew up near Walden Woods. I believe you're familiar with it, Professor?"

"Henry David Thoreau wrote *Walden* there."

"That's correct. My father wanted me to see where he had spent so many hours of his childhood, so he took me camping in some secluded grounds nearby. It was late at night and my father was sitting alone outside the tent, watching the stars, searching for the constellations the way he loved to. He considered himself something of an amateur astronomer. I was in my sleeping bag in the tent waiting for him when suddenly I heard a maniacal growl, like a crazed bobcat on the prowl. Then I heard my father scream, the most horrible sound you can imagine coming from a grown man." Hempel pulled a handkerchief from his jacket pocket and dabbed at the sweat on his forehead.

"I was terrified, but I wanted to know what was happening so I peeked through the slit at the front of the tent. That's when I saw him, a white-skinned, blond-haired man-ghost gnashing his teeth into my father's neck. Actually, the vampire looked a lot like you, Professor. There he was with my father in his arms, sucking the blood right out of him. By then my father wasn't struggling any more. His life was gone along with his blood. If it hadn't been so horrible it would have been almost tender the way the vampire looked like a newborn suckling from its mother. Do you know what it looks like to see a vampire drinking from a loved one?"

James couldn't look at the reporter.

"There was nothing tender about it," Hempel said. "My father was dead but his eyes were open, gazing lifelessly at me, seeing somewhere far beyond the forest. His face was frozen into the mask of horror he wore when he saw what was coming. I don't know why the vampire didn't attack me. Maybe he was satiated after feeding on my father. He didn't seem to notice me." Hempel dabbed at his forehead again. "I have been haunted by that night ever since. When I told my mother how my father was killed, she didn't believe me. She was so upset she brought me to see a psychiatrist. He prescribed medication, but when I still insisted that a vampire killed my father he admitted me to the mental hospital. He had to treat my delusions, as he called them. I was telling the truth, I had seen it myself, but no one believed me. So I have dedicated my life to studying vampires, understanding them, hunting them, and now I can begin to prove they're not merely legends or delusions, but real and here among us. People need to know so they can protect themselves from the evil ones, the ones that will kill your father right in front of you. I have proof now, so people will have to believe me."

James waited while the reporter seemed to struggle against the violent memories. He had to speak when he could no longer stand the silence.

"Not seeing someone during the day doesn't mean he's a vampire. Neither does not seeing him eat or drink. You don't see other people use the restroom, but you know they do. Is that next? Are you going to follow me into the restroom?"

Hempel said nothing. He looked like an attorney in a court case where he expected the suspect to confess after a particularly moving testimony.

"During the Salem Witch Trials," James said, "innocent people were falsely accused of witchcraft. Some were coerced into false confessions, and others who weren't witches were hung for witchery. What will happen if you're successful starting a new hunt? You're just like the magistrates from 1692. Your decision about who is guilty has already been made no matter what anyone else has to say. You've made your decision about me and declared me guilty without allowing me to defend myself. That makes for a dangerous environment where lies and madness breed. I don't want any part of it."

"You seem to know a lot about the witch trials, Professor. Were you there?"

"I'm thirty years old."

Hempel remained unmoved. James knew it was time to play the one hand he held that could make this nightmare go away.

"I have to go to class," James said, looking at the time on his cell phone. "Meet me here tomorrow and we'll figure out how to settle this amicably so I can prove my innocence to your accusations and we can both walk away satisfied and be done with this."

"I have meetings and a deadline tomorrow," Hempel said. "How about Friday night?"

"I don't have time Friday night. Friday during the day would be better."

Hempel sat upright on the stone bench. He crossed his arms in front of his chest. "You would meet me here during the day?" He looked like a boy who just learned that his best friend was imaginary, air in his head, never really there.

"Have I ever said I wouldn't meet you during the day?"

Hempel thought a moment. "Very well, then. I'll see you here at the library on Friday. At noon."

James laughed. "Very well, Mr. Hempel. Friday at noon. But on one condition: after you see me during the day you'll stop this nonsense."

"Yes," said Hempel, extending his hand, "I'll agree to that." James hesitated, but he stretched out his hand. Hempel studied the sallow, blue-toned flesh. "You're still cold, Professor. Did you know vampires are cold?"

Hempel walked away, though he turned back as if he had an afterthought.

"By the way," he said, "I recently reread *Dracula* and I realized I made a mistake when I referenced Van Helsing on Halloween. You're aware of the mistake, I assume."

James nodded. It didn't pay to deny what he knew about the story.

"And what was my mistake?"

"Though Van Helsing is known as a vampire hunter, he was indeed a vampire slayer. He killed the three vampire sisters living in Castle Dracula."

The reporter nodded as he disappeared into the shadows the campus lights traced on the ground. James felt a crashing wave of melancholy sweep over him. Friday at noon was not far away. He felt himself pulled in deeper when he realized he didn't know how he was going to tell Sarah. He saw her through the tinted glass doors of the library and couldn't bring himself to go in. He couldn't face her yet. While he paced outside he called Jennifer and told her about his plans. Jennifer did everything she could to talk him out of it.

"It's the only way," he said.

When he walked into the library he saw Sarah behind the librarians's desk. He went to her, kissed her lips, trying to seem casual, as though there was nothing that could be wrong in the world because she made everything right. But Sarah must have sensed something was bothering him because he saw her worried eyes.

"It's nothing," he said to her unasked question. "I'll talk to you after class. Don't worry."

Class went by quickly that night. It was Monday night, his poetry seminar. It was Timothy's turn to present, and the boy recited Langston Hughes's "The Negro Speaks of Rivers." The words meant something to anyone who wanted to understand, but to someone who had lived many generations, watching one civilization meld into the next, seeing wisdom passed from the tide to the shore to the people, it was particularly meaningful. Yes, James thought as he listened to Timothy, my soul has grown deep like the rivers. He hoped his river would not run dry on Friday. There could be no drought this time.

He waited until they were back at their house to tell her. She was frantic. She shuddered with the same barely contained frenzy he had seen the night she learned she might be the reincarnation of Elizabeth.

"No, James. No!"

In a matter of moments her frenzy turned into fear turned into melancholy turned into frustration. It pained him to see her so upset, and he almost changed his mind about meeting Hempel. Yet if he didn't go through with the plan the consequences would be palpable. The reporter had him in a trap and wouldn't let go.

"We just found each other again," she said. "How can you do this now? You promised you'd never leave me ever."

"I'm not leaving you, Sarah. I'm going out in the sun. You do it every day."

"But you could die."

"I'll be fine." He led her to the sofa and helped her sit. "I'm sorry," he said. "I should have told you sooner. I kept hoping Hempel would give up, but he hasn't. I can't let him tell the world the truth. It's too dangerous."

Sarah sat with her head in her hands, leaning forward, as if she were trying to stop herself from falling over. He waited for her to say something, but she couldn't speak. Finally, she looked at him and held out her hands, pleading. He sat next to her and took her hands in his.

"There has to be another way," she said.

"There isn't. I have to prove to Kenneth Hempel that I'm not what he thinks I am."

"But you are."

"That makes it harder, but not impossible. Meeting him at the library during the day is the best way to do it. He seemed surprised I'd agree to it, so I think I have the upper hand by going through with it. And he agreed that if he saw me during the day he'd stop harassing me."

"Can't you eat or drink something in front of him? We could have him over for dinner one night."

"I don't think that would be enough by itself. Think about it: you could drink blood if you wanted to. You wouldn't like it, but you could do it. It's the same for me with food. I don't know if people think we can't eat food. They think we don't because we drink blood. Being outside during the day is different because that's the first thing people think about—we can't be in the sun—and either I'm in the sun or I'm not. That must have been the hook that got him to agree to leave me alone."

"Would it really be that bad if people knew the truth?"

"Imagine the madness of the witch trials with twenty-first century technology."

He could tell she was suffering. She trembled as if she were cold, as if the cold were coming from inside herself. He wanted to put his arms around her and pull her close, but he knew there was little he could do to warm her.

"All those nightmares I've had look like rainbows and ice cream compared to the visions flashing behind my eyes right now," she said. "I keep seeing you contorted in agony, going up in flames, reduced to a mound of ashes, suffering in horrible ways. James..."

"Sarah, listen to me. If Hempel makes it public, about me, about Jocelyn, or Timothy, or anyone else, he'll unleash panic everywhere. There are others watching to see if he goes public with his proof, whatever it is, and they may try to retaliate in their own way. Hempel could start a new hunt that will be so much more far reaching than the witch hunts because the world is so much smaller now. You know as well as I do what happens when hysteria breaks loose in a society. People will become afraid and start seeing vampires in every nook and shadow. And they may catch some. What do you think they're going to do to the ones they catch? And then people will start looking at their friends and neighbors and wonder if they're vampires too. It will be bad enough if some real ones are implicated, but what's going to stop innocent people from being accused? And if innocent people are accused, how will they help themselves if people fabricate evidence against them? They won't be able to be helped any more now than I was able to help you then."

Sarah stood up, shaking her head as if she were pushing the memories away. "I can see them," she said. "The pointing fingers.

The false accusations. The hysteria. The hangings. Dying for no real reason at all."

"Then you know what I say is true. What if I can stop it this time? What if I can convince Hempel his whole hunt is a waste of time?"

"But why does it have to be you?"

"I think he thinks catching me would be like catching the vampire that killed his father."

"Why?"

"He thinks I look like the vampire that killed his father."

"Did you kill his father?"

"No. His father died about thirty years ago. I was long past hunting by then." James paced the room, venting his nervous energy. "Besides, you're assuming the worst will happen. I went out in the sunlight once and I didn't die."

"No, but you ran back inside in agony and you haven't been out since."

"But I'm still here. And I'll be here Friday night. I can stand a lot."

"You can stand anything but sunlight."

"For you, I can stand the light of a hundred suns at noon on the equator in June if that's what I have to do to come back to you. I've been waiting over three hundred years to see your face again. I'm not leaving you now." He grasped Sarah's hands and held them to his chest. "Don't you see? I'm doing this for you. What will happen to you if everyone learns the truth about me? They could accuse you too. How can I subject you to that again?" He tried to wipe her tears from her cheeks, but she pulled away. "I couldn't help you the first time, Sarah. I won't let that happen again."

"Are we back to that? Are you still blaming yourself? Please, let it go. It wasn't your fault then, and what's happening now isn't your fault either."

James didn't know what to say. In fact, he had been feeling like the whole mess with Kenneth Hempel was somehow his fault. He must have trusted one person too many with his secret, done some unhuman thing when he thought no one was looking, used too obvious a food source at the local hospital, crossed one line too many. He wasn't human. No matter how human he challenged himself to be, no matter how well he controlled his natural instincts and basic cravings, no matter if he assimilated so well he was virtually undetectable in their society, he was a natural predator of humans and he would never be welcome in their world. For centuries he had lived on the fringe, moving frequently, creating few ties anywhere. Now, with Sarah in his world, he wanted to engage fully in life again. She gave him a reason to wake up every evening. He wanted her to be his wife again. But as long as Kenneth Hempel wanted to expose him he would have to live in fear of having his newfound happiness pulled like a trick tablecloth from under him. He didn't want to live that way. He didn't want Sarah to live that way. She suffered enough before.

"If I don't do everything I can to stop him, then this time it will be my fault. You have to trust me. I'll be all right."

Sarah slumped forward, her shoulders limp. "There's nothing I can say to change your mind, is there? You've decided. No matter what I say, you're going out in the sunlight, Friday at noon, a western-style showdown between the vampire and the vampire hunter, both of you ready to pull the trigger at the first sign of movement from the other."

"I'll be all right," he said again.

When she finally calmed enough, James carried her to bed and she fell asleep in his arms. She slept fitfully, tossing and turning. He heard her pull herself out of bed about an hour before dawn.

"Sarah? Are you all right?"

From his desk in the great room he watched her come out of the bedroom with the blanket around her shoulders. It was spring and warmer in the house, but she shivered as she pulled the cover closer. He thought she looked like she would never feel warm again.

"Did you have a bad dream?" he asked.

"No."

She walked to his desk and stood behind him, rubbing his shoulders as he shifted through the papers in front of him. When he felt her hands on him he leaned back into her, allowing her warmth to comfort him. "What are you doing?" she asked.

"Attempting to grade midterms. I've been teaching for two hundred years and every term the students get lazier. What's wrong with this picture?" He showed her the paper.

"The student didn't even take the web links out."

"I remember the days when students used to at least pretend to read the books they were assigned." He picked up his pen, drew a zero, then crumpled the paper and tossed it into the trashcan. "I'm starting to think I need another line of work. You need help at the library?"

He saw how uncomfortable she looked standing there shivering with the blanket around her shoulders. He put his arms around her and pulled her onto his lap. She put her arms around his neck and her head on his shoulder.

"What is it, honey?" he asked.

Sarah sat up and looked into his eyes. "Why do you live here?" she asked.

"Is there somewhere else?"

"Maybe. Somewhere you could live as you're meant to."

"I can't live anywhere else. Or any other way. Not now."

He thought for a moment, pulling the words together, trying to make sense of a time when sense didn't matter. "I lived as a hunter for a number of years, but then I decided it wasn't for me. I'm not even sure how many years I lived like that since my life wasn't ordered by calendars or timepieces then. After I was turned I didn't know what I was, and I hated that I was forced to live this limbo life of immortality, not that I knew I was immortal then. But I knew I needed blood."

"What did you do?"

"In those early days I stayed mainly in the Massachusetts forests, dodging the Wampanoag and Narragansett tribes. Some natives noticed me, but they seemed unafraid of the nighttime blood-drinking man-spirit frequenting their woodlands. They called me Maske, their word for bear, and left me alone to wander as I would. As a white European settler I had been taught to fear the natives, and when I was alive I saw their beaded buckskin clothing, their seashell and bear grease decorations, their animal skin robes in winter, and I was afraid. After I was turned I was still more nervous about them than they were about me.

"Even in those first years, when I was all blood and fire, I knew I loved my wife." He kissed Sarah's cheek. "I knew I loved my father, and I guessed he was distraught with grief over my disappearance. I wanted to know he was well, and some nights I wandered as close to Salem Town as I dared, hoping to overhear some word of him. One night I heard a woman calling my name. As she came closer I remembered her name, Prudence Stapleton."

Sarah tapped her temple with her finger. "My cousin," she said.

"That's right. 'Oh, James,' Prudence said. 'Richard said he saw you here the other night and I didn't believe 'twas so, but he brought me here and now I can see with my own eyes. 'Tis you.'

"I nodded, afraid to speak or do anything that might reveal that I wasn't as I was.

"'Your father is coming,' she said. 'When we saw for certain 'twas you Richard ran to fetch him. Oh, James, where were you? We were afeared you'd gone mad after Lizzie died.'

"Suddenly I heard my father's panting breaths and running footsteps, and I saw him sprinting toward me. Prudence and her husband backed away, leaving us our reunion to ourselves.

"'Oh James,' my father said. 'I was afeared you'd run off to another colony, or gone back to England, or...' He couldn't finish the thought. 'Why didn't you come to me? You know I would do all I could for you.'

"'I'm sorry, Father,' I said.

"My father didn't understand my meaning. He thought I was apologizing for disappearing, but really I was apologizing for my weakness, for the fault in me that allowed me to become this unnatural thing.

"'You needn't apologize,' my father said. 'My Prodigal Son is home.' He recited the passage from the Bible: 'Son thou art ever with me, and all that I have is thine. 'Twas meet that we should make merry, and be glad: for this thy brother was dead, and is

219

alive again, and was lost and is found. You are found, James, and I shall rejoice.'

"He clasped my hand and tried to lead me forward. 'You're cold, Son,' he said. 'Come home. I shall warm you with tea by the fire.'

"'I cannot come home,' I said. 'I cannot be warm. And I am dead and alive again, Father, I am.'

"My father stroked my hand, trying to warm me, trying to soothe me the way he did when I was a child. It was nearly a starless night, so he leaned close to my face. Even in the darkness he could tell my eyes were wrong. Though I found comfort in his presence, I knew I couldn't stay with him. I felt diseased, like lepers from Biblical days yelling 'Unclean! Unclean!' to warn passers-by from drawing too near lest the passers-by become contaminated themselves. I didn't want to contaminate my father with my uncleanliness. Even newly turned I loved him too much to hurt him.

"'I cannot come home,' I said again. 'I am not myself, Father, and I cannot stand for you to know me as I am.'

"My father looked afraid, not of what I was, but of losing me again. 'You shall come home, Son,' he said. 'I insist upon it.'

"I tried to scare him into letting me go. I spoke with my most growl-filled voice. 'I am a demon now. Do you hear me? I am one of the evil specters the people in Salem have been searching for. I have been a demon since the time Elizabeth died. This is why I wanted you to believe I died, because I am dead, Father. I didn't ask to be this way, but I am, and now I am a danger to you in more ways than one.'

"'You shall stop speaking nonsense, James, and you shall come home with me.'

"'I can tell by your look you know what I say is true.'

"'Even so, you shall come home with me.'

"'Are you certain? Even as I am?'

"'You are my son.'

"'Yet what if I truly be a demon?'

"My father looked me steadily in the eyes as he had always done. 'Then my son is a demon,' he said. 'And yet I love you still.'

He pressed my cold hand in his. 'Come home, Son, and we'll see this through. Please, I beg you, come home.'

"I followed him to the house where I had lived with him, worked with him, shared my love for you with him. The house looked different to my far-seeing eyes where details are etched like sharp pencil drawings into my corneas. Things looked darker, sadder than I remembered, though it might have been my preternatural vision projecting gloominess where before I had seen only contentment and light. I hoped he had changed his mind and he would lock me out and never see me again, but he opened the door and stepped aside. I hesitated, but I went in. My father lit a fire, poured water into a pot, and placed the pot on the hook inside the hearth.

"'The tea shall soon be ready,' he said.

"'I do not drink tea,' I said.

"'You love tea.'

"'No longer. I have a thirst for something stronger.'

"'You want ale? I may have other spirits here as well.'

"'I have a thirst for something stronger than ale.'

"My father stared at me, waiting for an explanation. The water boiled, he poured himself some tea, and then he sat in a chair by the hearth. Though I wouldn't look at him, I sensed him studying me, seeing how changed I was in this paranormal body I didn't understand.

"We sat in silence for some time. Finally, my father asked, 'So what has become of you?'

"'I know not what I am,' I answered. 'Truly I don't.'

"'How have you come to be this way?' he asked.

"I explained about that night outside the jail, how the long-faced man with the smirking grin lured me and bit me, how when I woke up I was changed into something unnatural and left to fend for myself.

"'I've done things, Father, terrible things. If I am not already in hell then I shall be there soon from the demonic things I've done. I would hardly believe it of myself except 'tis scratched into my memory. I wish I were dead, truly dead, Father, because I want to be human again and I know I cannot be. I cannot live like this.'"

"Demonic things?" Sarah asked.

"I didn't always get blood from the hospital, Sarah."

After a pause, she asked, "How did your father react?"

"At first he didn't seem to believe me. 'Don't say that, Son,' he said. He leapt from his chair and kneeled before me, taking my hands, trying to soothe me, but there was nothing he could say to take the burden of this preternatural life from me. I pulled away and flashed to the other side of the room. My father's head jerked as he watched me.

"'All shall be well,' he said.

"'Nothing is well! Nothing shall be well again!'

"''Tis not you, James. None of this is you.'

"''Tis me. 'Tis what I am now. I'm dead, Father. I walk but I'm dead.'

"To prove my point I took my father's hand and pressed it to my chest. He gasped aloud and tried to pull away, but I wouldn't let go.

"'Look at me!' I yelled. 'I am a demon! My eyes are black and my skin is cold and I do not breathe and my heart does not beat! I drink blood, Father. That is why I do not want your tea or ale—they do nothing for me. I need blood! And you do not want to know what I do to get it. Look at me and know me for what I am, man! How can you see me this way?'

"My father closed my face between his hands. 'You are my son, James, and you are still in there. Though your body be changed I look into your lightless eyes and I see your truth still fighting to live. And no matter what has become of you, I shall help you. I am your father.'

"'I am the son of Satan,' I said.

"'No. You are my son. *My* son!'

"I began to cry from the frustration of having to control my rage. The sight of the blood streaming from my eyes upset my father more than anything else he saw that night.

"'Are you hurt? Are you ill?' he asked.

"'No,' I said, wiping my face with my hand, streaking my cheeks demon-fire red. I began pacing the floor, my arms flailing around me. "''Tis blood now, blood yesterday, blood tomorrow.

222

Blood to drink, blood to weep. 'Tis always about blood.' I held my bloodied hands to his face. 'Blood is all I have.'

"My father finally saw me for what I was. He turned away and dropped his head into his hands. There was nothing left for him to say.

"'I must be on my leave,' I said. The sight of my father grieving for a son standing before him was too much. 'I cannot be here. Imagine the difficulties you'll face if others discover your son the demon in your home.'

"'The witch hunts are past,' he said.

"'The hunts shall never truly end. Humans shall always search for a way to lord their power over others. They shall always lie about others to protect themselves.'

"'But I shan't allow you to run because you are afeared of what others might do. You shall stay with me and I shall help you however I can. You cannot leave me. I have lost so much already—your mother, Elizabeth...'

"'Me.'

"'I haven't lost you. You're here.'

"'Am I? Sometimes I'm not even certain. Sometimes I think I'm dreaming in my death's imagination of a demon life I recall from a nightmare. 'Tis all just a nightmare, is it not? An unending nightmare? Tell me 'tis all a nightmare that shall end and then I can sleep peacefully at last knowing I have died human.'

"My father couldn't speak, and I couldn't stand to see him so miserable. I looked out the window and saw the light of the new day peeking through the low-sitting clouds.

"'I must be on my leave,' I said again. ''Tis nearly daylight.'

"'Don't mind the daylight,' my father said. 'No one shall come round this day. You're safe here.'

"'I cannot be in the sunlight,' I said. 'It pains me.'

"My father looked at the sun breaking through to day. He grabbed some quilts and used them to block the light coming in through the window. 'Do you stay indoors while the sun is high?' he asked.

"'I sleep,' I said. 'While the sun is high I sleep like the dead, and when the sky is dark I am awakened with life again.'

"He gathered more quilts and bundled them on the floor along the wall farthest from the window. It was an amazing act of love, this devoted man making a special bed away from the sunlight, his only wish to keep his demon boy safe from harm. He didn't seem at all afraid that this bloodsucker he let into his home would attack him and drain him dry. He gestured toward the makeshift bed. 'Sleep, James,' he said. 'Sleep now and we'll talk more this night. Just know that I shall do all I can for you. All shall be well.'

"'Nothing shall ever be well again,' I said. 'I miss my Lizzie.'

"'I know, Son. I know.'

"I was weary, it was my time to rest, so I did as my father said and I lay on the quilts and fell asleep."

James stopped when he heard Sarah sobbing. He pressed her head to his chest and stroked her hair. He kissed her tears away.

"Poor John," she said. "How he must have suffered seeing you so changed. He always had such a loving heart."

"My father was the epitome of unconditional love, and there was a lesson for me that night that was a long time coming. Even after that time with my father I was still intent on acknowledging only what was wrong with all humans, not what was good about some." He kissed the top of Sarah's head and pulled her closer. "I don't think I fully grasped the magnitude of that lesson until I met you."

"What lesson?"

"There are good things, sweet things, beautiful things in the world if you open yourself enough to see them. Even I, turned as I am, can see them."

"Yes," Sarah said, "I can see them too."

He kissed her lips, softly at first, then passionately. She slid her arms around his neck, tousled his hair with her fingers, pushed her lips into his. He couldn't get enough of her warm softness. Her body temperature was soothing to him, such a contrast to his cold-blooded skin. In his entire life, all the many years of it, he had never held another woman in his arms. No one else would do. Now just being near Sarah made all that lonely time worthwhile. Basking in the scent of strawberries and cream, feeling her responsive heat, made him feel alive. As they sat there intertwined he realized that it might be one of their last nights together, one of the last times he could touch her, but he pressed that thought away.

Sarah pulled away first. "Tell me more," she said.

James had to shake the memories back into place. He was too distracted by her lips.

"After I left my father's house I lived alone in isolated rural areas where I could hide easily and hunt unnoticed. After a time I realized I could no longer live like the mindless hunter I had become, driven only by instinct and not by reason."

"How did you decide which people to hunt?"

"I hunted people who were alone."

"Oh."

"I haven't hunted for a very long time." He looked at Sarah and wondered how much she really wanted to know. But Sarah, like his father, was the epitome of unconditional love, so he didn't edit his words. He didn't worry about saying too much. He knew she loved him, all of him, the good and the bad of him, and he decided to tell her things he had never told anyone. The honesty was thrilling to him.

"There were years when I spent my nights as the quintessential hunter, jumping out from the shadows. I would find my prey, stalk them soundlessly, effortlessly, better than any predatory animal in the wild. I had to feed myself. Besides, I thought, all humans were weak, selfish, and willing to sacrifice innocent others for their own personal gain. Then I realized I was no better than the people I despised for so long. I felt the painful pangs of human emotions again, and I realized, with a long-lost shudder, that I felt ashamed. I knew you wouldn't be proud of what I had become. That was the revival of my humanity."

"So you stopped hunting?"

"I remember the night like it was yesterday. I saw a young family, a father, mother, and child. They were mountain people living in a lonely log cabin beneath the deep green foliage in the Great Smoky Mountains. The Smokies are one of the oldest mountain ranges on earth, more than a million years old, and I felt better about myself among the ancient stones and time-telling trees. There were times when I felt like the oldest being on earth, and in the mountains I was surrounded by things even older than me. They're called the Smokies because even at night you can see the gray-blue fog settle like an ethereal veil over the mountains."

"It sounds beautiful," Sarah said.

"The mountains are a great cathedral of hardwood trees like sugar maples and shrubs like hydrangeas, wildflowers, and too many species of birds and wild animals to count. I liked it there because I could get lost in the maze of the forest, think my thoughts, and wonder at what I had become.

"That night I was hungry, I hadn't fed in some time, and I saw the family. My instincts began singing attack songs between my ears—there is your next meal, they sang. Though the family was together, I was so hungry I didn't care. The mother was stirring a pot over the fire burning in a pit outside the log cabin, and she had a smiling baby on her hip. The father was dragging in wood he chopped. Suddenly I heard the wife's laughter at something her baby did and the memories flooded back, like tidal waves crashing into my skull, knocking me back into consciousness after staying numb so long. I saw you standing before me as you used to, and I remembered how happy we were before the madness overwhelmed us. I realized how that family was just like us, how we could have been if our child was born and we were allowed to remain happy. Whether I took all of them or just one or two of them, I would be stealing their happiness the way our happiness had been stolen."

"I don't think I could do that," Sarah said. Her voice was serious, as if she had spent some time considering it. "Hunting."

"You don't need to be anything other than what you are, Sarah. I wish I could be the one to change. I wish I could be human again."

"But..."

He pressed his finger to her lips. "We have time to worry about such things."

"James..."

"Hush." He kissed her lips to stop her from saying any more. "Another time."

He didn't want her to spend that night worrying about what he knew they would have to come to terms with one day. He had learned over time that it didn't pay to waste today away consumed by tomorrow's problems. Tomorrow would come soon enough.

He hugged her closer as he continued. "After I saw that mountain family I knew I couldn't do to them what had been done to us. I left at such a rapid speed I was miles away by morning, and I had to find a place to hide until night. That's when I challenged myself to be more human than some humans. There have been times when humans were better predators than any lion in the wild or any vampire on the prowl. Like the way Kenneth Hempel is hunting me right now."

"I still don't want you to go out in the sun."

"I know, honey, but I have to. It's the only way."

He kissed her again, lost once more in her warm softness. He could lose himself in her lips forever. For a moment he forgot how much time had passed. He was transported to the days before the Salem Witch Trials, a time when there were no problems in the world when they were connected that way. He carried her to bed, but when he looked at her face he saw her closed eyes so he covered her with the blanket. He would let her sleep that night. They would have other nights to enjoy connecting again. When he stood up to leave, Sarah grabbed his arm and wouldn't let him go.

"Stay with me," she said.

"I'm not going anywhere, Sarah." He put his arms around her and held her until she fell asleep again.

CHAPTER 22

The hunt. The hunter. The hunted.

Hunting is an innate state for animals in the wild, for vampires, even for humans. The first tribes of human civilization were hunter-gatherers where men hunted wild game and women gathered edible fruits and berries. To aid their hunting skills, humans invented arrowheads to bring the animals down. Vampires are closer to wild animals in their hunting skills, to lions in the jungle for example, than to humans who need weapons, strategy, and skill to conquer their game. We do not need arrows, traps, or guns, James thought. We need only our predatory instincts and natural abilities. To human eyes a vampire hunt might seem gorier than a lion attacking an antelope because vampires hunt humans, but most vampires are only looking to feed like the lion. Lions in the wild are not sadistic. They are feeding to survive. Yet vampires are different from the hunting animals, too, because while they are driven by the same primal instinct to lunge at their prey, feed, and satiate themselves, they were human once, and the human emotions were still there, even if they were so long forgotten they were nearly undetectable in some.

Some humans hunt for reasons other than survival, though, and sometimes the human hunt is more subtle. The Salem Witch Trials are also called the witch hunts. They were seeking and searching for anyone guilty of witchcraft. This wasn't a blatant hunt where the hunters brandished their bows and arrows. Instead, the witch hunters brandished their accusations and condemnations. Instead of hunting for sustenance so they could live another day, they were hunting to inflate their egos and wield power over those weaker than themselves. Hunting is always about overpowering someone weaker than you, James thought. When you are the weaker one then you are the hunted. It is a law of nature. Humans, like vampires, are guilty of giving into their baser instincts, survival of the fittest, there isn't room for all of us, better me than you. Everyone wants to be at the top of the food chain, the hunter instead of the hunted. Everyone, humans, animals, and vampires alike, are entrenched in this endless cycle. James knew only the strong would survive.

As James thought about Kenneth Hempel and the reporter's own hunting games, he wondered who would prove to be the stronger of the two. Who would be the hunter and who would be the hunted? Who would walk away standing, the victor in this battle of wills? Hempel had flushed James, his prey, out of hiding in the dark night into the sunlight. To counterattack, James had to lunge at him, unafraid, and bare his fangs, figuratively speaking, and show that he wouldn't surrender. He wouldn't be the prey. He would be the final link at the top of this chain. His only solace was knowing that this miserable hunt would soon be over and he could go back to his new life with the woman he loved.

The night before he went to meet Hempel he watched Sarah as she slept. Everything he ever loved, then and now, was sleeping there. Those last few nights he spent his late night hours with his arms around her, watching her sleep, watching her breathe, her chest rising and falling to the rhythm of her heartbeat. As much as he didn't know what would happen when he stepped into the sunlight, he was prepared to endure whatever pain he must, that and tenfold more, to be back safe in their home Friday night. He would not say good-bye again. Not now. Not after everything that had to happen in exactly the right way at exactly the right time for them to be reunited. He had endured one long endless night waiting to see her again. And suddenly there she was, Sarah, sweet Sarah, beautiful Sarah, and he was determined to remain there for her. To know that she loved him, even as he was, to know that she still smiled whenever she saw him, that sweet, beautiful smile, those were the images he would see in his mind when the glare of the sun made him blind. He would do what he needed to do.

That night he wrote a note for her:

Sarah,

I could write for days and never get to the depth of how I have become a better man since that night you first stood in front of this house, wanting to know it better because it looked familiar to you. It should have looked familiar to you because it is your home. You have made me happy again.

I will come back to you on Friday. It is more than a coincidence or an accident that we found each other again. It is fate. It has to be. It is our destiny to be together. Just know that I love you and I will be with you forever.

Forever.

James

CHAPTER 23

Sarah had a plan. It was a good plan, deceptively simple, so simple Kenneth Hempel wouldn't notice or even suspect it. Sarah, Jennifer, and Olivia were going to help James make it into the library while exposing him to as little sun as possible. The sun couldn't be completely avoided, it was James in the light Hempel wanted to see, but they could keep him out of it as long as possible. Jennifer offered to cast a spell so the heat wouldn't hurt him, but James said no, he would do this on his own. He could stand a lot, he reminded them. But they were still determined to see him through his mission.

Olivia suggested using the keys to let him inside the library before dawn. "We can hide him in his office until Hempel arrives," she said.

"No," said Sarah. "Hempel will be looking for any tricks James might try to play."

With the exception of this one, she hoped.

The next morning, the day James would go outside in the sunlight for the first time in three hundred and nineteen years, Sarah drove his black Explorer to the library and parked it in its usual spot in the faculty lot. It was early when she arrived, not yet eight a.m., and she sighed with relief when she scanned the campus and saw only a few scattered students and some birds perched in the trees. She expected to see Kenneth Hempel jump out from behind the bushes lining the parking lot and yell, "A trick! I knew that man wasn't human!"

The library wouldn't open for another hour, so Sarah let herself in. Dim and silent inside when closed, it felt strange to be alone when the place usually whispered sound and movement.

233

She checked behind the librarians's desk, around the computer terminals, besides the stacks, still looking for the reporter. She glanced at the camera perched on the ceiling and imagined Hempel sitting at the security desk, his feet up, his hands behind his head, watching the monitors, seeing her every move. She thought she heard footsteps overhead and stopped. When she listened again and heard nothing, she brushed off the terrible chill, tasting the paranoia like sour grapes in her mouth, waxy and bitter. She had to stop worrying about how this day would play out and stay focused. For James.

She let herself into the closet where the maintenance workers left their supplies. She grabbed the long metal bar with the hand-like claw and closed the blinds on all the windows. When she turned the lights on, it wasn't obvious that the blinds were closed since enough fluorescence glowed to illuminate the room.

She took the elevator up to the third floor and closed the blinds closest to James's office. Standing alone in the hallway she paused, certain she heard movement near the storage room, though she dismissed it as her paranoia rising to the surface again. She used James's key to let herself into his office and she closed the blinds in there. She thought about covering his window with black paper, but she was sure Hempel would look for tricks like that. The blinds were tattered, old, the ends sticking out in different directions, and streams of sunlight played patterns like checkerboards on the wall. She tried to bend the ends back into place, but they were stubborn. She put her hand on the first checkerboard and nodded when she didn't feel any heat. That was good, she thought. For some reason she thought the heat of the sun was worse for James than the light.

As she turned to leave she noticed the brown paneled icebox sitting under his desk. She had seen James place the red-filled medical bags in there. She opened the icebox, removed the two bags, and brought them to the refrigerator in the third floor faculty lounge. She hoped no one looked in there since she wasn't sure how to explain the donated blood in the vegetable drawer. It could be for the science department, she thought, for a biology lab or a pre-med class. But there was yogurt on the shelf that had expired over two months before, so she wasn't too concerned that anyone would look that closely. Besides, no one had seen her put the bags in there, so as long as no one checked the security cameras no one should question her. Later, before the library opened, she filled James's icebox with cans of diet soda and candy bars from the vending machines. Just in case.

It was morning but it was dark inside Jennifer's house. The blinds were closed, the curtains drawn, and over that were four layers of black velvet pinned with thumbtacks. No sunlight was getting through that day. James had been there since four a.m. so he would be inside before sunrise, and soon after he arrived he fell asleep on the sofa. Jennifer and her mother stayed away, letting him rest, whispering to each other when they needed to speak, getting Jennifer's car in the garage ready for the three-mile drive to the library with their light-sensitive cargo. The windows of Jennifer's white Toyota were tinted, but she was afraid they were not dark enough and she tacked some black velvet around all four sides of the backseat.

Jennifer let James sleep until a little after eleven a.m. He was disoriented when he woke up, but he would be strong that day. He shook away his lethargy and stood up, wandering to the window. Daylight peeked into the living room where the velvet curtains had come unhooked. He stared at the splash on the wall, more sun than he had seen in over three hundred years. As he stood there he realized the few beaming streams weren't hurting his eyes at all. It wasn't anything like the flash of agony he remembered from 1692. In fact, he felt comforted by the radiating warmth. Jennifer jumped between him and the light, pinning the corner closed.

"No peeking," she said.

"What is it with witches and black velvet? Isn't that something of a cliché?"

"I like black velvet, that's all. Aren't you supposed to burn to ash in the sun?"

"You need to be careful about getting your information from nineteenth century novels."

"But it could be true."

"I was just standing near the light and it didn't bother me."

Olivia interrupted them. "Would you like me to warm some of that drink you brought with you, dear? I can put it in the microwave. You need all your strength today."

"Yes," he said. "Thank you."

Jennifer wrinkled her nose and shook her head as she walked into the kitchen. She grabbed a bowl from the microwave, a spoon from a drawer, and sat at the dining room table. "That's disgusting," she said.

James looked in the bowl of oatmeal she was eating. "You have the nerve to call what I drink disgusting? That looks like samp, the corn mush we ate in the seventeenth century."

"It's better than what you drink."

"No, it isn't."

Olivia put the warmed coffee cup in front of him.

"Now, James, you know what to do," Jennifer said. "We'll drop you off as close to the library as we can. Sarah will keep Hempel talking inside so he won't be standing by the door watching for you. He'll be by the librarians's desk, and he'll be able to see you walk in from there."

"What if Sarah can't keep him from waiting in front of the library?" Olivia asked. "What if he sees James get out of our car?"

"I don't know," Jennifer said. "We'll have to figure out how to explain that if we need to." She looked at James. "So all you have to do is make it a few feet in the sunlight."

"I can do that," he said.

Jennifer seemed surprised when she saw the time on the clock on the oven. "It's 11:30," she said. "We should get going." James followed her to the garage door. With her hand on the doorknob, she turned to him. If he didn't know her better he would have thought she was about to cry. "It's not too late to change your mind," she said.

"I'm not afraid."

There were no windows in the garage, so he was in no danger there. Jennifer opened the car door, and she checked the fastenings of the black velvet curtains while James sat in the backseat.

"It looks like a coffin back here," he said.

"At least you're used to it," said Jennifer.

"Why would I be used to it?"

"You sleep in a coffin, don't you?"

"Of course I don't sleep in a coffin. I sleep in a bed like everyone else. Why would I sleep in a coffin?"

"Because you're dead."

"I'm not that dead."

"Never mind you two." Olivia pulled the black velvet curtain aside so she could see James. "Do you think we should put some sunblock on him?"

"Sure, Mom. You have any SPF 400 laying around?"

"I don't think the sunscreen will be necessary," James said. "I don't have far to walk."

Jennifer and Olivia climbed into the front seat. "Are you ready, James?" Jennifer asked.

He pulled the black velvet curtain into place.

"Let's go," he said.

He leaned against the car seat, and as he looked at the black lining he couldn't shake the gloomy concerns brought on by the makeshift coffin. Hopefully they won't be bringing back a corpse today, he thought. But he wouldn't allow himself to dwell on that. He thought about Sarah instead. He would see her soon in the library. She was already there paving the way for him.

"Okay," said Jennifer. She opened the garage door and turned the key in the ignition, but she didn't pull the car out. "The garage door is open. Are you still okay back there?"

"It's still dark. Start driving."

Jennifer made her way down the tree-lined streets to the Central Campus at Salem State College the same way she had for over five years. James pictured the route in his mind, down Lafayette Street, past Pickering Wharf and the Dodge Street Bar and Grill, past Harbor Street and the Pioneer Village. He pictured the overhanging leafy trees, the spring-fresh flowers, the quaint shops, the historical landmarks. He felt the hum of the car as Jennifer drove as quickly as the ebb of Salem car traffic would allow. The town had been settled so long ago that the small-town streets didn't seem suited for modern vehicles. As Jennifer pulled onto the college campus she described the students with their backpacks swinging from their shoulders, laughing and carefree as they sat on the lawn or walked to their classes. She spoke as if James had never seen such things.

"Do you think they can tell Professor Wentworth is in the backseat separated from the day by a width of black velvet?" she asked. "Can they guess why he needs to be kept away from the light?" James heard the strain in her voice. "You can still change your mind."

"I'm immortal and I'm strong."

"James is immortal and he's strong," she repeated, the mantra over and over, "James is strong, James is strong, James is strong is strong is strong..."

"Oh no..." James heard Olivia rattle through her handbag, shuffling her keys and her wallet. He heard the panic in her voice. "I didn't bring the sunglasses. I set them on the dining room table and I forgot to put them in my pocketbook."

He heard Jennifer sigh. "Do you want to turn back, James?"

"No," he said. "I can't be late."

"Are you sure? Your eyes..."

"There's no time. Keep going."

They arrived at the library fifteen minutes before noon. Jennifer drove through the parking lot looking for Kenneth Hempel's car, a green Buick. She read the license plate of the first green Buick she saw.

"Yes," James said from behind the black velvet curtain, "that's his car."

"That's good," Olivia said, "he's already here."

Jennifer pulled the car along the curb as close to the library as she could where Loring Avenue crossed the bike path.

"Good luck, dear," said Olivia. "It's not that far."

I'm coming, Sarah, he thought. He slid on his wire-framed eyeglasses, silently cursing the absent sunglasses that might have helped him that day. After he opened the car door and stepped into the light of the noontime sun, Jennifer sped away, leaving no evidence of how he arrived.

Immediately, he felt blinded by the light, like someone was pricking pins into his eyes. But he was determined to make it to the library where Sarah was waiting. The closer he stepped the more he could hear her voice, the worry that he should have been there by now. She was patiently refuting Hempel's bizarre claims. Yes, she saw James drink water and soda and wine. He doesn't like beer. Yes, she saw him eat. She cooked for him almost every day. What did he like to eat? He liked whatever she cooked. Yes, he'll be back any moment. He went to the dining hall to get something to eat. No, you don't need to look for him.

Using his stubborn will as a crutch, despite the sharpness behind his unseeing eyes, he walked down the bike path. One foot in front of the other, he kept saying to himself, just one foot in front of the other to the library. His eyes felt liquid in his face, as if they would melt away, but there were just a few more feet to go and he would be inside. Even seeing Kenneth Hempel didn't matter then. He was going to see Sarah.

Suddenly, despite himself, for a reason he didn't understand, he glanced up to see it. The sun. He saw it the way he might see a parent who had abandoned him years before, with longing and awe. Even after he looked away the warmth pulled him in and embraced him. He felt comforted, as if the sun were an illuminated manuscript that held the answer to every question he ever had. He had missed the sun for so long after he was turned, over one hundred years, and for over three hundred years he had seen only the moon and the stars in the darkest sky. Glimpsing the sun again, knowing the brightness, feeling the heat, wanting the light that had been worshipped itself as a god in earlier civilizations, sent him into a dream-like stream of consciousness. He forgot time and place. For a moment he thought he was an ordinary man standing in the bright light of late spring. For centuries he tried to convince himself that the moon and the stars were as good as the sun, beautiful in their own ways, but they always seemed too far removed, unfamiliar and cold, the moon an estranged aunt, the stars distant cousins. The sun was always mother. He had been without his mother so long.

As quickly as the confusion struck was as quickly as it left. When he came back to himself, he felt warm and flushed, and he was reminded what he was. He felt like he had to get inside or he might die. He felt himself falling, his legs weighted down like overflowing bags of blood, but he heard Sarah inside the library, still talking with Hempel, her voice tinged with an anxiety only he could hear.

"Here he comes," she said.

He put one foot in front of the other, right, left, right, left, he said to himself through the chaos in his muddled mind. He knew Sarah was waiting and he would do this for Sarah. Somehow he made it to the door. He paused, disoriented, but he knew he couldn't look strained or Hempel would see he wasn't himself. He would do this for Sarah.

Right, left, right, left, he thought as he walked across the foyer. Just a few more steps. How many times had he crossed that foyer, hoping to see Sarah, wanting to be with her, smiling when she was there, he had lost track. Now she was there waiting for him the way he had waited for her for over three hundred years. He saw the worry on her face, which she tried to conceal from Hempel, but he knew that face so well. He had dreamed about it for oh so very long.

Kenneth Hempel stood in front of the librarians's desk, watching James with wide eyes which he quickly reigned in, as if he were trying to hide how surprised he was to see it: James Wentworth, the man he had been hunting, walking into the library in the spring sunlight at noon. It was as if he couldn't believe that James hadn't exploded into a puff of smoke or withered into a mound of dust.

Right, left, right, left, James thought as he walked to Sarah.

"Hi, honey," he said.

He leaned over the librarians's desk and kissed her cheek. From her wide eyes to her open mouth, the concern everywhere in her face, he thought she must feel how warm he was. But he wouldn't be swayed. He had come to beat Kenneth Hempel at his own game, to be the hunter instead of the hunted. The persistent reporter wouldn't bother his new life with Sarah any more. James wouldn't let on about how weak he felt, like his flesh would slip off his bones and melt away. Hempel wouldn't suspect a thing.

"Good afternoon, Mr. Hempel," James said. "How are you today?"

"Just fine, Professor. I see you're well."

"Never better."

For the first time since their acquaintance began, Kenneth Hempel was lost for words. Good, James thought. This is working even better than I hoped.

"Would you like to join me in my office where we can speak more privately?" he asked.

"That would be fine."

Right, left, right, left. James pushed his legs front and back mechanically, like a wind-up doll. He held himself upright and Hempel didn't seem to notice if he looked stilted as he moved. They took the elevator to the third floor, and James kept his eyes on the buttons to keep himself focused. He was afraid that if he looked too closely at Hempel, his eyes, which still felt like fireballs in his skull, would give something away. When they reached the third floor he unlocked his office door and stepped aside so Hempel could go in. He gestured to the chair where his students sat when they visited him during office hours.

"If you'll excuse me a moment," James said. "I need to use the restroom. You're welcome to join me if you'd like to watch."

Hempel shook his head. "That won't be necessary. I'll wait for you here."

"As you wish."

James closed the office door behind him and walked down the hall to the faculty men's room. He went to the sink and turned the water on as cold as it would go, splashing his face, trying to feel heatless again the way he had for three hundred and nine-teen years. The warmth made him oh so very tired and he wanted to lie on the cool linoleum floor and sleep. Suddenly the room slid as if the earth had tilted off its axis and everything tipped diagonally, over the hills and far away. He gripped the sink with such force he nearly tore it from the wall, but he steadied himself. He looked in the mirror, the first time he studied himself that closely in years. Who needed to see when he always looked the same? He sighed when he saw the flushed red spots on his cheeks and neck. He pressed his glasses against his nose and stared deeply, willing himself to stay strong. Just a few more minutes, he thought, just a bit more time with Hempel and it will all be over. He could endure this and a hundred times more for Sarah. This is all for Sarah.

He limped back to his office, right, left, right, left. Hempel was flipping through a thin volume of Transcendentalist poetry when he walked in.

"Interesting collection of books you have," Hempel said. He took a sip from a can of diet soda. "I hope you don't mind, but I helped myself while you were gone."

"Excuse me?"

"I took this can of soda from your refrigerator. I hope you don't mind."

"Not at all." James looked at the icebox beneath his desk.

"And it's such a lovely day I opened the blinds to let the sunshine in. I love these later days of spring when the weather gets warmer before the humidity hits."

James saw streams of sun land in a circle of light on his chair, but he wouldn't stop now. He was nearly done. He could hear it in the resignation in Hempel's voice. He sat down, the light of the sun illuminating the dust in the air, and he swiveled around to face his hunter. He sat up straight, his shoulders back. He wouldn't give into the tumultuous tipping of the world he felt before. He would win this round with a full deck in his hand, his Queen of Hearts intact, his king stronger than ever.

"So what were we talking about the other day?" he asked.

He was surprised at how steady his voice sounded. Maybe everything else was a hallucination and he was fine now, the worst of it behind him. He had every reason to feel victorious. After all, Kenneth Hempel would no longer be a problem. He could feel it.

"Here I am in the daytime at noon, in the sunlight streaming through my window. I haven't exploded. I haven't withered away. I'm not melting. I'm sitting here the same as you. Would you like me to share a soda with you so you can see me drink something too? I'd be happy to oblige."

He opened the icebox door and looked in. He almost laughed out loud when he saw the cans of diet soda and candy bars filling the two short shelves. Sweet Sarah. Beautiful Sarah. You may have saved my life today, he thought. He removed a can and popped the top.

"That won't be necessary, Doctor Wentworth. I made some misguided assumptions. I got some faulty information from a source I trusted. I apologize for wasting your time."

The reporter stood up to leave.

"Are you going to stop hunting now, Mr. Hempel?"

"Not at all. I'm still on the hunt. I still have leads on others who might be vampires, but you're off the hook. I can see I was wrong about you."

"But why would you keep hunting? If you're so sure vampires are real and one killed your father then you must find them frightening. Aren't you afraid you're putting yourself in danger?"

"I've always known hunting vampires is a dangerous occupation, but I'm prepared to make the sacrifice if that's what I need to do. Have a good day." He extended his hand, which James shook. Again, Hempel wouldn't let go.

"You're warm, Doctor."

"What did you expect?"

Hempel nodded. He looked at James, as if this last glance would confirm or deny whether or not James Wentworth was guilty as charged. He must have decided that the young-looking professor sitting in the ribbon-like streams of sunshine with a healthy flush to his cheeks couldn't be anything but human. The reporter left without another word, closing the door behind him.

James sat without moving. He heard the heavy, plodding steps of the reporter as he walked to the elevator, went in, and disappeared down the shaft. He continued waiting, stone-like, like the carved statue *The Thinker*, afraid that the slightest movement would bring Hempel running back, pointing his finger, exuberant like a hunter bagging his prized game, or Ahab netting Moby Dick. James waited longer, then longer after that. Finally, when he felt safe from prying eyes, when the sunlight on his face felt like someone had run a blowtorch along his skin, he stood up to close the blinds. And then it began again, the world falling away, the axis tilted on the wrong diagonal. He felt himself slipping down an inward spiral where he would never reach the end until he found the bottom of the darkness, the darkness calling his name, after all those years, calling him home. All the fist-held stubbornness that kept him strong that afternoon was gone, dropped down the elevator with Kenneth Hempel. Oh Sarah, he thought, I came so close to saving us today.

And it was the thought of Sarah, her face, her smile, her love that gave him that final push forward. He staggered to the door and stepped into the hallway. He just had to make it downstairs, he thought, and then he could see her again. He smelled her...strawberries and cream...*right, left, right, left, Sarah where are you, right left right left, I can hear you Sarah, I can hear you talking to Jennifer and I know you're afraid but don't be afraid Sarah, right left, I will always be with you my strawberry Sarah, Sarah you saved me today Sarah, sweet Sarah beautiful Sarah, rightleft, Sarah I love you...*

CHAPTER 24

Sarah heard him collapse from the first floor. Everyone inside the library heard him collapse. It wasn't just a man falling to the ground but the roar of thunder, an earthquake, or an apocalypse echoing from the third floor in booming waves. Students yelled and ran for cover. Library staff wanted to call security, but Jennifer calmed everyone, saying not to worry, they were reorganizing some things on the other floors, they must have dropped something heavy, don't panic. Everyone settled down, everyone but Sarah because she knew what the crash meant. She raced to the stairwell because the elevator would have been too slow. Jennifer was right behind her.

When they got to the third floor they saw him, Timothy, his chest heaving as though he were desperate to breathe again after suffering from empty lungs too long, an unconscious James in his arms. Sarah had to stifle a scream when she saw them.

"James?" she cried. "Jamie?"

But he couldn't hear her. His face was blushing red, not ghost white, and he was so still.

"Bring him in here," Jennifer said. She already had the faculty lounge on the third floor ready in case there was an emergency. The blinds were down and black butcher paper was taped over the windows. Timothy laid James on the sofa, then stepped back and looked at his friend.

"How did you get in here during the day, Timothy?" Jennifer asked.

"I snuck in last night. I've been in here all day, hiding in the storage room down the hall. I wanted to be here if he needed me."

"How did you know he was going to be here today?"

"I overheard him talking to Hempel the other night. I told him to call me so I could help him. He never called, but I was worried so I came anyway. He sounded fine while they were talking. I didn't know anything was wrong until I heard him fall. Why didn't he call me?"

"He didn't want to put you in danger," Jennifer said.

"But he needed me. Look at him."

Sarah sat on the table in front of the sofa, stroking James's hand, brushing his gold hair from his eyes. She would have cried, but she was dry inside. She was afraid to ask Timothy if her worst fear had come true because she didn't know what she would do with herself if it were. She held James's hand to her cheek. "He's so warm," she said. "He's burning up like he has a fever."

"Then let's cool him down." Jennifer took the ice cube trays from the freezer. "Let's start with this." She cracked the trays and dropped the ice over James's still body. "I'm going to run to the store to buy a few bags of ice. Maybe that will help."

While Jennifer was gone, Sarah and Timothy waited. Sarah couldn't look at the boy because that would make this real and she couldn't pretend it was a bad dream. She would have gladly spent every night for the rest of her life trapped in a nightmare if it would make this waking terror go away. She took one of the ice cubes and rubbed it along James's face, along his forehead, across his temples, down his neck and chest. The blush on his cheeks reminded her, through Elizabeth's memories, of his human days. He looked like he was sleeping with his head turned, his chin tilted. She wouldn't take her eyes from him because she was afraid that if she stopped seeing him, even for a moment, then he would disappear, like he was never there. Maybe this was one of her famous nightmares. Maybe she was still living in Los Angeles married to a man she didn't love in a city that didn't agree with her. Maybe James was too perfect to be anything but a dream. She kissed him, his forehead, his cheeks, his lips, trying to wake him. Wake up, Sleeping Beauty, she thought. I need you.

Jennifer came back with Olivia, both carrying two bags of ice, which they placed around James's still body. Olivia locked the door from the inside so no one else could get in.

Too much time passed with no change. Jennifer pulled a corner of the black butcher paper from the window and peeked outside. "It's dark," she said. She pulled the paper down and opened the blinds. She stared at the stars, the lights in the sky staying respectfully distant and dim. Then she turned to Sarah. "Why don't you take some time for yourself. If there's any change I'll call you."

"I don't want to leave," Sarah said.

"You need to take care of yourself. You need to stay strong for James."

Sarah didn't want to go, but Jennifer pressed her until she left. She stumbled away, checked the hallway to be sure no one was around, and closed the door behind her, softly, as though a slam would disturb James from his sleep. She didn't go far, just to the women's faculty lounge to wash her face. Then she sat on the floor in the hall. Through the closed door she could hear Jennifer talking to Timothy.

"Why don't you go stretch your legs?" Jennifer said.

"I don't need to stretch my legs."

"But you need to stay strong too. You're crowding James hovering over him like that. You need to pull yourself together."

Timothy walked into the hallway. He didn't seem to see Sarah as he disappeared into the stairwell. After a few more minutes, Sarah decided that the only place she needed to be was near James. When she walked into the lounge she saw Jennifer's face set in determination as she spoke to her mother.

"I'm going to cast a spell for James. I'm going to cleanse the weakness from him, give him strength." Olivia began to speak, but Jennifer used her hand as a stop sign. "I know you're the one who tells me we can't use our spells to interfere in people's lives. And I know James isn't conscious and can't give his consent, but I'm going to do it anyway. This is for James, Mother, our friend James, the first one you called the day I was born, the one who has always been there for us, for our whole family back generations. If I can't use my magic to heal him, then I don't want it any more."

"I was just going to ask if I could help, dear. I'm the one who taught you how to cast spells, remember? Did you bring the sage incense and the white candles?"

"Of course."

Jennifer saw Sarah and nodded, saying, "I'm going to cast a spell for James. He can't give permission, but you can. Do you give me permission to cast a spell for him, Sarah?"

"What kind of magic spell?" Sarah asked.

"Sometimes we can help when people are ill," Olivia said.

Sarah stared at them with fear and awe, then nodded her consent.

From her bag, Jennifer pulled incense, white candles, and a glass she filled with water from the tap. She took matches from her bag and lit the incense and the candles.

"Do you think it will work?" Olivia asked. "I've never cast a spell for someone like James."

"I hope it works, Mother, because I don't know what else to do."

Jennifer took her mother's hands, and the two witches stood over James and closed their eyes, whispering, "Angels of protection, angels who clear, remove all weaknesses that don't belong here."

Jennifer put her hands on James's temples. "Heal James's spirit. Make him well. Give him power and strength. Make him endure as he is made to endure."

She took the glass of water in her hands and held it over him, her eyes shut in concentration, pressing the glass as if she would shatter it, as if she directed the negative energy in the room, in James, into the water. When the water bubbled and steamed, Jennifer poured it down the drain.

"It's okay, James," she said. "Your weaknesses have been flushed away. You can be well again."

But he didn't move. He looked exactly as he had, flushed, unstirring. Dead. Jennifer shook her head and wrung her hands in circles, over and over, rubbing until her skin was red. The three of them hovered around him, waiting for some sign that the spell had worked. Sarah looked at the counter near the sink and saw the candles still flickering, and her lungs burned from the spicy incense. Jennifer and Olivia wouldn't look at her. She saw their melancholy faces and understood what they were trying not to say.

"It didn't work," Sarah said.

Jennifer shook her head. "I'm sorry, Sarah."

Sarah was heartbroken, torn outward from the soft organs inside. While she was washing her face in the women's lounge, feeling like the mirrors would shatter around her in jagged teardrops, she felt the resignation settle over her, not unlike the resignation Elizabeth had felt in prison when she knew she was dying. She didn't want to die, but it didn't matter, she died anyway. Sarah wasn't ready for James to die, but she knew that didn't matter, either, if it was time. Sometimes events turned away from you so quickly there was nothing you could do to try to reel them back and send them in the direction you wanted them to go. She wanted to be with James. She wanted to live out the happy lives they had started over three hundred years before. The more she and Elizabeth melded into one woman, the more she knew there was nowhere else for her to be but there with him. And he was already leaving her again. It didn't make any sense. But life would do what life would do, and she never felt like she had complete control over the direction of her destiny. She could only wish there was still some way she could keep him with her. Unless there was some universe-driven practical joke that had gone badly wrong and was never meant to be funny but only tragic, then it couldn't be possible for them to go through everything they had for such a brief reunion. There had to be more.

Suddenly Timothy burst through the door. "I know! Let's feed him!"

"Whatever gave you that idea?" Olivia asked.

"I saw it on television. That's what the vampires do when they're hurt. They drink."

Sarah thought she should go to the refrigerator for a bag of blood, but she couldn't bring herself to leave James's side. She sat on the edge of the table and stared at him. Most of the ice had melted, so she took one of the last cubes and rubbed it down his temples and across his forehead.

"Wake up, Sleeping Beauty," she said. "You're my dear and loving husband. I'll never leave you ever." She kissed his lips.

Then she felt it, the cold that made her lips tingle. Not from the melting ice, but from James.

"He's cold!" she said. "Jennifer, he's cold!"

Olivia took James's hand and held it between hers. "He is definitely colder," she said.

Sarah tapped his cheek with her fingers. "James? Jamie? Can you hear me?" When he opened his eyes she began to cry. "Oh James," she said.

He blinked a few times, saw everyone watching him with hopeful smiles, and he sat up as if he had woken up from a nap. He looked like nothing strange had happened, he hadn't gone out during the day, he hadn't seen the sun. He hadn't tricked his hunter and sent the man limping away. He looked like it was an ordinary way to spend the afternoon after finding his way in the nighttime world so long.

"What's wrong, Sarah?" he asked. "Are you all right?"

Sarah ran her fingers from his temple to his chin. "I'm fine. Are you all right? I thought you were leaving me."

James brushed her tears away with the back of his hand. "I promised I'd never leave you ever. I feel fine. I'm just a little wet. Why am I wet?"

"We were trying to make you cold again so Jennifer and Olivia put ice on you."

"Ice. Great idea." He pushed the bags of water onto the floor and saw the worried faces. "Why do you all look like you've seen a ghost?"

"Actually," Jennifer said, "you looked more like a corpse until you woke up just now."

"You always look a little dead, dear," Olivia said, "but today you looked really very dead. I'm glad you're feeling better. You had us all worried."

Sarah patted James's hands. "Do you want something to drink?" she asked. "I put your bags in the refrigerator in here in case Hempel looked in the one in your office."

James nodded. "Yes, and yes, he looked in the fridge in my office. He seemed very happy with the diet soda he found. He may have even taken a candy bar."

Sarah pulled a medical bag from the refrigerator. She sliced open the top with a knife she found in a drawer, pulled a styrofoam cup from the cupboard, poured the red liquid into the cup, and put it in the microwave.

"That doesn't gross you out?" Jennifer asked.

"It's what he drinks."

"You really are the right girl for him."

"I know."

As she brought James the warmed cup she heard Timothy speaking to him like an irate parent lecturing an unruly child.

"Next time you need to let me help you." Timothy wagged a frustrated finger to emphasize his point.

"What could you have done?" James asked.

"I could have done something. Promise me next time you'll ask for help."

"Very well, Timothy. The next time I'm stalked by a relentless hunter I'll ask for help."

Timothy seemed satisfied with that answer. Seeing that James was well, Sarah was calm, and Jennifer and Olivia were content, he looked ready to leave. It was too much for the boy, Sarah thought. He hadn't slept all day. From outside, Sarah heard a dog, or was it a wolf, howling a long, lonely low. She looked through the window, saw the full moon hanging in the sky, and she shuddered, afraid of what might be waiting for them. James didn't seem concerned. He listened to the howl and turned to Timothy.

"Your dad's here," James said. "Sounds like he's worried about you."

Timothy nodded. "He's worried about you too." The boy listened to the wolf's bark, short and sharp now. "Coming Dad," he said. He smiled at James as he walked away. Sarah looked through the window again and saw a large gray wolf with gold glowing eyes sitting outside the library door. She was sure the wolf bowed in her direction, one front paw behind the other, its head bent in a courtly manner, when it saw her. Though she was curious, she would ask James to explain another time. At that moment, all she cared about was James.

Outside the library, Jennifer threw her hands into the air when she saw the parking ticket on her windshield. She had left her car by the curb along Loring Avenue after she ran to buy ice. She didn't want to waste time running from the parking lot, and she hadn't been back since. She took the ticket from the windshield, crumpled it, and threw it into the backseat.

"I told you it was a no parking zone," Olivia said.

"You didn't tell me it was a no parking zone. You said no such thing."

"I did. I said it was a no parking zone. You should try listening to your mother sometimes."

"It's hard to listen to your mother when she insists on communicating through telepathy. You need to speak in words like the rest of us."

"But you work here, Jennifer. You should know it's a no parking zone."

James nodded his head toward the car. "Where's the casket drapery?"

"I took it down as soon as you got out," Olivia said.

"Do you two want a ride somewhere?" Jennifer asked.

"No," said James. "The moon looks beautiful tonight, and I still need to dry off. We'll walk."

Jennifer looked at him and smiled. "Don't forget, I promised you three wishes. You still have two more to go."

"Don't worry. I may take you up on that."

James and Sarah watched while the witches drove away. When the car disappeared around the curve, he took her hand.

"Do you think it was Jennifer's spell that made you well again?" she asked.

He brushed a dark curl from her cheek. "I don't know. Maybe my body needed time to recover from the heat. I am immortal after all, and I don't think it's been forever yet."

"I thought it was my kiss that woke you up."

James laughed. "I felt your lips on mine when I opened my eyes, so perhaps your kiss did heal me. We better not tell Jennifer and Olivia that your magic is more powerful than theirs."

Sarah nodded, leaning her head against his arm. "All right, Sleeping Beauty. I won't say a word."

James and Sarah walked home under the light of the full spring moon. They walked without speaking, casting shy glances at each other, like people in love. He was happy to see the moon lighting the night sky, solid and patient as always.

"I think that white glow will do just fine for me from now on," he said. "I'll never dismiss it as an estranged relative again."

He held Sarah's hand tightly, afraid to let her go. He had the unnerving thought that if he lost touch with her he would lose her forever, and perhaps they would never reconnect again. She grabbed his arm, tugging on him until he looked at her.

"Jennifer told me once that you helped her family in ways I can't imagine, but she never said what you did. How did you help them?"

"Her ancestor helped me first, in 1693, and then I helped her family during the Great Depression and World War II." Sarah looked as if she wanted to know more, but James shook his head. "I'll tell you everything you want to know, but not tonight. We have time." He grinned from ear to ear with the thrill of the victory. His hunter had been vanquished, and he was certain Kenneth Hempel would no longer be a problem for them.

"What happened when Hempel left the library?" he asked.

"He seemed eager to get away. Did he agree to stop harassing you?"

"He did."

"Is he going to stop hunting?"

"That he wouldn't agree to."

"So what do we do now?"

"For now we hope he doesn't find any more evidence against anyone else."

"But what about the others? Won't they be watching to see if he goes public?"

"I don't know." He needed to change the subject, and he smiled at her. "Was that your idea to fill my refrigerator with soda and candy bars?"

"I thought he might want to see what you kept in there."

"I think that brilliant move saved the day."

"I didn't save anything. You did it, James. You convinced Hempel to leave you alone."

Had it only been a few hours since that happened? It already seemed like a dream from another century. His life seemed so settled all of a sudden. The scattered pieces had been gathered and fitted together, creating one whole. Still, there was one part slightly out of place, one last thing he needed for everything to be just right. He looked at Sarah and saw her gentle glow of love. He saw the peace, the contentment that comes only when you are fulfilling your destiny. In her eyes, he saw their future as well as their past. In her eyes, he saw the one last thing he needed.

He put his arm around her shoulders and held her close while they walked the last block. He stopped a few feet in front of the wooden gabled house, and Sarah laughed as he pulled her close. She threw her arms around his neck and pointed her face up, ready to be kissed. He couldn't resist that look and he acquiesced, gladly. Then he stepped back to look at her.

"Are you certain about this?" he asked. "About being with me, now, the way I am?"

Sarah shook her head. She stood on her toes so she could take his face between her hands. "James, how many times do we have to go over this? I loved you as you were then, and I love you as you are now. I told you, I'm here and I'll never leave you ever."

He kneeled while he held her hand to his lips. He wanted to start their future together, all the happy nights, months, and years they would have together. It was the way it had happened then, in front of that very house, the one his father had built for them when he knew she would be his wife. A few hours earlier it all could have ended for another century, or millennia, or forever. But that night he was there, he was willing, and he was asking her to marry him. He knew how lucky he was then to marry for love, and he knew how lucky he was now.

"Yes, yes, James, of course I'll be your wife. You're my dear and loving husband. I love you."

"You see," James said, "second chances happen. If you're lucky."

"We are lucky," Sarah said. "Everyone should be so lucky."

CHAPTER 25

How long would you wait for the one you loved? James had waited over three hundred years.

Their second wedding was different. The first had been an afternoon affair after harvest season, a simple ceremony where they pledged their commitment, knowing in their hearts that their love would span eternity. Their second wedding took place in the luminous warmth of an early summer night at Jennifer's house, a Victorian-era home where the rose-filled backyard glowed with white Christmas lights, candles and incense burning all around. Jennifer presided over the ceremony like an ethereal princess in her flowing robe, her long auburn hair loose around her shoulders. Their guests stood in a sacred circle holding white tapered candles, sending light across the night. Sarah wore a crown of flowers, James a crown of ivy.

This was a traditional Wiccan hand-binding ceremony, and their friends had important roles to play. Martha stood to the north and held a fan to represent air since it was her connection to unseen things that helped Sarah realize all of who she was and who she could be. Olivia stood to the south and held a red candle to represent fire. Sarah's mother, who came to Salem from Boston after all, stood to the east and held a blue crystal to represent earth. Jocelyn stood to the west and held a glass of water. One by one they put their items on the altar, which the loving couple knelt before, their hands bound by a woven cloth rope. The rope was not a life-stealing binding as the iron chains had been. This was a warming, loving connection. It was right that they should be tied together that way. Jennifer waved a bouquet of fresh scented herbs around them to ward off evil spirits. Then, before she began the giving of the rings, she slipped the rope from their hands with the knot still intact, signifying that husband and wife would always be bound in marriage.

Jennifer said, "Now you are bound one to the other with a tie not easy to break. Grow in wisdom and love so your marriage will be strong. So your love will last in this lifetime. And beyond."

Timothy began sweeping with a straw broom, pushing away bad luck and impurities, leaving the sacred circle fresh and new.

Jennifer said, "I take you my heart at the rising of the moon and the setting of the stars. To love and honor you through all our lives together. May we always be reborn so that we may meet and love one another again. And remember. May we always remember."

To end the ceremony, James read Anne Bradstreet's poem. Sarah couldn't stop the happy tears as she heard the words that expressed their love, then and now:

> ...*Then while we live, in love let's so persever*
> *That when we live no more, we may live ever.*

After the ceremony, Sarah pointed out that it was just like the end of a Jane Austen story since Austen's novels end with the happy couple getting married.

"Is this the end of the story?" James asked.

"Of course not," she said, smiling that smile he loved to see. "This is only the beginning."

The only pause of the night was when he saw his wife looking over the top of Jennifer's fence, scanning the empty street. She seemed anxious somehow, almost frightened.

"What are you looking for?" he asked.

Sarah shook her head. "I'm still expecting to see Kenneth Hempel jump out at us from behind the bushes. I keep thinking I see him there. My imagination must be getting the best of me."

James brushed her curls from her face, leaning close and wallowing in the sensuous joy of strawberries and cream. He kissed her forehead, both of her cheeks, her lips. He lingered on her mouth a long time.

"What was I worried about again?" Sarah said.

James laughed. "I don't think you need to worry about Kenneth Hempel right now. He won't be bothering us again any time soon."

Sarah looked at their guests, saw them happy and laughing. "What do you think he would say if he could see us tonight? Do you think he'd change his mind about his hunt?"

"I doubt it. His vengeance is not against those like Timothy, Jocelyn, or me. He wants retribution against the wild ones like the one that killed his father. But you can't tame unruly vampires any more than you can tame unruly humans." He kissed his wife's lips again. "In just a few short weeks Kenneth Hempel has become a distant memory, like a story told ages ago."

"Like a fable or a legend."

"That's right. Tonight I remarried the only woman I have ever loved. In over three hundred years there has been no one in my heart but you, and that is all that matters now."

"And if Hempel comes back?"

"As long as we're together, everything will be fine. Remember, I'll never leave you ever."

"And I promise you the same."

As their guests mingled, James introduced his wife to others who came to celebrate the night, friends he had known, some for generations, and she was happy to meet them and know them. He even invited Geoffrey, who seemed pleased to be there, proud of his vampling. James laughed when he heard Geoffrey boasting to a white-skinned friend: "I turned James. That's right, I turned him. He's my vampling."

When Sarah stepped away to speak to her mother, Geoffrey grabbed James by the arm and pulled him to the far end of the yard. "When are you going to turn her?" he asked.

"Who?"

"Don't be daft, James. That perfectly nice little human person you're married to, that's who. If you leave her be she'll die."

"Tonight?"

"Of course not tonight. But soon. A human life is like a snap of our fingers."

James watched Sarah. Sweet Sarah. Beautiful Sarah. She was laughing, joyful, stealing glances at him. He closed his eyes and savored the sweetness of strawberries and cream. She was perfect. He didn't want her to change.

"She doesn't want to be like us," he said.

"You don't need people's permission to turn them."

"I'm well aware of that. But I would never do to Sarah what you did to me. If this isn't what she wants then I'm not going to force her to it."

"James."

"We have time before we have to worry about it."

"Humans always think they have time. Then before they know it they're eighty-five years old, eating through a tube, shitting in a diaper, and what do they have to show for it?"

"A lifetime of memories."

"Will that be enough for you when she's gone again?"

James clutched Geoffrey's shoulder. "It's my wedding, Geoffrey. Give us this one night to be happy. You can sing your tale of woe for us some other time."

James stepped away, shaking aside the hollowness he suddenly felt. But he refused to dwell on the sadness Geoffrey's words could bring. There would be only joy and light that night. He and Sarah had decided. And as for the rest of their time together, they would take each night as it came, appreciating what they had while they had it. They would know not to take their love for granted this time. There were no guarantees in a human's life. They were not guaranteed health. Or wealth. Or time. Or happiness. But right now, that night, he and his wife were married again, caught up in the bubble of joy they could find only with each other. They were fulfilling their destiny with the only person they could. When you love someone and cannot exist in any form, human or otherwise, without her, when you're sure you were created for her and she for you and no one else, you will always love her. No matter how many centuries pass, despite whatever comes, you will always love her. And, if you're lucky, you will find her again. Even in Salem. Especially in Salem.

He found his wife, grabbed her hand, and led her across the yard to introduce her to Howard Wolfe, a biology professor at Salem State College and Timothy's guardian. She seemed happy to meet him.

"I've seen you in the library near the human physiology section," she said.

As they chatted James waited for her to make the connection between the wolf that howled for Timothy and the man they were speaking to, but she needed some prompting. After Howard was called away, James pulled her close.

"Have you noticed how he always cancels classes the night of the month when there's a full moon?" he asked. He saw the recognition in her eyes.

"Timothy called that wolf Dad," Sarah said. She watched Howard as he laughed with his vampire son. "He's a werewolf?"

"Yes, but he won't be any trouble tonight."

Sarah looked at the slice of the crescent moon hanging above them. She didn't look worried, James thought. Perhaps a bit apprehensive.

"Are you sure there's no such thing as Frankenstein?" she asked.

"There is no such thing as Frankenstein. That I'm aware of."

Everyone moved from the backyard into Jennifer's house, drinking or eating and talking and hugging each other. Through the window, barely visible against the shadows of the night, James saw a wisp of streaming light that beckoned him. When he looked again he was certain he saw his father standing there, looking him in the eye as he had done so many times before, smiling, his hands pressed together as if in prayer, joy in his kindly eyes. He seemed happy for James and his new bride just as he had been oh so many years before. As if no centuries had passed since his death, James ran outside to greet him.

"Father!" he said. But his father was no longer there.

Sarah followed him out the door. "James? What's wrong?"

"I just saw my father standing here. He was smiling."

"Your father was always smiling."

James put his arms around Sarah and pulled her close. He thought he was hallucinating again the way he did the day he was in the sun.

"Do you think he was really here?" he asked.

"These days I'll believe anything."

He held his wife even closer and kissed her.

"You're right," he said. "Anything is possible."

The next night James was shaken awake by his wife. She stood over him, Sarah, just as she did when he called her Lizzie, poking his shoulder, shaking his arm, laughing.

"James? Jamie? It's been dark for over an hour. It's time to wake up."

She walked to the window, threw aside the blackout curtains, and raised the blinds. The sky was well dark, the moon clearly visible, the stars winking at them from the distance. They had seen this dance between James and Sarah many times before in years gone by. James was awake, but he loved how she was playing with him and he didn't want it to end. It felt right for them to be that way again.

She pulled the blanket from him. "James Wentworth, it's over three centuries later and you are still the laziest man ever born!"

He pulled her into bed with him and kissed her. They dissolved into each other like no time had passed and they had been together that way every night for three hundred and nineteen years and they would be there still for three hundred and nineteen years more.

Some things never change.

ACKNOWLEDGMENTS

I remember the day, three years ago, when one of my students handed me Stephenie Meyer's *Twilight* and told me how much she loved it. Having never been one for vampire stories, I read the book solely on her recommendation. While the student shall remain unnamed, I thank her.

Laurin Wittig, who read an early draft of the novel and pointed me in the direction this story needed to go.

My mother, who has always supported me in my endeavors.

The editors and staff at Copperfield Press.

The contributors, authors, and devoted readers of *The Copperfield Review*. I hope *CR* continues for many more years.

As I said in an earlier work of historical fiction, I am not an historian, though I ride on the coattails of talented historians who do the hard labor digging through layers of the past to find the facts. While my intention was to remain true to the history of the Salem Witch Trials, and to the town of Salem, Massachusetts itself, in the interest of full disclosure I admit to taking some creative license in the representation of both. As a former history teacher, my hope is that readers will become intrigued enough by the Salem Witch Trials that they will seek out historical accounts of the era. *The Salem Witch Trials: A Day-by-Day Chronicle of a Community Under Siege* by Marilynne K. Roach is a good place to start.

As to the history of vampires, I'll leave that for Book Two, *Her Loving Husband's Curse*, to comment on…

ABOUT THE AUTHOR

Meredith Allard received her B.A. and M.A. degrees in English from California State University, Northridge. Her short fiction and articles have appeared in journals such as *The Paumanok Review*, *The Maxwell Digest*, *Wild Mind*, *Muse Apprentice Guild*, *Writer's Weekly*, *Moondance*, and *CarbLite*. She has taught writing to students aged ten to sixty, and she has taught creative writing and writing historical fiction seminars at Learning Tree University, UNLV, and the Las Vegas Writers Conference. She is the executive editor of *The Copperfield Review*, an award-winning literary journal for readers and writers of historical fiction. She lives in Las Vegas, Nevada. Visit Meredith online at www.meredithallard.com.

Her Dear and Loving Husband is Book One of *The Loving Husband Trilogy*. Book Two, *Her Loving Husband's Curse*, will be available April 2012. Look for more titles from Copperfield Press coming soon.

CPSIA information can be obtained at www.ICGtesting.com
Printed in the USA
LVOW080243110313

323613LV00001B/53/P